Tales from Lachmuirghan

Tales from Lachmuirghan

Madeleine Oh
Pandora Grace
Xandra King
Maristella Kent
Clarissa Wilmot
M. A. duBarry
and
Isabo Kelly

A Samhain Publishing, Ltd. publication.

Samhain Publishing, Ltd.
577 Mulberry Street, Suite 1520
Macon, GA 31201
www.samhainpublishing.com

Print ISBN: 978-1-59998-983-9

Digital ISBN: 1-59998-842-9

Editing by Jennifer Miller
Cover by Anne Cain

First Samhain Publishing, Ltd. electronic publication: December 2007
First Samhain Publishing, Ltd. print publication: October 2008

Table of Contents

Introduction to Lachmuirghan
~7~

The Public Houses:
~11~

A Night at The God
by Madeleine Oh

Over the Sea to Skye
by Clarissa Wilmot

The Monolith and The God
by Madeleine Oh

Hali's Rescue
by Isabo Kelly

Loch Larg, the River and the Beach:
~61~

Eileen's Tale
by Maristella Kent

The Gro'ach
by Madeleine Oh

The Guesthouse:
~89~

Kirsty Muir and the Guesthouse
by Xandra King

Kirsty Muir and the Bondage Cellar
by Xandra King

Caleb's Tale
by Maristella Kent

The Museum:
~141~
Ben's Tale
by Maristella Kent

The Castle:
~153~
Bed of Roses
by Clarissa Wilmot
The Return of the Prince
by M.A. duBarry
Adam's Tale
by Maristella Kent

The Teashop—Sweet Cream and Honey Cakes:
~191~
A Teashop Tale
by Madeleine Oh
Rainy Day Encounter
by Madeleine Oh

The Book Shop:
~211~
Shapeshifter
by Pandora Grace
The Ride of Your Life
by Clarissa Wilmot

Afterward
~243~

Introduction to Lachmuirghan

You may have trouble finding Lachmuirghan on maps and atlases. And you would be quite right, because Lachmuirghan doesn't exist—except here and now. So come with us on a stroll around our secret valley...

Imagine a sheltered valley and loch somewhere in the west of Scotland. At the head of the valley is an ancient circle of standing stones; at the lower end stands a ruined castle overlooking the village center of Lachmuirghan.

Among the narrow streets and the gray stone cottages, you'll find a cluster of shops: a general store, a butcher, a greengrocer and a narrow shop selling curios and antique jewelry. Up the street a little way, just past the garage, is the village bookshop that in these times also stocks DVDs, tapes and CDs. Up the hill, you'll find The God in the Valley, one of two village pubs. The other is The Royal Rescue, on the riverbank. The God in the Valley is the larger and caters to visitors and locals alike. Upstairs are three bedrooms which the landlord rents out when the fancy takes him. Very fortunate indeed is a visitor who spends a night at The God in the Valley. And if a weary visitor passes by The God, at the top of the village, surrounded by heather gardens and rockeries, is the Lachmuirghan Guesthouse: a large, imposing stone building.

Why these quaint names? Local legend claims The Royal Rescue was used as a hiding place for the Young Pretender during his escape to France, and the oldest part of the building does indeed date from the early eighteenth century. The God in the Valley refers to a much, much older legend. Some say that millennia ago the whole valley was constructed by a sea god for the human woman he loved. He set the stones at one end to serve as her calendar, provided a sweet freshwater stream, blessed the land with extraordinary fertility so she would never hunger, and surrounded the valley with magic to protect her from ills. But cruel fate intervened, she drowned in the river, and as she had refused the gift of immortality he had offered her, the god could not save her. Brokenhearted, the god wept for five years, flooding the valley where he'd buried his love, and then left, never to set foot in the valley again. But many say the magic remains...

Who knows if this is truth or myth? Certainly the loch is slightly saline, but the river leading off it is freshwater—an anomaly that has long mystified scientists and geographers. The fields and hills around are extremely fertile, the climate warmer and more temperate than the surrounding areas. The villagers are healthy and long lived and the air is clear and invigorating. You notice this particularly as you stroll through the village. You pass several villagers who smile and wish you a good day: a young woman pushing a toddler in a stroller, two women talking in front of a cottage, a good-looking, dark-haired man carrying a knapsack, who smiles at you as you pass. A dog barks through a garden gate.

Walk up through the village, towards the hills. Once past the last cottages, pause and look around you. In the shifting light, it seems the village changes. Is that a ruined church, not a stone circle? And are those dark shapes along the loch rocks or caves? It seems the mountains are closer and grayer—

perhaps the mist plays tricks on the eye.

Or does Lachmuirghan change as you watch? The abandoned manor house you passed at the end of the village now appears to be a castle, complete with battlements and a ruined tower. The road back towards the village surely has more twists and turns than you remembered. Where did that farmhouse in the distance appear from? Surely it wasn't there a moment ago?

Returning to the village, anticipating a glass of something alcoholic at The God in the Valley, you notice a small teashop offering honey cakes and sweet cream that you missed on the way up. In front, two women stand talking, but their skirts are long and one wears a bonnet and the other a knitted shawl. A little way on, you meet the young woman, no longer wearing blue jeans and T-shirt, but long skirts and pushing a large pram. She smiles as before, and mentions that Angus is waiting for you at The God in the Valley.

Before you can ask who "Angus" is and how he knows you, she turns down a narrow side street and disappears. Meanwhile you notice the garage is a smithy and farrier, and several more shops have appeared: a baker, a wool and haberdashery shop and McGreerly's Apothecary.

Lachmuirghan has changed and so have you. Your hair is longer, tied back with a ribbon. You're walking faster, and as you go along, you catch sounds and scents you missed before: bread baking, soup simmering, roses in a garden, a kettle whistling on a stove, a child singing, a baby crying and a man telling his love what he plans when the bairns are fast asleep. Blushing a little, you walk on feeling a trifle envious, until you remember the mysterious Angus waiting for you. Ahead the sign for The God in the Valley rocks in the breeze. Outside sits the man you passed earlier, watching you. Is he what you want? Do you dare? Would it be safer to duck into the bookshop and get lost among the stacks and shelves? Or why not nip down a narrow side street which catches your eye? A side street that appears to lead down to the shore where the sun glints on the water. As you stand trying to decide, a voice calls your name from a window across the street.

Where will you go? And to whom? The choice is completely yours. Explore the village with us, and live out your fantasy.

One:
The Public Houses

Lachmuirghan boasts two public houses: The God in the Valley and The Royal Rescue. (We won't consider the rather disreputable establishment down on the river.)

Both pubs have a lot to recommend them.

The God in the Valley is the oldest, largest and most imposing: an ancient stone building fronts the road, with two bars, a restaurant and rooms overhead to let to suitable travelers. It's not everyone gets a room at The God but those who do wake up smiling, relaxed and contented.

The Royal Rescue—so named because Flora MacDonald supposedly met the Young Pretender here before spiriting him down the valley to the coast and off to Skye—is smaller and was built in the last century but, so tradition holds, on the site of a much older dwelling. Much smaller than The God, The Royal Rescue has only one room to let: a large corner room up in the eaves, with three dormers giving a magnificent view of the loch, the castle and the standing stones. The room at The Rescue is often booked weeks in advance and many visitors return time after time.

ଓ

A Night at The God

By Madeleine Oh

The wipers swooshed back and forth at top speed, barely managing to clear the windshield before the driving rain obscured visibility once again. Beth swore to herself. Why in the name of sanity had she agreed to drive to the back of beyond and meet Ian for the weekend? Heck, she wasn't even sure she wanted a weekend—and the inevitable rather boring sex—with him. The last half hour of howling wind and driving rain had definitely put her not in the mood. She might even arrive with a genuine headache.

"You'll love Lachmuirghan," Ian had whispered in her ear as they lay naked and sweaty between tangled sheets. "It's magical."

He'd omitted the bit about the village not being signposted and invisible on the damn maps. Yes, he'd given detailed directions, but somehow she'd missed some vital landmark. She drove on because it seemed marginally preferable to trying to reverse in the narrow lane. She was actually getting used to the rain beating a tattoo overhead. As long as Lachmuirghan wasn't farther away than a quarter of a tank, she'd be okay.

As if in answer to a silent plea, she turned the next bend and a weather-beaten board announced *Welcome to Lachmuirghan.* Bingo! Just when she'd been wondering if the entire place wasn't a figment of Ian's imagination, she was here. Almost. The road headed downhill, and through the dark and rain, Beth noticed lights in cottage windows and the dark outlines of roofs. The road leveled out as she approached the first houses. The street was the next best thing to deserted, but there on the left, just as Ian had described it, was the pub—The God in the Valley—with a swinging sign and a welcoming beam of light streaming from the open door.

Beth parked under a shuttered window. Stopping only to grab her overnight bag and lock the car, she sprinted through the puddles and through the front door.

The light and warmth greeting her put her in mind of a warm drink, a steaming bath and a nice soft, cozy bed.

“Welcome,” the gray-haired man said from behind the bar. “You’d be Miss Adams. Young Ian said to expect you.”

That was a mercy. If she’d come all this way and not been expected, she’d be hard-pressed to be very gracious about it.

“Super!”

“You’ll be wanting something to eat and a dram to warm yourself after your drive.”

All she really wanted was a hot bath and a soft bed, but the idea of a dram rather appealed. “I don’t really need dinner, but a sandwich and a warm toddy would be more than welcome.”

“We can manage that for you,” the landlord said, stepping around the bar to take her coat and overnight case. “Have a seat by the fire until everything’s ready.”

When he came close, Beth noticed how short he was—barely her own five feet. She took a seat by the log fire and only then noticed the bar was deserted except for a large spaniel asleep by the fire. Odd, that. More than odd. But so what? With no audience, she could kick off her wet shoes and dry her feet by the fire.

She was comfortably warm to the point of drowsiness when the landlord reappeared with a tray of sandwiches and a steaming glass and invited her to follow him upstairs. Brilliant suggestion.

"If Ian arrives, please tell him I'm upstairs."

The landlord nodded. "When he comes." He didn't sound entirely optimistic.

"Here you are, Miss. Hope you find the room comfortable. It's the only one we have available tonight for visitors."

Might be the only one, but who'd complain? She hadn't expected a wide, four poster bed, deep blue Turkish carpets and a vast tiled bathroom with an enormous claw-foot bath that was clearly intended for two.

Oh well, Ian wasn't here but she was and the steaming water that poured out as she turned on the taps wasn't to be wasted. She dropped her clothes on the floor and reached for the bottle of heather and wild herbs bubble bath on the shelf. This might be the back of beyond, but it was definitely civilized. She'd thank Ian—when he finally appeared.

Putting her tray of provisions on the round table she dragged in from the bedroom, Beth stepped into the bath and let the water run until the bubbles reached her chin.

It was sheer heaven. She picked up the glass. Whatever was in it smelled of whisky and some sort of herb or spice, and it tasted of honey and peat fires and long-forgotten dreams. And a couple of glasses of this and she'd be out cold. Alcohol on an empty stomach wasn't a good idea. Beth reached for a sandwich. Had she ever tasted ham this delicious? If she so, she didn't remember. Amazing what hunger did for the taste buds. Maybe she should have taken up the offer of dinner, but two rounds of sandwiches more than satisfied.

She was halfway to dozing off in the warmth and the alcohol-induced relaxation, when a distant clock struck eleven. Cripes! Ian wasn't here yet, and to be honest, she hadn't missed him, but she was feeling a trifle randy and would be more than ready for him, if he walked through the door.

He didn't.

But warm water and creature comforts were their own seduction. Beth shut her eyes, inhaling the scents of heather and green life and wild rain. And was she glad to be out of the rain! The wind seemed to amplify as it buffeted the walls and slashed against the windows. Relaxed in the hot water, Beth listened to the thrum of rain overhead, sipped her toddy and decided the landlord had been a bit too generous with the whisky, but what the heck? She closed her eyes and prepared to dream of warm sheets and hot sex.

Strong hands rested on her shoulders.

"Ah, Ian, I didn't hear you come in. I'm so glad you got here."

Beth lay still, glad of his touch. He had a new aftershave, woodsy and fresh.

"That feels wonderful. Where've you been? I had a terrible time finding this place."

"Shhh." His breath came warm on her shoulder as his hands stroked and eased out the tension of the evening. "Relax. Shut your eyes and forget the rain and the drive. You're safe from the fury of the storm."

As if on cue, wind buffeted the outside walls and rattled the shutters, but Beth relaxed under his touch. She let out a slow, contented sigh and eased a little lower into the warm water. Beth savored the frisson of excitement that settled deep in her cunt. The warm water rippled as he dipped his hands in and stroked droplets of water across her chest, cupping her breasts and gently caressing until they felt heavy and swollen. He lifted them, bouncing them lightly as ripples of water lapped her chin. Beth lay still, enjoying the growing sensations in her body. Anticipating more.

Beth watched his long fingers moving through the green water, or was it green fingers in clear water? Did it matter? Not while he touched her like this. She sighed with contentment and the lights went out.

He chuckled at her cry of surprise.

"Not to worry. The fire's inside you."

His hands slid down her belly towards her pussy and a sweet itch rose in her cunt.

"Kneel up," Ian whispered, "I'm getting in with you."

The water swooshed as he settled behind her. The rough hair on his legs caressed the soft skin of her thighs and his cock pressed hard against the small of her back. She leaned into him, rocking to stroke his erection along her spine. His hands steadied her hips.

"Keep still. The storm is easing. Listen."

He was right. The wind was scarcely noticeable and the rain beat gently overhead.

"I'll have you with the storm," he said. "When the wind blows easily, I'll caress you and taste the beauty of your skin." He paused to run his tongue up her neck from between her shoulder blades. "When the storm rages harder, I'll fuck you, and as the thunder claps and the lightning flashes across the heavens, you'll scream your satisfaction."

This was not the Ian she knew. Must be the fresh mountain air that set his imagination roaring. She was not about to complain, not when his lips brushed the back of her neck and his fingers teased her nipples.

Her mind tried to shape the argument that there was no thunder, just rain and wind. How important was that while he kissed and nipped his way down her shoulder? She wanted to turn and face him, to rub her breasts against the rough hair on his chest and press his erect cock into her belly, but he held her steady. As he reached for the soap and slowly lathered up her breasts, she thought of nothing else. Never before had Ian caressed her with such infinite and teasing slowness. As he opened her pussy and sent waves of scented water breaking against her clit, she leaned back against his chest and moaned.

"You like that."

She'd be a liar and a fool to deny it—if she could find the words. All her mind registered were his hands on her breasts and his fingers working her nipples hard, while his lips fluttered over her shoulders and neck. She dropped her head forward and his mouth kissed a trail up the side of her neck to her ear. He nipped the lobe, holding her fast as she jerked with shock.

"Easy, I'll kiss it better."

He suckled her earlobe until trails of desire skittered over her skin.

He took a washcloth and squeezed water over her breasts and belly so rivulets ran down her body. She was throbbing and he'd yet to touch her cunt with his fingers. She needed Ian's strong fingers opening her and penetrating her slick cunt in preparation for his cock. Instead he splashed and teased her with scented water. She angled her hips to send more water against her aroused pussy.

Rain hit the roof in a wild tattoo. A loud gust of wind against the windowpanes was followed by a great crack and a thud. Beth jumped but his arms wrapped her close.

"Be calm, it's just an old tree falling to the power of the wind."

Power indeed she felt around her, the force of the storm and the strength and might in the arms that held her. She paused, inhaling the green country scent and rubbing her breasts against the rough hair on his arms. She wanted more.

Needed more. She rocked against his erection.

"The storm increases. Stand up."

She obeyed without thinking, his hands steadying her. She expected to shiver as cool air hit her damp skin but the air around seemed warmed by the heat between them. He pressed her hands flat on the cool tiled wall.

"Brace yourself."

She balanced, shin-deep in water, as her heat inside burned with a building need. His hands marked her body as his. He stroked and caressed, pulling her nipples between two fingers, tracing wild circles on her belly, teasing trails up and down her back, cupping the aching heat of her pussy, tugging at her pussy lips and teasing her clit with soft flicks.

It wasn't enough.

She wanted his fingers penetrating her and his cock deeper, but he made her wait, running wild kisses across her shoulders in a rhythm that matched the wild beat of rain against the panes. He rubbed his cock between her thighs, stroking back and forth until she moaned for penetration.

He paused—but only long enough to gather handfuls of water and trickle warm trails down her back and breasts. She groaned. Was he going to make her wait forever? His slick touch on her thighs and arse meant he'd soaped his hands again. Or had he? It didn't feel like soap. She tried to look but in the dark, she felt rather than saw his fingers open her pussy while his other hand stroked her arse. Now he had two hands on her, caressing and gently massaging and parting her cheeks as his fingers skimmed between them.

"Trying something new, Ian?" Beth asked.

He replied with a slow kiss on the side of her neck and gentle pressure of one finger against her puckered arsehole. She took several slow, deep breaths. She was tight, but his steady pressure opened her until she felt the easy intrusion of his fingertip. He waited. His free hand stroked up and down her spine, soothing her, settling her apprehension as she was stretched and filled. He didn't move until her muscles relaxed a little. Then, he gently moved his finger back and forth until she sighed and rocked in rhythm. Her tightness eased as her passion soared. The rain came in harder gusts and lightning flashed as he pressed deep. She stood there, hands splayed on the tiled wall, presented for his intrusion, as her body let out a soft moan halfway between ache and need.

"Soon," he promised and withdrew.

"More," she gasped. Bereft and ready to cry out at the loss.

His deep, husky laugh sent warm ripples down her spine. One arm snaked round her waist, holding her steady as his free hand parted her arse cheeks. His hand rubbed along her crack, easing something smooth and cool into her now not-quite-so-tight hole. His cock pressed between her crack as he fluttered soft kisses across her shoulders. She gave a little sigh of pleasure as the head of his cock pressed against her opening. He rocked gently, just enough to stimulate but not stretch. Another lightning flash, and he pressed easily and insistently as her muscles slowly opened and her body surrendered her last virginity. Her moan was lost in the thunder. He paused. Waiting as his fingers stroked her breast and his other hand crossed her belly to cup her pussy. She sighed as his fingers nestled between her curls and opened her. Wet and soaking as the world beyond this steamy room, she yearned for his deep penetration. She rocked her hips, but he moved with her, keeping the head of his cock just inside her.

"Wait," he whispered as his finger softly tapped her clit.

She would go wild with waiting. Another flash of thunder and he drove in deep, her shout masked by the thunder. He was vast and filled her with his strength and male power. She was stretched and invaded and possessed by wildness as he moved in cadence with the driving rain.

Sighs of pleasure became moans of need as her passion mounted and his grunts of power echoed in the small room. If was as if they were locked together and one with the storm outside. His fingers still played her clit but now her cries rose above his. Like two animals locked in a primal embrace, they pushed each other towards the brink. His thrusts came fast and furious with the rising wind. Her cries came louder and keener as thunder came immediately after lightning. His finger gave one final flick and sent her over the edge. As she climaxed, he drove even deeper as he pumped his jism into her depths. Her legs wobbled as her climax spent. Only his cock and his arms kept her from falling.

As he withdrew, he lifted her out of the tub. Her toes sank into the deep pile rug as he wrapped a towel around her. The dark didn't slow him as he dried her and carried her into the bedroom. Lightheaded and spent, she felt his hands smooth and tuck in the covers. She sensed rather than felt a kiss on her forehead, and she sank into exhausted sleep.

She woke to sunlight streaming through the window, clear blue skies and voices in the street outside. Ian had to be up already, his side of the bed was smoothed and his pillow plumped up. He'd been gone a while. The sheets were cold. Beth stood, still relishing the sweet sensations deep in her body, and crossed over the window.

Puddles sat in low points among the cobblestones. A brewer's lorry was drawn up to the door, and a red-faced man with sleeves pushed up huffed as he unloaded wooden cases of bottles. Ian's red Citroen rounded the corner and pulled up in front of the pub. He got out, took his bag from the boot, locked up and walked into The God.

Beth sat down on the lumpy armchair with a thud, and leaped up again. So he'd popped out, maybe to get a paper. But why the suitcase? Looking around the room, there was nothing of his here. No shoes kicked off. No shirt or trousers draped over a chair. She crossed to the bathroom door. No shaving things by the sink. No towel on the floor.

Determined to sort this out, Beth pulled blue jeans and a sweatshirt from her case and pulled them on over her warm and sex-scented skin. Not stopping for shoes, she ran down the dark oak stairs barefoot.

Ian stood in the deserted bar, his suitcase at his feet and his jacket over his arm.

"She were fine," the landlord was saying. "Got in late because of the rain, but we took care of her."

Damn right, they had.

"Darling!" Ian said, looking up as Beth called his name. "The road was flooded and I backtracked and spent the night in Largs. Sorry you were stuck here all alone."

Little did he know or suspect, and Beth thought it politic to leave in that way. But she couldn't miss the knowing look in the landlord's eye as she and Ian sat down to breakfast.

☙

Over the Sea to Skye

By Clarissa Wilmot

"And this is the very room where Flora stayed," Gavin MacDonald, owner of The Royal Rescue, declared. "In Flora's time, it was divided in two, the prince's bed was next door, and there was a connecting door between the two rooms. When the redcoats came, Flora led the prince out through a secret passageway hidden somewhere in this room. Did I tell you my family was descended from her clan?"

And the rest, thought Mary. During the course of her research into Flora MacDonald and Bonnie Prince Charlie for the book she was writing, *Over the Sea to Skye and Other Stories from Scottish Folklore,* she had lost count of the number of places claiming to have put the fugitives up, and the number of people claiming to be living descendants of Flora MacDonald. The conventional story told of Flora spiriting the prince away from the isle of Benbecula to Skye, without stopping along the way. However, Mary had discovered evidence to suggest that at some point they may have been forced to land somewhere along the Scottish coast. She had begun investigating, and when the name Lachmuirghan had come up, well, she couldn't resist. She had had to come back.

Lachmuirghan. Just the sound of the name made her whole body tingle. Her last visit here had been different, to say the least. The very least. Wild, passionate, exciting, *erotic,* were also words that sprang to mind. She had never quite worked out whether the incredible sex she'd had with a perfect stranger had actually happened. And what a stranger! She blushed to think about it, but her mysterious lover could turn into a horse for God's sake. Did other people have sexual encounters with sea kelpies? Or had the whole encounter been a product of her stressed state? After all, John had only just left her at the time. She had been pretty flaky round that period—perhaps she had just imagined it?

Mary had concluded in the end that she had. And yet it

had seemed so *real...*

Even now, thinking about her sea kelpie made her feel hot all over, particularly in the parts that no other man had ever reached. And somehow ever since that strange trip here a couple of years back, life in Edinburgh had seemed to lack color. She had reached out and taken a bite of forbidden fruit, and normal life had lost its luster as a result.

And now she was back. Investigating another Scottish myth and wondering whether anything interesting would happen to her this time. No, not wondering, *hoping.*

"*Ah, Flora my love...*" The softest of whispers in her ear, like a tree blowing in the breeze. Then, sure she hadn't imagined it, she felt the sweetest of kisses brush past her cheek, filling her with a sense of hopeless yearning and making her long for more. She whirled round to see—nothing. There was nobody there but herself and Gavin MacDonald. He was standing by the window pointing out a hill in the distance, way beyond the castle that dwarfed the town.

"There's an old croft up there," Gavin was saying. "Legend has it, the couple spent the night there, but who knows if it is true."

"Did you just hear something?" Mary asked.

"No," said Gavin. "Unless it was the ghost of Bonnie Prince Charlie. They do say he haunts this place."

"Do they indeed?" asked Mary, laughing. That was typical. The prince was supposed to haunt nearly every other place she had visited, too. She must have imagined the whisper. And the kiss. The romantic associations of the room, and her memories from her last visit, were fueling her imagination. That was all. But why then, did she feel that quickening of desire, and what was making her heart beat that little bit faster? It couldn't be the presence of Gavin, who was stolidly unattractive to her, but something about this place was stirring her dormant sensuality once more. Maybe Lachmuirghan had other pleasures to offer her. Mary rather hoped so...

"Flora, you must awaken!"

Mary woke to the sound of a fierce banging on the door. She had gone to bed late, and had been reading letters Gavin had passed to her—he claimed they were Flora's, although she couldn't be sure they weren't fakes. But they certainly made for interesting reading.

Her dreams had been jumbled and confused—she was with the prince in a boat, and redcoats chased them. The oarsmen decided to shelter in a creek for safety, and she realized they were near her kinsman in Lachmuirghan. She and the prince agreed to lie low there for a couple of days and arranged to meet the boatmen again when the coast was clear. And so she took the prince to her cousin's tavern, and they slept in adjoining rooms. Flora meant to stay awake but eventually exhaustion overcame her.

Flora? Mary sat bolt upright. Her clothes felt unfamiliar—she was wearing a long linen shift, and her hair tumbled down her back in brown ringlets. *Ringlets*? Since when had she worn her hair in ringlets? What was happening to her? Was Lachmuirghan working its magic once more?

"Flora! The redcoats are coming, you must leave now!"

She was out of bed in an instant. Heart pounding, she ran to the window and looked out to see a column of light—men with torches—making its way down the path towards the inn. The door flew open, and her cousin, Donald, stood before her, torch in hand.

"You must hurry," he said. "You can leave this way." He

pressed a panel in the wall and it creaked open to reveal a dark passage. "I will keep the soldiers at bay. I'm sure they can be persuaded to take a wee dram with me after all their hard travails."

"I will waken the prince," she said.

The prince's soft French accent came from the doorway. "He is awake."

Flora curtseyed and, as usual in the presence of her prince, she felt awe, affection, and...something more. His eyes were of liquid green and his voice was like the wind on the water. The sound of it sent ripples over her whole body, shaking her to the core, and made her think of things it really wasn't proper for a young lady to think about.

Proper or not, there was no time for such thoughts now. Flinging clothes on as fast as they could, they took the torches offered by Donald. Heeding his instructions about making for the abandoned shepherd's croft high on the mountain, where they would find shelter and supplies, they hurried down the passageway and out into the night, and safety.

It was hard going on the mountain. They walked all through the night and the best part of the day. In places, they weren't even able to walk but had to scrabble in a most undignified manner. But now the threat of immediate danger was over, Flora rather began to enjoy her adventure. She was climbing a mountain with her prince and lord, the man they called the Young Pretender. Who could not be excited by that? Especially when he was such a handsome prince—even disguised as he was in the clothes of a woman, he couldn't hide his innate charm. She wasn't sure if it was the exertion of the climb that was making her heart pound, or her closeness to the prince. He was not just handsome—he had an almost animal magnetism, which made her feel that she would do anything he asked. Anything at all.

How much further?" The prince was panting. He looked utterly exhausted. No wonder, considering the ordeal he had recently undergone. The weeks of hiding had taken their toll, and though still handsome, he was much thinner then the debonair figure she had seen from a distance in the crowds who had come out to cheer their hero on his arrival in Scotland. Now he was a wraith, and while his too-thin face gave him a gaunt romantic beauty, he was a shadow of what he had been Added to which, the sight of him in women's clothing should have repulsed her, but somehow, oddly, it added to the attraction—making him seem that little bit more exciting. And he had such presence—even dressed as an Irish maid. He was her prince, way beyond her reach, but something about his plight tugged at her very heart.

Here on the Scottish hillside, they were no longer prince and subject, but two fugitives from the law, bound together by a common purpose. When he took her hand to help her over a root, or took her arm to propel her forward, his very touch thrilled her to the core. No one, not even her beloved fiancé Allan, had ever made her feel like this. When he turned those beautiful green eyes on her, he made her melt into pools of liquid desire. She knew she should dispel such thoughts, but she couldn't help wondering what it would be like to touch his naked body...

"Not too far, sire," she said, somewhat more positively then she felt. "Come, lend me your arm."

"Is it come to this, Flora MacDonald, that the King of England should be reduced to leaning on a woman?" He smiled at her weakly, but even in his feeble state, the look he gave her sent a shiver down her spine, and his touch as he took the shoulder she offered was so soft, it made her think once more of the whisper in the trees on a summer morning. She had a sudden longing to feel his gentle caress, but pushed it away. The prince was weak—she had to get him to shelter and fast.

"Come, Your Majesty, we must hurry," she said, half pushing, half dragging him up to the top of the next peak. The croft Donald had talked of could not be far now.

It wasn't. She reached the brow of the hill. Standing in front of her were two redcoats, pistols drawn.

Now what should she do?

"Who goes here?" the first of the redcoats demanded.

"Two weary travelers seeking shelter in the village over the hill," Flora said with a confidence she didn't feel.

The redcoat didn't seem satisfied. "Have you seen anyone suspicious on your travels?"

"No, nothing," Flora said.

"What about your companion? Cat got her tongue?"

The soldier made towards the prince, who had been keeping his head down as much as possible.

"My maid is not well," Flora said. "Which is why we are seeking shelter."

"Maid, is it?" The soldier looked suspicious now. "Strange that, considering as we have heard tell that the Pretender is going about these parts dressed as a maid, along with some chit of a girl."

Flora swallowed hard, wondering what to do next. She glanced at the prince, but the exertions of the morning had taken their toll. He looked exhausted and on the verge of collapse. Weighing up her options, she decided it was time to take control of the situation.

"Well, kind sir, I don't know who you could mean." She simpered slightly, and blushed. "I am no supporter of the Jacobites. God bless King George—he is the true and protestant King of England."

The soldier looked a little uncertain, so Flora pressed home her advantage. "You surely cannot believe that a young girl like me can have spirited the prince away from under the noses of the English army?"

The soldiers looked at one another, less cocky now.

"I did hear rumors that a whole troop of rebels had landed down the coast at Dunrae. It was the talk of the village from whence we have come. If you head straight there, you might reach them before anyone else does. Think what it would be to be known as the two who captured the Pretender!"

"Well thank you, ma'am." The soldier was completely won over, and he and his companion hurried to their horses and rode off down the mountainside.

"Quick, sire," Flora said, "we must hurry to the croft and find the supplies Donald spoke of. We cannot tarry here for long."

They staggered into the croft, and the prince collapsed on the floor. Flora found him some old furs to lie on, and scrabbled around until she found the food Donald had told her would be hidden behind the chimney. She dared not light a fire for fear of drawing attention to them, but she poured the prince some brandy and thrust it to his lips. This made him revive a little and he looked at her and smiled.

"You are my savior, Flora MacDonald," he said, taking her hand and raising it to his lips. The kiss was so gentle she barely felt it, but the sound of wind whispering in the trees filled the room, and made every fiber of her being quiver.

"I merely did my duty, sire," Flora said, in some confusion.

"Ah, Flora, what a queen you would make me!" He gazed at her, and she felt herself melting, every part of her body tingling with desire.

"Your Majesty, I-I—" She stammered, not knowing quite what to say.

"Hush, my bonny, brave lass," he said, and he brushed his lips briefly against her cheek before falling into a deep sleep.

Flora sat up all night, listening for the return of the redcoats. But her ruse must have worked, because they didn't return. Nonetheless, in the morning they would have to change their disguise. There were some rough laborer's clothes lying in the corner, and she put them on. Then, taking the prince's sword, she hacked off her hair. The redcoats thought they were looking for a young girl and her maid. They would not be looking for a laird and his manservant. When the prince awoke, she would tell him to take off the clothes of an Irish servant and wear the plaid and kilt of a highlander. Dismissing the image this conjured up of the prince once more restored to his masculine glory, she sat and waited for the dawn.

"Flora, what has happened to your hair?" the prince's voice roused her from a troubled doze.

"I thought it better if I became a lad, sire," she said. "And I suggest you wear the clothes of a man once more. They will not be looking for two men."

"Ah, Flora, what you have done for me!" The prince leaned over and kissed her again. The effect was electric. Little thrills of desire shot over her body and she blushed once more. She was affianced to Allan McDonald, but oh, how she wanted this prince of hers!

"Your Highness—" she stammered.

"Hush," he said, stroking her face. "Call me Charles. And

as you have shed your curls, let me do the same." He took the sword and cut off the long, fair curls he was known for.

Then retrieving one from the floor, he searched around until he found one of Flora's brown curls. He entwined the two locks together and placed them inside a silver locket he wore around his neck.

"Now you will always be close to my heart, Flora MacDonald," he said.

"We must leave now," Flora said, bustling about and clearing away the evidence of their stay to overcome her confusion. "If Donald was right, there should be a horse in a field over the next ridge. We should take it and ride down to the coast. We dare not tarry here, in case the redcoats come back."

The morning was fair and bright. Having found the horse, they mounted it, Flora in front, the prince holding her firmly from behind. Their closeness thrilled her, but the prince seemed to have withdrawn somewhere into himself. Further kisses didn't seem forthcoming. Flora was disappointed but tried not to show it. He was a prince. He had been brought up in the French court. What would he want with a Scottish lass from the islands?

Flora directed them over the other side of the mountains, towards the beaches that lay to the north of Lachmuirghan. It was there that they had agreed to meet with their boatmen.

She rode with him, thinking how handsome he was in his Scottish plaid. He held her firmly against him, and she could feel the beat of his heart. Did he realize how much her own was pounding to be so close to him? Now that he had left Betty Bourke behind him, he seemed like more of a man again—and what a man! His presence conjured up images of his great-uncle Charles II, rather then the effeminate Stuarts of the past. How Flora longed for him to truly see her as a woman, not the boy she had become in order to keep them both safe.

They arrived at the beach by mid-afternoon. A warm spring sun shone down on them. They were both hot and thirsty from their journey. A fisherman's hut stood empty on the beach, and Flora scanned the horizon for the boatmen. They had said they would be here in two days. But there wasn't a boat in sight. Had they been captured? Or worse still, had they betrayed their prince?

"Who goes there?"

A man appeared from behind the hut.

"Two wanderers who risk safe passage to Skye," Flora said, bold as brass.

"It'll cost you." The fisherman spat on the ground and contemplated them sourly. His breath smelt of whisky, and he looked an evil sort.

"We can pay." Charles tossed a purse of gold coins on the sand.

"Who are you?" The man was suspicious now.

"I had heard tell the fisher folk of Lachmuirghan were more welcoming than this," Flora said. "We are two simple people who will pay for a boat to take us to Skye."

"Where do such simple folk get all that gold?" the man growled. "Are you thieves?"

"No thieves, we," Charles said. "I have a few trifles left to me by my mother. Nothing more. Now will you grant us safe passage to Skye?"

The man picked up the purse and counted out the money. He seemed satisfied.

"You, boy," he said motioning to Flora, "There's a boat over there by the nets, you can use. That should get you to Skye."

Flora followed him to the boat, which was hidden beyond the hut. She bent down to look inside it, when suddenly the fisherman grabbed her from behind.

"Unhand me, immediately!" she cried.

"Not until you tell me who you are," he said, "and who your fine friend is. Though I can make a good guess."

He pressed a knife to her throat, and she trembled with fear. Charles was out of sight behind the hut—would he see her plight?

"What have we here?" her assailant was feeling inside her pockets for money, and in the course of his explorations had discovered her true nature.

"A lassie, are you?" he said. "Then I was right. You're the wee maid who stole the Pretender away from under the redcoats' noses. I know all about you."

"You know nothing about me," Flora said, struggling to get out of his grasp.

"Don't move a muscle."

The Prince, *her* prince, was standing looking every inch a king, his sword poking straight into her assailant's back.

Flora nearly fainted with relief.

"Or you'll do what?" sneered the man.

"Have you arrested for treason. Now kneel before your king, or so help me God, I shall run you through."

Despite her predicament, Flora's pulse raced with desire. Charles *was* the true king of England, and he was doing this for her. Taking advantage of her enemy's distraction. She elbowed the man as hard as she could.

He moaned before collapsing to the ground. "You little—"

Charles' sword was still playing on his back. "Get up, you worm," Charles said. "Now tell us what you know."

"Nothing." The man looked surly. "There were some boatsmen here a few days ago. They told me to look out for you, it was too dangerous for them to stay."

"Did they give you money?"

"Maybe," he spat.

Charles' hand flickered downwards and cut the old leather belt round the man's waist. The belt fell to the ground, along with his trousers.

"Did they give you money not to betray me?" he said again, in stern tones.

"Yes." The reply was sullen.

"Then you shall earn your keep," Charles said. "And I shall take both my coins and your boat. But as I don't trust you to stay silent, I'm afraid you may have to be a little uncomfortable, until we are well away from here."

So saying, he marched the man towards the hut, kicked open the door, and calling to Flora to help him, tied him up with old fishing tackle. They used some wet cloth they found at the bottom of the boat to gag him, and then Charles marched out with a flourish, every inch a king.

Flora followed him—the sight of him striding down the beach, the sun streaming behind him, dazzled her. He was her king, well beyond her reach. She could never have him—she saw that now, yet perversely she had never wanted him more.

She followed him, resolving to put such thoughts aside, when he turned and pulled her roughly towards him.

Suddenly his mouth pressed hard on hers, and his hands were exploring her body, undoing the rough laborer's clothes of a boy to find the soft contours of a woman. He pulled up short.

"Flora, I thought I might lose you," he panted.

"Oh, Your Majesty," she said, "I am so unworthy of you."

"Unworthy?" He held her close to him, pulling her closer still. "Of all my subjects, you are the most worthy, the most brave—and the most beautiful."

Flora blushed and looked into those liquid green eyes. She knew she was lost, absolutely lost. Gently now, he peeled off her clothes layer by layer, his mouth pressed hard against hers in a passionate kiss. All thoughts of decorum and modesty were gone as she drew him to her, guiding his soft lips to her private places. His hands caressed her and his lips touched her breasts, her nipples, her stomach, sending her mad with desire.

Flora caressed his back and let her hands wander over his body in a voyage of discovery. Soon she found what she was looking for and was rewarded with a sigh of pleasure from her royal lover. She caressed his manhood until it grew firm and strong in her hand, while his hands and kisses reached to the base of her belly button and his quick and clever fingers found the place where her desire pooled into little whirls of ecstasy.

Gasping, she pulled him to her, and lay down, a willing victim on the beach while her king and lord took her to the sound of a lapping sea.

"They will sing of our adventures in years to come," Charles said to her softly as the boat gently touched on the shores of Skye.

"Mayhap," said Flora, tears stinging her cheeks. The adventure was over. Here she knew they must part.

"I'll no' forget you, Flora MacDonald," he said, kissing her once more on the mouth, reawakening the desires he had quenched in their passionate union by the shores of Lachmuirghan.

"Perhaps we could tarry a while longer," he said "No one knows we are here and safe."

His hands, experts in her body's secret places, brought her quickly to arousal, but reluctantly she pulled him away.

"Your Majesty, I need to bring you to safety. You must become Betty Bourke once more, and I shall be plain Flora MacDonald. But one day we will meet again in the Palace of St. James."

"Aye, Flora, one day." Charles smiled a sad smile and pulled her roughly to him, kissing her with a passionate intensity she had never felt before. Tears blinded her eyes as he pushed something into her hands, and she stumbled up the path to the home of her friend, Lady MacDonald. Was it her imagination, or did she hear him breathe the words, "*Ah, Flora, my love...*"?

When she got to the path, she turned to wave, and her last sight was of the prince sitting on a log, looking lost and lonely. Her heart yearned to join him, but she knew what she must do, and as she turned back towards the house, she opened her hand and saw what he had placed there. It was the silver locket.

Mary sat bolt upright in bed. She blushed to think of the dream she had had. First it was sex with a sea kelpie, now she imagined she had been rogered by a prince. And yet, her body felt loose and languorous, her whole being tingled with desire, and she could almost still feel hot, soft kisses pressing ever deeper into her very core. She must have been imagining it—it was reading all those letters of Flora MacDonald's that Gavin had given her before bedtime, swearing they were genuine. He had even claimed that Flora allegedly gave birth to Charles' bastard son—but Mary knew that couldn't be true. Soon after the prince fled, Flora was arrested and sent to London. Someone would have surely known.

But the last of the letters, addressed to Flora's mother and sent from Lachmuirghan, had been dated November 1746, and Flora wrote of having news of great import. Perhaps she had ended up going to London later than previously thought—her movements weren't very accurately documented.

No, this was nonsense. There couldn't have been a child. Someone would have known about it. Someone would have *said.*

She got up and looked out of the window. Down the path where in her dream she had seen the redcoats coming, up to the hill where the castle stood guarding the town.

Well, she had to hand it to Lachmuirghan, imagination or not, she would never forget her visits here.

There was a knock on the door.

"Room service," a soft Scottish brogue came from the other side.

Room service? Mary frowned—she hadn't ordered room service.

The door opened before she could reply, and there standing in the doorway was a sight that took her breath away. It was her Charles! Well—there were some differences—the fair curls were tied back in a ponytail and he wore jeans and a T-shirt. But there was the same animal presence and those liquid green eyes to die for.

Mary thought her heart had stopped beating altogether, and then there was a rushing in her ears and a familiar flood of desire rushed through her.

"And you are—?"

"Charlie," he said, with a smile that was heartbreakingly familiar. "Charlie MacDonald—I'm Gavin's son. Oh, and he asked me to give you this. It wasn't with the letters, but it's been in the family for generations."

He handed over an object wrapped in soft tissue. Mary opened it with wonder, and found herself looking at a silver pendant. She opened it, but knew what she was about to find. Contained within the locket were two curls, one brown and one fair, wound together in perfect harmony.

Author's note:

I hope my gentle reader will forgive me for the huge liberties I have taken with Scottish history in pursuit of a good yarn. But then again, this is Lachmuirghan, where anything can happen. Who's to say it isn't true...

☙

The Monolith and The God

By Madeleine Oh

Julia peered though the twilight and the driving rain. Coming here had been a big mistake. So much for a nice weekend in Scotland for a stress-free getaway! She was now lost in the bloody countryside.

The road forked. Decisions, decisions. She took the right hand one, following the single signpost she couldn't read in the blinding rain and, a few miles later, reached the outskirts of a small town.

As the windshield wipers dragged back and forth, Julia longed for a nice pub with warm rooms and a soft bed. As she rounded a curve, there was a pub on the right. Julia turned into the car park and almost crashed her car into an immense standing stone. Swerving around it, she parked and killed the engine. The rain had eased to a steady and miserable drizzle but the lights of the pub were cheerful and welcoming, and that was enough for Julia. She ran for the front door, skirting the standing stone. The painted sign over the door announced she was entering The God in the Valley, and by the wicked leer on his face, the God knew how to have a good time. She stepped straight into a large room with a beamed ceiling and a wide stone fireplace with a crackling fire. A young man sorted knives and forks at a side table. Julia walked up to him. "I'm hoping for a room for the night."

"Of course. Welcome. I didn't expect a visitor on a night like this, but come with me." He led her up wide oak stairs to a large room with an immense, carved bed. The air smelled of lavender and the sheets looked crisp and clean. There was no en suite bathroom but Julia wasn't about get picky. She had antique furniture, a stone fireplace, and was out of the rain. Wherever she was. "I found this place by accident," she said. "Where exactly am I?"

"No accident," he said, shaking his head, a light gleaming in his dark eyes. "If you found The God, you were intended. You're in Lachmuirghan. I'm Angus Wallace." He held out his hand. "Welcome to The God in the Valley."

His handshake was firm and his hand dry. A very nice hand, actually, and the rest of him wasn't half bad either. In fact, "bedworthy" might be a good description for Angus Wallace. *Whoa*!

"Any chance of dinner? I don't need a lot. Just something warm."

"I've some cock-a-leekie soup on the stove. I'll bring you up a dish in a while. Anything else you want?"

You seemed a bit presumptuous. "A nice pot of tea?" was a lot better, much less like a sex fiend. She wasn't sure what was getting into her, but Angus was certainly getting to her.

"I'll bring it up in a wee while. There's plenty of hot water if you want to get out of your wet clothes."

Angus headed down the stairs and Julia gathered up towels and soap and took herself to the bathroom. The bath was enormous, the water was hot, the towels large and the soap deliciously scented with herbs. She soaked in the warm water and washed away the worries of the last few weeks. The thick towels smelled of sunshine and fresh air, and Julia slathered her body with the scented lotion provided. This might be the back of beyond, but they understood comforts for travelers.

Pulling on jeans and a sweatshirt over her still-damp skin, Julia made a turban of one of the smaller towels and padded barefoot back to her room.

Minutes later Angus reappeared with a laden tray. A small tureen held the so-called cock-a-leekie soup that wafted savory aromas when Julia lifted the lid. Beside it was a plate of thick slices of buttered crusty bread, a chunk of cheese and a pot of tea.

Angus stayed long enough to light the fire in the fireplace, wished Julia a good night and left.

She rather missed him, but asking him to stay and keep her company would be a bit much. And a bit forward.

Besides, she had a crackling fire, warm soup and hot tea. Three cups of tea and a good supper later, Julia stretched out by the fire and watched the flames play over the sweet-smelling logs. Were they fruit trees of some sort that they gave of such an aroma? Magical, mythical trees that scented the air and her dreams?

Yeah! Right!

Julia watched until the fire died down. Then pulled on flannel pajamas, fished her book out of her bag and took herself to bed to read and listen to the rain on the window panes. Cuddling up with Angus would make a perfect evening, but she was not about to call him upstairs and tell him so.

She'd settle for a good read. Okay, a rather naughty read, but it was the best sex she could manage solo.

The storm strengthened with renewed force, smashing hard against the building as great gusts of wind tore at the outside walls. A clap of thunder vibrated off the windows, followed fast by a flash of lightning...and the lights went out.

Great! She'd hold her breath and count to ten for the lights to come on again. They didn't. Not even for fifty. There was just enough light from the dying fire to see but nowhere near enough to read by. She needed a flashlight. Damn, she had one. In the car. That wasn't stopping her. The house had gone quiet. With no one about, she'd slip out and back without any trouble. Julia stepped into her shoes and pulled on her raincoat over her pajamas.

Downstairs, Angus was nowhere to be seen. Julia opened the heavy door and stepped out.

Big mistake. Water bucketed down from the sky. The path to the car park resembled a small stream and she could barely see her car. Julia splashed down the path and squelched over the gravel. As she opened the passenger door, the rain came down even heavier.

She shoved the flashlight in her pocket. The rain slashed into her face, running down her neck and stinging her legs. She should have stayed dry and warm and put up with the dark. Pulling her raincoat over her head, she ran, barely able to see her way though the driving rain. A misstep on loose gravel pitched her forward. Reaching out to save herself, Julia slammed into the monolith. Wrong direction entirely.

Or was it?

The bulk of the stone protected Julia from the wind and the worst of the rain. Another loud clap of thunder and almost simultaneous lightning had Julia pressing closer for the shelter the vast stone offered. She had no idea how long she clung to the monolith. Her body throbbed with the cadence of the storm as a wildness streaked though her. She cupped her own breasts. Her nipples were hard with cold and her flesh soaking with desire. She was in a bad way. And liable to die of pneumonia if she didn't get inside. Fast.

Gathering her useless raincoat around her, Julia splashed back to the inn. Her feet were cold and wet—at some point she'd lost her shoes in the rain—but a wild heat flowed in her veins, her hands still tingled, her nipples throbbed hard under the damp flannel, and wetness ran between her legs.

The door stood half-open.

Angus stood in the doorway.

"The God called you," he said. "Come on back in."

She had no idea what exactly he meant by that, but the "come on back in" sounded like a very good idea.

Except Angus was bare chested and barefoot, wearing only jeans that he'd obviously just pulled on. The waistband was still unbuttoned.

Julia was doubly, triply, aware of the wet flannel plastered against her breasts and legs and the sodden raincoat flapping round her ankles. Didn't seem to bother Angus.

"Coming with me?" he said.

Why not? This whole place had a touch of unreality about it.

Julia smiled and held out her hand.

Angus pulled her inside and closed and barred the great oak door. And turned to smile.

Was it the close warmth of the inn or the heat in her body that spiked her need?

"Okay, Angus," Julia said, heading up the wide staircase, Angus's footsteps heavy on the broad steps behind her. Her bedroom door stood open. Someone—Angus?—had built the fire up to a roaring blaze, a row of candles burned on the mantelpiece and four more flickered, one on each post of the bed.

Angus closed the door with a soft thud. He stepped close.

She rested the flat of her hand on his chest. Feeling firm muscle under the skin, Julia looked him in the eye and parted her lips.

He lowered his mouth.

Slowly.

His lips were warm and male and opened hers with a promise of sweet fire. Wet heat roared between her legs as his tongue swept hers. He pulled off the raincoat and her soaking pajamas. Then took one of her discarded towels and rubbed her down, kneeling at her feet to dry her wet legs, and then standing to run his hands over her breasts.

Yes, they both had the same idea!

His arms closed round her shoulders in a fierce grasp. Her breasts flattened against his chest, his thigh eased between hers, his erection pressing against her belly. He was more than ready. She wasn't. Not yet.

"Just a minute," she said. His breath caught as her fingers rubbed his nipples to stiff points. She ran her tongue over his left nipple, sensing his need and relishing her power. She moved back as he gave a little gasp.

He was watching her with glinting eyes, his broad chest rising and falling with each slow breath. "All right," Julia said, watching as Angus unzipped his jeans and stepped out of them.

He'd gone commando.

His cock was magnificent, jutting at her from its nest of dark hair, and was hers for the having.

She skimmed her fingertips over the erect flesh and circled him with her hand. He gasped as she moved up and down, easing back his foreskin to reveal the dark head of his cock. She squeezed.

Angus shuddered. A glistening bead of moisture gathered on his cock. He'd have stepped back, she was certain, but she had him hard in her hand. She stroked the head of his cock with her thumb, spreading his moisture, fascinated by the tender end of his erect cock and how his foreskin moved at her touch.

His fingers were rough but gentle. He caressed the full undersides of her breasts with cupped hands, slowly eased his thumbs over the swell of her breasts until he caught her nipples between thumbs and index fingers and tugged. He rubbed her areolas until the little nubs around them stiffened and she shivered with desire.

His hands eased down her belly as he knelt before her. She smiled. Heck, she grinned, as Angus gazed at her pussy as if she were the wonder of creation.

Warm air brushed across her pussy, ruffling her curls like a quickening breeze. His fingers opened her. Wide. His breath came closer as the flat of his tongue lapped her. She whimpered as his arms closed around her thighs and a gust of rain hit the windowpanes. If the glass had caved in, she'd never have noticed. Angus was devouring her with slow perfection. He covered her with his lips as his tongue narrowed and played her clit, flicking and teasing until she moaned with need. He paused and she grabbed his head to hold it to her. He could not stop. Not now. She would not permit it.

But he'd only paused to slide one hand from her thigh. The other held her as firmly as ever. His mouth continued its slow caress as he pressed one, then two, fingers inside her cunt. He played her, his fingers pulsing a beat that matched the thrust of his tongue.

She was lost. She was found. She was all and everything she'd ever longed for as a lover knelt in homage at her pussy. His fingers, slick with her arousal, smoothed her ass as his tongue drew her towards climax. Need blazed deep in her belly. She cried aloud as his fingers curved deep and his mouth worked her faster. He was merciless. He was magnificent. He was all. She clutched his head, thrusting her hips into his face, reaching for her coming climax. Her shouts increased as her need climbed. Until she came in a wild crescendo of joy and release that had her screaming aloud as her legs buckled.

Angus held her firm. Steadying her as his mouth fluttered little kisses up her belly. It was almost too much. She would never have enough.

He gathered her up in his arms as easily as if she were a lightweight. His mouth, wet and warm with her juices, met hers. A slow kiss, gentle as a whisper, that sent her body wild. Nothing could satisfy her but his magnificent cock deep inside. He grinned with knowing pride and male arrogance as he sat her on the bed and turned her onto all fours.

He stroked her ass, smoothing up her back as he dropped soft kisses up her spine to her neck. The mattress shifted under his weight as the power of his erection pushed between her legs. He grasped her shoulders. He was hard against her, pressing to meet her need. His hips rocked. His cock slid through her wetness. Julia cried out as he thrust. She was tighter than she'd expected and Angus filled her, stretched her and possessed her. Driving with grunts and animal need, pressing into her soul with his male heat. Pumping her, taking her, possessing her, giving all a man could. They melded in a need that took them both higher and harder through his grunts and her cries until, with a relentless thrust, he drove deep as she screamed aloud her triumph and he poured his jism into her heat.

She collapsed, his weight pressing her into the mattress, his cock embedded in her cunt, her mind drunk with joy and life, and her heart racing at one with the storm outside.

Through a haze of grogginess, Julia felt his weight ease off her. Angus shifted her so her head rested on the pillow. Lips pressed on her forehead, arms held her close and she passed from frenzy to satiated rest.

She woke to electric light blazing overhead. Damn! The power outage. She'd left the lights on. Padding across the room to flick out the switch, she realized she was naked, her night clothes lay in a crumpled heap in front of the last dying embers and she was wet halfway down her thighs.

She had just fucked a total stranger!

So what? It had been stupendous and her body still vibrated with the memory of Angus's tongue on her skin and his cock planted deep. She curled up between sheets that smelled of sex.

Bright morning sunshine awoke her later. Time to be on her way. She'd have to face Angus over breakfast but so what? He'd fucked a total stranger too. Her shoes waited, cleaned and polished outside her door, and breakfast was set at a lone table by a window downstairs.

Julia didn't usually have porridge, kippers, toast and buttered oatcakes for breakfast. But she was hungry. She must have burned up a million calories last night.

Angus carried her luggage out to her car. He seemed not the slightest embarrassed. She wouldn't be either.

"Thank you," she said, as he put her suitcase in the boot. "For everything."

He smiled. "You came because The God called you," he said. "You'll be back."

Julia hoped so.

ര

Hali's Rescue

By Isabo Kelly

"You need to get laid."

Hali Lukos dragged her gaze away from Dr. Julian McManus's retreating back—such a lovely broad back with such a nice firm butt displayed so well in his dress slacks—and scowled at her co-worker. "What the hell are you talking about?"

"You've been staring after that man's ass for six months now," Lydia said. "Have you gone out with anyone else since he started working here? Have you had one orgasm in the last six months that wasn't self-induced?"

"What does that have to do with anything?"

"You need to get laid. You need to relax. And you need to stop swooning over a man who doesn't know you exist. As far as he's concerned, you're a security guard, a uniform like any of a dozen other uniforms in this building."

Hali winced at the accuracy of Lydia's comment. They worked for one of the largest research and development conglomerates in the Consortium of Planets. Stationed on Earth, in London England, it was one of the most prestigious jobs you could get in private security. She'd worked her way out of poor gentility on a backwater planet to second-in-command of the day shift, making an excellent salary. She had succeeded beyond her own expectations in her chosen career.

But compared to the prestige and success of the scientists working for Roen Waters, Inc., she might as well have been an Andylican flutter bug. Hali looked at the console in front of her and groaned. Lydia was right. She'd been pining after a man she'd exchanged exactly ten words with. And while they'd been good words, words that let her know what a decent and sexy man he was, she obviously hadn't left enough of an impression for him to notice her a second time.

"I'm sorry, sweetie," Lydia said, patting her arm. "What you need is some good, hard sex to get over him."

"I can't afford to have a one night stand in this city," she said with a tired sigh. "I let a stranger pick me up in a bar, he could be anyone. You know how they are about corporate espionage at Roen Waters. I'd be sacked in a matter of hours."

"So get out of the city. You've earned a holiday. Put in for a couple of days off and go somewhere else."

"And where exactly would I go to avoid any hint of

impropriety?" She shook her head. "There are spies on and off planet, Lydia. There's nowhere I could go for casual sex without coming under suspicion." And that sucked most of all. Because Lydia was right. Hali needed to get laid. She needed a good hard fuck to get her mind off Dr. Julian McManus and her ever more elaborate daydreams. Maybe if she could find another man who got her as hot and bothered as the doctor, she could get past the idea that she felt more for Julian than just lust.

If she couldn't, she was in deep trouble.

"I have an idea." Lydia smiled, a particularly lascivious grin, and scanned the huge, marble-covered entryway they manned. "You've heard of Tantalizing Time Travels?"

"The company that'll send you back in time for a small fortune? I've heard of them. They are way out of my price range."

"I'm fucking one of the booking agents. He'll give you a really good deal. There's this place, in twentieth century Scotland, that you just have to go." She squeezed Hali's arm again. "People swear by this village. It's supposed to be gorgeous and quaint. And you're guaranteed to leave more relaxed than you arrived."

Hali raised an eyebrow at Lydia's wicked grin.

"Trust me. All of Kyle's women travelers swear by this place."

"I can only get three or four days off, though. This time of year..."

"That's all you'll need. And there is no way the paranoid heads can claim you were in cahoots with a spy. Roen Waters didn't even exist in the twentieth."

"It's safe?"

"Absolutely! Kyle sends hundreds of people to different time periods every year. They guarantee the stability of the wormholes."

Hali sucked in a breath. This did sound like a good option. But... "How the hell am I going to meet some random man I'll be attracted to in a small Scottish village? They're rare enough finds in the sprawl of modern London."

"Oh, sweetie, you are not going to have to worry about that."

"You sound like you're speaking from experience?"

Lydia winked. "Trust me," she said again. "You'll have fun."

Well, she'd always wanted to try one of the time travel holidays that were all the rage this decade. Once the scientists had learned how to stabilize a dozen or so wormholes to specific periods in time, entrepreneurs had seized the opportunity to promote a healthy tourist trade. She wasn't sure how they worked, or how they kept from creating time paradoxes, but she didn't particularly care. Not if the trip gave her a chance for some release. "Okay. Put in a call to Kyle. At the very least, I'll have a few quiet days' rest."

As Hali sat in the pub commons on her last night in Lachmuirghan, listening to a bunch of rowdy lads singing pro-Scotland, anti-English songs, she decided The Royal Rescue, and all of Lachmuirghan, had proved to be far more than she ever expected. Her room upstairs, the only room the proprietor let to travelers, was large and clean, and she had a brilliant view of the loch, the castle and the standing stones at the head of the valley. Actual standing stones!

She could hardly believe she was here. Twentieth century Scotland. It was so beautiful and quaint. The people had all been lovely so far, friendly and welcoming. The weather was cool and crisp but blessedly dry. The last two trips she'd made to Scotland, it had rained the entire time. Granted that was during the early winter and not spring. And four hundred years in the future. But she was still grateful for the clear weather.

There was only one disappointment. She had yet to find a candidate for a naughty night of sex.

Oh, there were several handsome men walking around the place. A couple of the lads singing now were cute and sexy. A few years ago, she'd have been happy to take one of them to her bed. Hell, even seven months ago, she probably would have taken one of them to bed. But now, not one man in the entire village caught her attention or made her heart thump and her thighs clench the way Julian McManus did.

She was losing hope that anyone ever would again. Which was more depressing than she cared to think about. Instead, she was determined to enjoy her last evening here, drinking good Scottish ale and listening to the sing-along. And she would go home tomorrow relaxed and content. Even if she didn't get the Lydia-prescribed night of debauchery and orgasms.

She grinned as two of the singing men stood, pints in one hand and their free arms draped on each other's shoulders as they sang something particularly patriotic. She didn't recognize the song, but almost every person in the pub came in on the chorus. Delighted, she applauded their efforts with everyone else, then looked at her empty glass. One more pint wouldn't hurt. After all, this was her last night.

She was just turning to find the waiter, when a voice from behind her shoulder said, "Will you have another pint?"

She glanced back to see the impossible. Julian McManus, standing in The Royal Rescue, grinning down at her.

Hali's mouth dropped open. The broad-shouldered, dark-haired, dark-eyed man couldn't possibly be Julian. But this man, whoever he was, was a dead ringer. From the slightly long cut of his thick hair, to the tightly muscled body, to the shape of his firm mouth. Even the slight tilt of his eyes reminded her of Julian's. For a moment, she had the crazy thought that maybe he was on holiday here too. That the Julian McManus she knew from Roen Waters had taken time off and come to the same holiday destination she had.

But that was impossible. Tantalizing Time Travels never sent separate parties to the same location. There was too much chance of an accident.

Maybe this man was an ancestor?

Whether he was or not, he had the same immediate effect on Hali's hormones. Her entire body started to vibrate with need, just looking at him.

She could picture removing the dress shirt he wore one button at a time and dragging the snug worn jeans over his lean hips.

She blinked and realized she hadn't answered his question yet. "Are you going to join me?" she asked, feeling brazen because she was four hundred years older than him.

"I was hoping you'd ask." His voice was thick with Scotland, unlike Julian's flatter accent, but the deep tone was similar.

When he sat down across from her with his fresh pint, she was struck yet again by the similarity to the man she'd been pining after for six months. Although, now that she could study him more closely, there were a few small differences between this man and Julian. The small scar cutting a pale white line along his forehead, just above his left eye. The bump on his nose that looked like it came from a break. The lines crinkling the corners of his dark eyes when he smiled. Each little detail, when taken as a whole, only added to the man's appeal. She was staring at her idea of masculine perfection, and she didn't even know his name yet.

"I'm Hali. Hali Lukos." She gave her real name just in case. She was confident enough that this man wasn't the Julian McManus she knew. That would be impossible. But just in case...

"Christopher," he offered.

She waited for a last name. And when she didn't get it, she shrugged. She wasn't sticking around this village long enough to need his last name. What she did need was to get him up to her room. She wanted him so much, so intensely, she was already wet.

A part of her realized sleeping with Christopher wouldn't help her get over Julian. In fact, it might make her obsession worse. But she was in a place, in a time that was so far removed from her reality, she might as well be living a fantasy. And if she was going to live a fantasy, she was going to live it to its fullest.

"You're leaving tomorrow?" Christopher asked.

Hali raised a brow. "How did you know that?"

"I've seen you in the village. I asked. Not a long stay, was it?"

"I couldn't get much time off work."

"Shame you won't be here a few more days."

"I'm still here tonight."

He smiled, a slow, wicked lifting of the lips that made her pulse pound. They talked while they emptied their pints, inching nearer with each passing minute, until they were leaning so close together, their foreheads almost touched. The main topics of conversation were the village, her sightseeing, the legends. She didn't ask anything personal. Neither did he.

And when she set down her empty glass, he took her hand, lifted her to her feet and walked her to the back stairs leading up to the only room in the pub. Her room.

Her face heated. The commons had grown quieter while they talked. There were only a couple of people left. But those last few patrons would no doubt know where she and Christopher were going. She'd never asked if he was from Lachmuirghan. But she got the impression he was a local. And that meant the others in the commons no doubt knew him. They would know she and Christopher had just met.

She took a deep breath and reminded herself that she wasn't in her own time. She didn't have to worry about gossip. She didn't have to worry about what other people thought of her at all. She was four hundred years older than the oldest old fart in the room. If she wanted to fuck a virtual stranger, who was here to judge? No one she knew or would ever see again. She wouldn't even see Christopher again after tonight—except in his similarities to Julian.

This was her night and her holiday. She would not be embarrassed, she decided as she opened the door to her room.

A fire crackled on sweet-smelling logs in the fireplace, giving the room a cozy glow. The proprietor made sure her fire was built up every evening, and she was grateful for his thoughtfulness. Despite the time of year, the nights were cold. The warmth of the room made her sigh in pleasure.

Christopher's hands moved to her shoulders, pulling her back against the solid wall of his chest. Without a word, he turned her to face him, lowered his mouth slowly to hers and kissed her. His lips were gentle and firm, testing. Teasing. She leaned close, gripped his shirt in her hands and fell into his kiss.

"I've been wanting to do that all evening," he murmured

against her mouth. "Actually, I've wanted to do that since I first saw you."

"Why did you wait?"

He smiled. "I had to be sure."

"Of what?" She frowned a little. If he was worried about her attraction to him, he needn't have bothered. She was nearly panting with desire. Her body pulsed. The feel of his muscled arms wrapped around her waist made her nerves hum. She could barely stand the clothing that stood between them. His erection was a hard promise against her lower belly. And her panties were already soaked in her own juices. Attraction was not an issue.

Instead of answering her question, he kissed her again. This time, his mouth was hard and demanding, his tongue plunging between her lips, no longer teasing and tentative. She groaned and started unbuttoning his shirt.

Clothes came off in a flurry of motion until she was finally, gratefully, skin to skin with him. She pressed close, flattening her breasts against his chest and reveling in the feel of his crisp hair on her peaked nipples. Unable to resist, she pushed him back a step and studied his naked body. Hard, rounded shoulders, a flat stomach and the most beautiful, thick cock rising from dark curls.

Licking her lips, she took his erection in her hand, caressing slowly as she studied the shape and feel of him. She cupped his balls as she stroked and his stomach muscles bunched in reaction. *Magnificent* was her only thought. He was magnificent. Better than she could have hoped. And she had to taste him. Dropping to her knees on the rug in front of the fire, she slipped the very tip of his cock between her lips. He groaned and dug his fingers into her hair. Smiling, she slid the full length of him into her mouth. He wasn't long, but he was thick.

The scent of him filled her nostrils as she sucked his cock, flicking her tongue under the hood before taking him fully into her mouth again. She played and tasted and teased until the fingers in her hair clenched tight, and he pulled her away.

"My turn," he said. He followed her down onto the rug and his lips closed over her nipple.

Hali arched up against his mouth. Her nipples were almost painfully sensitive. Each lap of his tongue set her nerves screaming and pulled a line of tension tight between her breasts and her pussy. As he kissed and nipped down her belly, he paused at her navel and tongued the small diamond she had there.

"This is very sexy," he murmured. "I wouldn't have guessed you'd have a piercing here."

"My little secret." She gasped as his lips moved lower, kissing her lower abdomen just above her curls. Then his mouth closed over her aching heat, and she could only moan.

He played her body well. His tongue teased her clit relentlessly, driving her to the brink of orgasm one moment only to move away the next, leaving her wanting and desperate. He licked up her slit, nibbled the skin of her inner thigh, and returned to torment her clit further. He continued this torture until she thought she might scream. Then he settled his mouth over her pulsing flesh and sucked hard, rolling her clit between his tongue and the backs of his front teeth. Her hips bucked. She clenched the rug tight and pressed her shoulders against the floor as her spine arched upward. Just as she felt her climax starting, he plunged two fingers into her pussy. She screamed, coming so hard she saw spots.

She was still panting and shuddering from the strength of her orgasm by the time he worked his way up her body. He kissed her jaw, her neck, then covered her lips with his and she tasted herself in his mouth. Framing his face with her hands, her senses swam in a moment of unreality. She could have been looking at Julian. And yet, she knew this wasn't the same man, couldn't be the same man from her time.

Then he plunged into her and her ability to think splintered under the perfection of his thick cock filling her completely.

"You're so tight," he murmured in her hair. "You feel so good."

His groan made her heart flip. The sound of his voice, so quiet and deep, sent another sharp jab of shock through her. His accent seemed thicker, and yet he sounded even more like the Julian of her dreams. How was that possible? Two men, in two different times, yet so much alike.

The crackling of the fire joined with the sound of their bodies moving together. His musky scent mingled with the sweet smell of burning logs. And every part of her body vibrated with fulfillment and want. She needed more from him, all of him, pounding deep inside her.

Wrapping her legs around his waist, she tilted her pelvis to take him deeper, urging him faster as he thrust hard into her. In the moments before her orgasm tore through her, time stopped. The face of the man above her blurred and blended. And she looked into the eyes of Julian McManus. She felt his cock pulse inside her, watched his dark eyes lose focus and his neck muscles strain. And then her own orgasm took her, forcing her eyes shut against the intensity of feeling rushing through her.

After, as she savored the weight of him pushing her into the rug, she tried to remember if she'd called Julian's name aloud or in her mind. When Christopher raised his head, he was smiling. He kissed her and then hugged her tight, a gesture so intimate her breath hitched. She couldn't have called

Julian's name aloud. No man would treat a woman so tenderly if she'd screamed another man's name during her orgasm.

The fact that this virtual stranger held her so lovingly made her head spin. She felt like she was living a fantasy. A fantasy she didn't want to wake from.

After a quiet bit of time before the fire, Christopher carried her to the huge bed and to her delight, fucked her again, thoroughly. She drifted off to sleep sated, content and more relaxed than she'd been in months. Lydia had been right. And Hali was sure she'd never hear the end of it after she got home.

Her return through the wormhole was uneventful. Christopher was gone when she woke on that final morning, but she wasn't upset by his absence. In fact, it added to the unreality of the night before, leaving her wondering if she'd really dreamed the spectacular evening. But her body ached in interesting places that hadn't been used in months, so she was pretty sure Christopher and her night of sex and satisfaction had been real. She spent her first day back at work smiling a lot. Something Lydia took every opportunity to point out and take vicarious credit for.

On her second day back, as she was doing a security round through the building, Hali came face to face with Dr. Julian McManus just outside his office. It was the first time she'd seen him since coming back from her holiday. Her breath caught and reality blurred for just an instant. She was looking at the man she'd spent a sweaty, erotic, magnificent night with just two days—and four hundred years—ago. Without realizing it, she grinned at Julian. Then the fact that he was not the same man she'd been in bed with hit her, and she swallowed her grin. Unfortunately, too late to escape his notice.

He stopped in front of her and tilted his head to one side. "Good morning, Hali. How was your holiday?"

For a full thirty seconds, she was too surprised to answer. Then she blurted, "Great. I...I went to Scotland. How did you...?"

"I love Scotland. I'm from there originally," he said, smiling.

And when he smiled, she realized his nose looked a little crooked, as if it had been broken. She'd never noticed that before. There were crinkles at the corners of his eyes too. She looked closer. On his forehead, just above his left eye, was the thin white line of a scar. She sucked in a sharp breath and met Julian's gaze again. She'd never had a chance to study him so closely. She'd never noticed the scar. Or the bump on his nose. And as he spoke of Scotland, his accent deepened.

Her heart thumping, she said, "I have a real fondness for the country now, too. I was in a village called Lachmuirghan."

He nodded, and something in his eyes danced with knowledge he shouldn't have had.

"I know the place," he said. "Beautiful. Very...relaxing."

She felt her mouth drop open and closed it with a snap. Her imagination must be working overtime, because he couldn't possibly be implying what she thought he was implying.

"Yes," she choked out around a dry throat. "It was very relaxing." She met his gaze and said, "Very satisfying." When his grin flashed again, her knees nearly gave out.

"I'm glad to hear that." He turned toward his office door, but stopped with his hand over the locking panel. "Hali, what are you doing after work?"

"Nothing much."

"Would you like to have a drink with me? I know this brilliant pub, not far from here. They serve the best Scottish ale outside of Scotland."

"I'd love to," she breathed, not quite believing her current reality.

"I'll meet you after your shift is finished, then."

She nodded, too stunned to talk. The man had exchanged exactly ten words with her before this moment. Now, he was asking her out after she'd slept with his look-alike four hundred years in the past? Something very strange was happening.

As he opened his office, she glanced at the nameplate on the door. Her heartbeat thudded, and she stopped breathing. Then, swallowing hard, she said, "I didn't know your middle initial was C. What does it stand for?"

She knew, though, even before he turned and flashed her that wicked grin. A grin she knew now was familiar because she'd seen it a lot two nights—and four hundred years—ago.

"The C is for Christopher."

Two:
Loch Larg, the River and the Beach

Lachmuirghan is blessed, so the villagers boast, by a warmer climate and more fertile surroundings than one might expect this far north. According to local legend, millennia ago a sea god made the valley for the human woman he loved. But cruel fate intervened, and she drowned in the river. The god wept for five years, flooding the valley, and then left, never to return. But some say the magic remains...

Another local myth tells of a sea kelpie which appeared to unwary strangers as a magnificent black stallion wearing a bridle of gold. Anyone foolish enough to mount the horse would find himself unceremoniously tipped in the water or worse, taken for a wild ride out to sea, and never heard of again. Local legend has it that the sea kelpie of Lachmuirghan fell in love with the daughter of the local laird, but when she became pregnant, her father stabbed her to death on the standing stones that sit high on the cliffs above the village, while the kelpie keened his wild lament below.

Of course these are just legends which help boost the tourist trade, but there is a strange anomaly in the waters round Lachmuirghan, which has puzzled geologists for years. The loch itself is slightly saline and yet the river leading off it is freshwater. And whether or not you believe the myths, there is something odd about the way the river snakes down to the sea. And when the sea mists come rolling in, if you are of a fanciful bent, you can picture the sea god out there somewhere, still lamenting his lost love. Or the screeching of the seagulls can bring to mind the sorrow of the sea kelpie. But these are merely stories; old wives tales to be told round a fire on a winter's evening.

Strange, though, that walking along the beach, you sometimes detect a sound on the wind like the whinny of a horse, or catch a glimpse of a black stallion pounding along the beach. And hear the wild keening of a man mourning his lost love...

☙

Eileen's Tale

By Maristella Kent

Eileen bent her head beneath the force of the shower and massaged the nape of her neck. Not for the first time she cursed the ancestors who had passed on the tight brunette corkscrews she was trying to condition. As her fingers worked at her scalp, she felt a forgotten tingle of awakening. Striving to ignore it, she maneuvered to wash out the last of the lotion, but the throbbing was as insistent as the pulse of the showerhead.

Half-smiling, she picked up the shower gel and lathered it over her breasts. Her nipples peaked as the stream of water washed off the foam. And the tingling intensified.

She gave in to the sensation and, cupping her hand, delivered another squirt of gel. This measure was destined for the darker curls around her sex.

It was bliss to know that Padraic would not be walking in on her. Her life was her own again. Her fantasies took over as she smoothed the gel into the delicate skin and foamed it in the surrounding hair. She imagined the fingers were those of a sensitive lover, one who had her interests at heart, one who would not cease until she had extracted all the pleasure she could from his actions.

She swirled one finger over the plump pad of skin above her clit, and then soaped her inner thighs and lips. How sensitive her skin felt, how satin smooth contrasted with the roughness of her hair.

There was no hurry, but there was an urgency.

Her body, long denied this sort of attention, craved for release. Unable to resist any longer, she leaned against the shower cubicle wall and gave her body up to the pounding water jet. As she approached her orgasm she imagined her fantasy man was with her, on his knees, worshipping her sex with his clever mouth, murmuring his devotion as he kissed and nipped at her. She added her fingers to the recipe and within seconds she was spiraling out of conscious control to a climax that left her all but screaming her fulfillment. And it seemed to her that she screamed out her fantasy lover's name as she came.

Later, wrapped in a warm, fluffy towel, she tried to recall the name she had cried, but was defeated. It certainly wasn't Padraic—the double-crossing cheat! Perhaps she really was over him.

She looked around her bedroom, sighed, and decided to leave the tidying up for tomorrow. Her suitcase was packed, and her backpack—the one she would be carrying throughout the trip—only needed the addition of a book and perhaps a bar of dark chocolate. On impulse, she searched the wardrobe for her pure silk nightdress. She would take it on the trip, and she would wear it in bed tonight. Tonight she was going to pamper herself. Tonight she was going to relax in those smooth linen sheets and sleep in utter contentment.

It felt odd to be on a journey like this on her own. In her childhood, her father had taken her walking many times. In young adulthood there had been a whole pack of teenagers camping out as they tackled the local hills and peaks. And recently, there had always been a close companion—sometimes a good female friend, sometimes a lover.

She looked around at the group. The tall, silent man, Adam, was a distance away, looking outwards at the loch, demanding solitude. The group of three middle-aged ladies—childhood friends, they had told her—were chattering with excitement about the castle visible on the hillside. The American, Caleb, had offered his help with the engine, but was now surrounded by the group of teenage girls. He looked up at her from time to time with a wry smile but she was in no mood to rescue him—not yet, anyway.

The couple in their thirties, Corinne and Dave, were holding tools while the coach driver, Ben, struggled to fix the engine. He had stripped off his jacket and shirt in the strong sunlight and was attacking the problem in his T-shirt. His muscled torso promised much.

Eileen wondered if any of the three men were actively seeking a partner. She was attracted to the self-confident and amusing Caleb, though there would not be much challenge in seducing him if those looks he kept giving her were anything to go by. Ben would no doubt prove an ardent lover, though he seemed shy and uncertain in the company of women. When the teenage girls had teased him earlier, he had flushed poppy red.

Adam was the one she found most attractive. But that might be because he seemed so remote. When addressed, he was perfectly polite but offered nothing more than the briefest of responses to the enquirer. She smiled to think what he might be like when his defenses were down. He was broodingly, darkly, stunningly attractive.

From the hillside she heard the sound of a distant hunting horn. Startled, she turned round hoping to see the hunter, but there was no sign of a hunting party. The sound came again, and this time it was nearer. But her companions gave no sign that they had heard the call. As she looked up into the heather, still luxuriant though autumn was in the air, she saw a magnificent stag looking down at them.

"Look!" she cried, tugging at the sleeve of the nearest of the three women, but when she turned again, the stag was gone.

The woman looked at her, bemused.

"I thought I saw a stag," she murmured, embarrassed, and though they all gazed upwards, the animal had gone.

She returned to her seat on the coach and grabbed her walking boots. The elderly couple sitting halfway back looked up briefly from studying their maps and smiled at her.

There hadn't been a planned walk before lunch, but the breakdown had changed all that. Though Ben had rung for an engineer, they had been unable to promise help immediately. Eileen was in summery clothing, having dressed with no thought but for comfort on such a hot day. Though she had walking shorts with her, she was reluctant to take the time to change. She wasn't planning to go far, after all, but a restlessness had overtaken her and she was desperate to walk into the lower hills surrounding the beautiful loch. She'd take her camera and a water bottle, and her fleece top in case it was colder higher up, but nothing more.

When she left the coach she realized she ought to say what her plans were, but she was reluctant to break in on any of the groups. Everyone was chatting. Everyone except Adam. Eileen walked over and touched his arm. He seemed startled, though he insisted it was nothing when she apologized. He was gripped, it seemed to her, by a deep weariness and sadness.

She explained her plans, and that she intended to be back within the hour. He said nothing, just looked at her.

"I need to get away from the group. Just for a short while," she told him.

Then he nodded. He held her glance but did not speak. After a second or two, as if satisfied by what he saw, he nodded again, as if he was giving her permission.

Strangely shaken, Eileen turned away and walked to a track through the heather leading up the hillside.

The track had been made by an animal rather more sure-footed than she was, and several times she stumbled before she found her rhythm and strode more comfortably up the hill. Bees buzzed between the heather flowers and the air was redolent with the unmistakable scent of late summer. The sun on her skin felt wonderful.

She reached the top of her hill and paused. There were bigger peaks beyond, inviting her to proceed, but she did not want to be tempted into missing her self-imposed deadline. Instead she spread her fleece on a corner of a small rock outcrop and settled herself. She untied her boots and took off the thick hiking socks, wriggling her toes with pleasure in the sunlight. Taking a drink from her water bottle, she wiped her mouth on the back of her hand and surveyed the stunning view of the loch. Although she knew her coach party was down there, they were out of sight, hidden by the undulations of the territory. In the distance were the lilac hills on the far side of the water. How peaceful it seemed now, but she imagined she felt the deep vibrations of a turbulent history. The castle far away to her left gave the lie to the sense of eternal stillness.

She lifted her camera and took some photographs. She smiled as she put the camera down and lay back on the fleece. This was a time for making memories.

Suddenly her body was fully alert. No sound had disturbed her, but she sat up, peering out towards the loch. And then from behind her, above her left ear, came a deep male voice.

"Don't worry, I mean you no harm."

He was standing there, behind her. Some stranger who had managed to creep up silently. Resisting the impulse to leap up and run, especially in a place that she did not know but this man might, she stared out onto the water and pretended indifference.

"I can defend myself."

He laughed, but it was a sound without malice and she felt her instincts relax their guard. Just a little.

"It's a fine view," she offered.

"That it is."

She tried to place his accent, but it was not one she knew. Her subconscious was responding to the mellow timbre of the tone. She leant back a little and her shoulder bumped into a solid wall of male chest. He responded immediately by steadying her with his hands. Before she could jump up, he spoke.

"Share just a few minutes with a fellow traveler. There's enough room for us both on your rock."

She wanted to turn to look at him, but his grip was so soothing, so persuasive, that she hesitated to break the contact. And there was a thrill in not knowing what he looked like.

Eileen tried to put a picture in her head to the voice. She would look around when it was finished and see if she was right.

He was no boy, but a grown man. Mature. Powerful—though that was a given when she could feel the strength in the hands that held her so gently but so firmly. Taller than her, but by how much? What was he wearing? A kilt? Walking shorts?

If he was the hunter she had heard earlier, would he be wearing special clothing, would he be carrying a gun? She shivered and the gentle hands stroked down her bare arms. Not a hunter, surely. His touch gentled her as she drew in a deep breath and prepared to turn round to face him.

"Don't look at me." His voice was urgent, compelling.

Immediately she stilled. She wanted to look, but what if he was horribly disfigured?

"Why shouldn't I look?" Her voice trembled a little.

"It is better that you do not."

It was obviously all the explanation he was going to give and, though he released his hold so she could easily have turned, she did not.

When she did not move, he rewarded her by placing his hands on her shoulders and massaging away the tension. As he felt her relax he stopped and she moaned quietly with disappointment. He was such a skilled masseur. Then his hands were back on her shoulders. He must have swung one leg over the rock so that he was sitting astride the outcrop, directly behind her now, because this time his hands were firmer, more compelling. And they did not stop at her shoulders. His warm palms stroked down her naked arms, bringing the pale hairs to tingling attention. He cupped one arm and worked his magic with both hands, massaging deeply. And then he cherished her other arm.

Eileen sighed. This was bliss.

He began work on her back, caressing the length of it, then working deeply on a small area, then gentling once more until she thought the whole of her body would drown in the languor he had produced. And then he concentrated on that special place in the small of her back that instantly aroused her. How did he know? Perhaps her breathing was giving her away. She found herself taking quick, deep breaths. She knew that liquid heat was pooling inside her, waiting for release.

She was so close to a climax that she almost came when one of his clever hands moved round her body, caressed one aching breast, and tugged gently at the nipple. And then she felt his mouth nuzzling at the back of her neck and stiffened in ecstasy. He nibbled at her ear, tugging at the lobe with his teeth with the same gentle pressure he was exerting, in synchrony, on her nipple. She gave herself up to pleasure and convulsed against him.

As her breathing slowed and she came back to full consciousness, she realized that she was snuggled into his chest. He had pulled her back into the cradle of his arms and seemed content to have her head resting on his left shoulder. His arms were bare, like her own. And then she realized that he was massively erect. With her body pressed so close, she could feel the hard strength of him through the thin summer dress. But he made no demands. He seemed content just to hold her gently and to nuzzle her hair from time to time. Without knowing how, she was certain he was smiling.

"Welcome back," he murmured.

Eileen felt herself blushing. She had let herself climax in this wonderful man's arms without knowing his name or seeing his face, and without him removing a single item of her clothing or even touching her sex.

"Please," she said, "I have to know your name. Mine's

Eileen."

"Eileen." After a few seconds he told her, "You can call me Cerne."

Cerne. Not a name she knew. Again she wondered at his accent.

He moved against her, probably just to settle himself more comfortably on the rock, and she felt a jot of arousal course through her body. What would it be like to have this man inside her?

She looked down to her side and for the first time registered that his legs were as bare as his arms, and covered with reddish brown hairs. A walker, then, though she could not see his feet without lifting her head.

She sighed and snuggled into his chest, turning her head to nuzzle against him. And as she did so she realized that he was not wearing a shirt. There were springy hairs over the pelt of his chest. After a moment of surprise she also realized that he must have been enjoying the sunshine, just as she had, and had removed his top. His heartbeat was strong and fast.

She relaxed against him, and as she moved again, she felt him adjust his lower body against hers. Hell! She had taken her pleasure without one thought for the frustration he must now be feeling. She was ashamed.

"Do you...?" She couldn't find a way to voice her thoughts. "Would you...? Shall I...?"

There was a deep rumble against her back as he laughed.

"Are you suggesting what I think you are suggesting?"

"Um, well, it seems rather unfair that I should have had all the pleasure..."

"Trust me, Eileen, there was pleasure enough for me in seeing you pleasured."

"But still..." She wriggled a little to show that she knew he was still so aroused.

He gasped and she stopped.

After a few moments he said, "I have a proposition."

She waited, tacitly, to hear him out.

"Would you consent to my covering your eyes with this material?"

He removed the silk chiffon scarf she had knotted around her hair and draped it over her shoulder.

Perhaps he was a celebrity. He certainly wanted to guard his identity. Eileen nodded her agreement.

He took the material, folded it, and tied it around her head so that she could no longer see the heather or the faint ripples on the loch's surface. Then he stood, raising her with him, and urged her forward a little. He was so much taller than she had imagined. Trusting him, Eileen allowed herself to be turned to face him. He took her hands in his and bent to kiss her. At first it was a tender kiss. Eileen gave herself over to the sensation of it. It was extraordinary how her other senses came into play when her eyes were covered.

She reveled in the warm cushion of his lips, the muskiness that was his smell, the hot and heady arousal that was hers. When he opened his mouth and hers and tasted her with his tongue, she nearly wept with the power of the sensation. She tried to sway against him, to feel his arousal once more, but he held her away. She felt his fingers undo the buttons, struggling a little with their size, one by one down the front of her dress.

She heard his intake of breath when he realized she was not wearing a bra. His fingers strayed as he cupped her breasts and worshipped each nipple in turn with his mouth. Then he undid the rest of the buttons and pushed the fabric down over her arms so that the dress dropped to the ground and she stood, revealed, in front of him. All that was left between her and nakedness was the small silky covering over her sex.

"Let me." She reached to tug at it, but he stopped her. He must have knelt in front of her because she felt his warm, heavy breath, and then his teeth gently nipped at her mound through the silk as his hands caressed her. She had thought she was aroused, but this drove her almost to insanity. He licked up her thighs towards the center of her pleasure, teasing her by stopping—though she cried out for him. The silk was sodden with her wetness and his.

When she was gasping his name and pushing herself shamelessly towards his face, he turned her once more, and reached round her. He was making a cushion of the fleece she had brought with her. Gently he removed the silk and then, facing away, she knelt in front of him on the fleece as he urged. Tremulously she felt him push her legs further apart and knew he was looking, admiring her secret self, wetly and hotly aroused and ready for whatever he chose.

And then she felt his arousal once more, brushing against her. This time it was seeking her center. She abandoned herself to his desire.

As he stood behind her, started to enter her, brushing against her clit, she came, crying out, "Cerne, oh, Cerne."

But he held on, waiting until her waves of pleasure began to abate. Only then did he push into her. Oh, the length of him! He sheathed himself slowly, groaning at the joy of uniting them.

"Eileen!" he cried, as she knelt submissively before him and allowed him entry. Glorying in the power she had over this man she contracted around him and he responded by surging forward to fill her completely. And then he paused, probably just to lick his fingertips, because she felt them—slick on her nipples—as he urged them into ever tighter peaks as he drove himself into her. With each stroke he pushed her nearer to another climax, something she had not thought possible.

The heat of the sun warmed them both and Cerne's musky scent was so seductive that she felt enclosed in a bubble outside of time, outside of any emotion other than this driven need for him. Just him.

She felt her body spasm and joyfully reached out for the orgasm, feeling his seed spurt inside her as she convulsed around his cock and he shouted. Later she found that she had been laid gently on the ground and that Cerne was behind her, one strong arm thrown protectively over her. She had no idea how much time had passed. On an impulse she brought his forearm to her mouth and kissed the sun-warmed skin. She left one kiss in the middle of his palm.

"Thank you."

"I'm sorry that I must leave, but I have to go."

Startled, she turned her head towards him, forgetting she was wearing the fragile blindfold. The trailing ends caught between them and pulled it slightly awry. He was looking out at the loch, and not at her, so he didn't know that she had seen him. Glimpsed what had been forbidden.

There was no disfigurement, and he was nobody she recognized from the media, but certainly he was magnificent, auburn-haired and so masculine. She shut her eyes and turned her head away, knowing she would never forget what she had seen.

It occurred to her for the first time that he had not taken any of his own clothes off, that he must already have been naked when he came to her and sat behind her. She wondered what other secrets he had.

"I must go too," she told him. There was regret and resignation in equal measure.

"Let me go first." He gathered her to him, his arms went round her as if he would never let her go. He kissed her neck, then he released her and stood. It was a few seconds before she realized that he was no longer holding her. She pushed off her blindfold as she levered herself off the ground and looked around, blinking in the strength of the sunlight.

He really was gone, leaving no trace.

She tidied herself as best she could, pulling on the dress and hoping that she could pass off the crumples as nothing more than the result of a good walk. She was too shaken to make up an excuse.

Her watch showed an hour had already passed. They would be getting anxious. She picked up her water bottle and camera, stuffed her underwear into a pocket of the fleece and zipped it closed. Struggled to tie her bootlaces with unsteady fingers. Made her way carefully down the hillside in a daze. Nothing seemed quite real.

As she walked the last few paces she felt Adam looking at her. Quizzically.

Please don't say anything, she thought, willing him to remain silent. *I can't bear to talk about it. It's something I will never forget. Something I will never quite understand.*

There was a cheer from the students as the coach engine burst into life. Gratefully Eileen made her way onto the bus and sat alone in the double seat, looking up at the hillside, waiting for the last leg of the journey.

But how would she ever be able to come to terms with the fact that, when she had seen those auburn curls covering Cerne's head, arising from the center of them had been a pair of magnificent antlers?

ᏈᏒ

The Gro' ach

By Madeleine Oh

Becky Archer eased off her rucksack and sat on the soft grass. It had been a climb and a half. So much for that old codger in the book shop saying it was just a "wee walk" out to the lake. Either she'd gone soft with town living or they had very different ideas of what constituted "wee".

Her feet ached. Hell, they throbbed inside her walking boots. Just as well she had worn them, though. The going had been rough and the path uneven, but the old boy had been right about the fantastic view down the valley to the ruined castle and the village of Lachmuirghan. It was a beautiful spot, peaceful and deserted and just a few meters to her right, a fast-flowing stream ran down to a little beach and into the lake.

Was it really salt, as the guidebook suggested? And what about the creatures that the rather fanciful legends claimed inhabited the waters around here? If she had more energy she'd clamber down and find out. Later maybe, after her feet stopped protesting. After she had a rest. And after she had lunch. She had all day and no reason to hurry. She was booked into The Royal Rescue for another night and already had several dozen photos to illustrate her story. Lachmuirghan might not be exactly the romantic getaway her editor had suggested, but it was picturesque and after all she was a writer, wasn't she? She'd manage her five thousand words of romantic atmosphere and implied passion.

Right now, time to satisfy other appetites. She reached into the bag from the village baker, spread the contents on her rucksack and broke the seal on the bottle of ginger beer. Did anyone else in the UK seal bottles with red sealing wax these days? Lachmuirghan was in another age. She tilted the bottle to her lips and gulped. The cool liquid tasted wonderful—spicy and with just enough fizz to tickle her taste buds. The cheese and onion turnover wasn't half bad either—flaky and buttery with lots of sharp cheese and masses of onion. She half wished she'd bought a couple, but it was definitely on the generous side and one was more than she normally ate for lunch. Must be something about the brisk Highland air and sunshine, because she had no trouble polishing off the sausage roll and the blackberry tart.

Hunger assuaged, Becky stretched out on the soft grass, settled her rucksack under her head, closed her eyes and let the sun soak into her skin.

She'd been dozing a minute or two when a hand nudged her shoulder. Not even opening her eyes, Becky rolled on her side, away from whomever or whatever wanted to rouse her.

"Don't turn away, Golden Hair. Do you not know me?"

Not in the slightest, but with a voice like that... Becky let out a slow breath and lay still, realizing she was dreaming as the hand eased across her shoulder and cool fingers ruffled the hair at the nape of her neck.

"I've waited long for you," the voice went on, "but now my waiting is over." Lips brushed the side of her neck and a sweet shiver skittered down her back.

"Awaken, my love," he continued, "awaken and come with me. Join me. Join with me."

In her dreams, the voice was impossible to resist. Becky turned, propping herself up on one elbow to get a good look at the speaker. Her mouth dropped open. He was male. A fact hard to miss since he was naked. His pale, golden skin gleamed in the sunshine. Long hair the color of ripe blackberries covered his shoulders, brushing his dark nipples. He had no navel, an oddity she noticed but accepted, realizing he was another being, not human but a creature of the hills, the sunshine and, judging by the webbed hand he rested on her arm, the waters.

"Who are you?" she asked, not entirely certain she really wanted, or needed, to know.

"I am the Gro'ach."

Becky sat up. Her grandmother always said eating cheese before going to bed brought on bad dreams. She'd been right about the dream bit, except there was nothing bad about this one.

"You're what?"

The Gro'ach. The Lord of Streams and Lakes. Come with me and learn the pleasures of the waters."

Yes, there'd been something about a legend in the guidebook but... Blinking, she took a good look at the Gro'ach. He wasn't the least bit hard on the eyes. She'd always had a thing about men with long hair and this particular head of hair was beyond magnificent. His smile wasn't half bad either. It lit up his pale eyes and suggested all sorts of naughty possibilities on the way through the water. She couldn't help staring at his rather splendid cock rising from between his impressive thighs. In fact, his not-far-from-erect cook was hard to miss, given his belly, groin and legs were completely hairless. Remembering it was rude to stare, Becky made herself look away from his cock and up at his eyes. They were pale gray, like the loch before the clouds cleared and left a blue sky, but it was his mouth that fascinated her. His wide lips begged to be kissed, and would, she just knew, kiss back with skill and expertise.

Time to stop ogling. Remembering his last words, she asked, "What pleasures?"

"Come and I will show you." He held out a webbed hand.

Why not? She wasn't likely to get any better offers before she got home.

"All right, but I've got to get back to Edinburgh in the morning. Editors don't like missed deadlines."

His wide forehead creased as a little knot formed between his heavy, dark eyebrows.

"Editors? Why would you answer to a mere mortal?"

Seemed no point in bothering to explain that this particular mortal was paying her handsomely to lie on the grass and ogle the best specimen of manhood she'd seen since the stripper at her cousin's hen party.

"Why would I, indeed?" she replied, reaching out to touch his arm.

His skin was firm and warm and smooth under her fingertips. She smiled up at him, tempted to see for herself if those lips were as worthwhile as she imagined. A soft breeze ruffled his hair; she reached out and caught one of the tresses. His dark eyebrows shot up, but he said nothing as she ran the lock of his hair through her fingers. It was soft as silk but thick and heavy and smelled of fresh air and sunshine and life. She let the tress fall and ran her hand over his chest, stroking his dark nipples and glancing lower. Yes, he was definitely interested. She paused, wondering how far she should take her hand. This was a dream, right? She could be utterly shameless. So, she ran the flat of her hand down his chest, and skimmed his flat belly.

His touch stopped further exploration.

"Not here, my queen. Too many mortals come this way, come to my haven."

He held out his hand. And smiled.

She'd be nuts to refuse.

She placed her hand in his.

Closing his fingers over hers, he stood, raising her to her feet.

"I will take you to the land of dreams, and show you joy beyond mortal imagining."

Didn't sound half bad. There was the little matter of a deadline, but wasn't she supposed to be writing about a romantic getaway? So far there hadn't been much to pad out her word count.

"All right, but what about my things?"

She looked around at her rucksack and sweater. Silly to be worry about them, she supposed. They'd be safe enough. There was no one else about.

"Come!"

Might as well.

He led her down to the flowing stream.

"This is my world," he said as the water lapped over her boots.

It wasn't hers, but heck, it was just a dream after all, wasn't it? The stream was cool and fast moving and much deeper than it looked. To Becky's surprise, the Gro'ach led her upstream, not towards the lake. She was thigh deep in the cold water, but felt no discomfort. After clambering over a waterfall, they reached a wide pool, secluded on three sides by banks of heather.

"Here," he said, "is my world, my haven. Will you stay awhile and let me feed your soul?"

What she had in mind was bit more physical than that. If he'd brought her all this way for conversation and spiritual elevation, she'd have a moan or two. Judging by his cock (which seemed not a jot affected by the cold water) she doubted that was a worry; but best get things straight.

"Just my soul? I had other hopes."

She reached over and rested her fingertips on his belly.

His hand covered hers, pressing her palm against his skin and the muscle beneath.

"All is hope and dreams," he replied, his dark hair falling like a curtain around his head as he bent and kissed her.

She been hoping, waiting, for this, but the reality surpassed her imagining. His lips were firm, cool, soft and yet utterly determined. It was more than a mere kiss. Her lips opened to him and as his tongue touched hers, it was as if he entered her mind. She not only felt his kiss, she felt her own kisses on his lips, her own need melding with his. She whimpered as his mouth came down harder. His kiss was fierce now, as his naked arms pulled her against him. His hand, flattened between her shoulder blades, drew her closer, then slid down to the small of her back and pulled her against his erection. His all-too-apparent need pressed into her belly like a promise.

She muttered into his mouth, sighing as she stood on tiptoe, wrapping her arms around his neck and angling her hips to bring herself closer. Her clothes were in the way, a soaking-wet impediment to feeling him skin to skin.

As if reading her mind, he stepped back a little, breaking their kiss to ease her T-shirt out of her jeans and over her head, before tossing the discarded garment on the bank. He frowned at her bra as if mystified, running his hands over the lacy cups and slipping his fingers inside until her nipples rose to tight points against the lace. He pulled the straps off her shoulders, pushing down the cups so her breasts spilled out, and he smiled with satisfaction.

"Such abundance," he whispered, "such beauty."

Admiration, while appreciated, darn well wasn't enough. All this was doing was getting her more and more aroused until her breasts ached, caught as they still were in the edges of her bra.

"Hang on."

She reached back and unhooked her bra.

He stared at it as he took it from her, frowning as he turned it over.

"Why do you wear this?"

A question she'd often asked herself.

"So I can take it off!"

He laughed. "Better without it." As if to make sure, he tossed it over his shoulder. Becky watched the pale lace cups fill with water and the damn bra sink. It was one of her prettiest, true, but darn, it felt so much better with the breeze on her skin.

And as far as she was concerned, he could run his hands over her breasts as much as he liked. She'd had lovers with nimble, sensitive fingers, but nothing, ever, had equaled the rush of sensation from his smooth, webbed hands.

Time for her turn. She leaned in, pressing his hands to her breasts as she kissed his chest. His skin tasted of salt and sunshine and...something hard to define...a freshness and a strange, almost magical, taste.

Well, she was dreaming wasn't she?

"My jeans are getting very heavy."

He took the hint.

He grasped her waist and lifted her out of the water. Holding her over his head, he kissed each nipple in turn, before striding through the pool to the bank. The heather was rough against her bare back, but the sharpness stimulated and excited her. Or perhaps it was his hands making fast work of her snap and zip. The damp denim clung to her thighs, but with a sharp, swift tug, her jeans were around her ankles. What happened to her socks and hiking boots, heaven, or the Gro'ach alone, knew. She was naked, flat on her back, looking up at her dream lover as he quite openly feasted his gaze on her naked bod. By his appreciative smile, he had absolutely no problem with her none-too-flat belly, or less-than-C-cup boobs.

The Gro'ach knelt, pulling her close to him, spreading her thighs wide with his broad chest as her knees bent and her legs dangled in the water.

She tried to sit up, but he held her down. "Be still! This is my domain. Here, you are mine!"

Before she could come up with an appropriate response to such a blatantly overbearing comment, he bent forward and put his mouth on her pussy.

Now she almost did rise off the ground! His mouth was magnificent! First he kissed her—sweet, gentle kisses covering her sensitive flesh, before he slid his hands down over her belly, parted the folds of her vulva and eased a finger inside. She was wet and ready and wanted more than a finger but oh, that one finger worked wonders. Stroking, penetrating, curling inside her, igniting a line of fire.

"More," she demanded, not caring who heard. "Please, more!"

"Oh, yes," he replied with a hint of a chuckle, as his mouth came down again.

He lapped her slowly, setting nerve endings tingling as the tip of his tongue found her clit. She let out a shout and a sigh and a long, drawn-out moan. As his lips tugged her clit, his hand slid up her body to her breasts. His fingers played her nipples, his lips drew up her need and her hips rocked of their own volition.

Little moans rose from deep in her throat, whimpers of pleasure and groans of rising need. She muttered, moaned and cried out as the power deep in her body surged. She moved her hips, pressing them into the heather. The roughness spurring her on, the sensation adding to the wildness flooding her mind and body.

He never faltered, never slowed, as her hips pitched and her shoulders heaved and rocked. With a shout, Becky climaxed, her entire body roiling with sheer joy. As the ripples of pleasure abated, he shifted.

"Ready?" he whispered.

Ready? She was just about done for, but seemed a bit rude to say so. After all, judging by the state of his cock, all but pulsating against her thigh, there was plenty more to come.

In fact...

"Just a minute," she said, wiggling so he shifted. "My turn."

"Your turn?" he asked. "Was that not satisfaction enough?"

"Oh! Yes!"

Darn it! Men, even ones with webbed hands, were so touchy about these things.

"Let me show you what I can do."

He stood, an interested expression on his face, as Becky slid off the bank and knelt at his feet. The sand was firm under her knees and the water up to her breasts, but she was the perfect level to appreciate the finer points of his particularly impressive cock.

Being so smooth was something different. No risk of stray hairs in the mouth with the Gro'ach. She ran her finger up his cock, noting how wide he was, although not much longer than most men she'd seen. He had no foreskin and the head of his cock was narrow and pointed and glistened in the afternoon light as if tipped with silver or crystal, but when she closed her lips over him, his cock was warm and alive with the promise of male potency.

He gasped, angling his pelvis so he pressed deeper in her mouth. With a great surge of desire and anticipation, she swallowed him to the root. Against her lips, she felt the tension in his body. As her tongue curled around his glorious erection, her heart lurched at the awareness of the sheer male power between her lips. She closed her mouth, easing along the length of his erection before swallowing him deep again. Slowly, she drew her mouth back, only to take him deeper as she pressed her face against his smooth groin. She caught the scent of male desire, and paused to savor the taste of his skin, the touch of his hands in her hair, and the cool water stimulating her still-sensitized pussy. She wanted him, needed him, and sensed the self-same desire in every fiber of his body. Slowly she drew back, looking up at him and smiling.

Soon.

Neither of them could last much longer. He was hard and ready. She was needier than ever. Seemed her earlier climax had increased, rather than sated, her desire.

"I need..." she began.

"I know," he replied.

He closed his hands on her forearms and with gentle pressure, raised her to her feet. Water ran down her chest and belly as he opened his fingers and his webbed hands stroked her breasts and skimmed over her ribcage. Their eyes met. He smiled. Closing his strong hands around her waist, he lifted her. She gasped, the breath catching in her throat, as he lowered her onto his cock.

She was impaled, filled. She whimpered and sighed as she tightened herself over his erection.

Now it was his turn to groan. The light in his pale eyes gleamed with joy as she caressed him with her inner muscles. He gasped, as if close to climaxing, but took a deep breath, easing her off him a moment before driving back with renewed force. Becky cried out as he penetrated to the very neck of her womb, stirring wild sensations, holding her close as his hips pistoned with his mounting passion.

She tightened her legs around his waist, wrapping her arms about his wide shoulders, pressing her hips into his to bring him even deeper. She was past reason, beyond thought. Nothing mattered but his cock, the wild gyrations of his hips and the touch of his webbed hands.

Joined, they fucked in the sunshine, the cool water swirling around their legs and the breeze tempering the rising heat of their bodies.

Seemed they were locked in a timeless embrace, destined to fuck forever, eternally enmeshed in their mutual aura of sexual need. She lost track of time. Hours, seconds, all blended into one endless fuck as he forced her mind and body higher and higher in need and desire. Becky flung her head back, exposing her breasts to the sun above, and let out a string of sharp of cries as her desire peaked. With a succession of wild thrusts, he drove her to the edge of her climax. Mind and body soared to the peak as she screamed aloud her joy. His climax followed hers as he pressed hard and furious, taking her to the peak again and again as he sated his desire in her body. She sagged in his arms. With his incredible strength, he stood firm and steady as he gently withdrew and lowered her to her feet. She clung to him, uncertain if she could stand on her own. Not really wanting to.

"That was incredible!" she muttered into his shoulder.

"Yes," he replied. "Never forget the Gro'ach."

"That's hardly likely!"

He chuckled, his hands stroking her back as he kissed her forehead.

She leaned into him. "You wore me out."

"Yes." Given what they'd just enjoyed, she forgave the smirk. He was indeed splendid and judging by the pressure against her belly, ready for more. That thought had her legs wobbling.

He caught her, lifting her off her feet and holding her close against his smooth chest. She wanted to speak but lassitude overtook her. She closed her eyes as he strode through the water. Naked, the breeze brushing her damp skin, she should be chilled, but all she felt was warmth and glorious satiation. She sighed and nestled closer as he tightened his hold. Might as well doze a moment as the Gro'ach carried her to the bank.

A shout woke her.

Dazed and drowsy, Becky opened her eyes and half sat up. On the road above, a man driving a tractor was calling to another man with a dog. They were too far to see her and she was alone. Completely. She pulled herself upright and looked around. The sun was low in the sky. Her rucksack was as she'd left it, but a bit squashed by her head. Her book still lay on the grass, beside the empty ginger beer bottle. She ached, presumably from lying on the ground for hours.

That had been some dream. She gathered her belongings together and perched on a rock to pull on her boots. She couldn't help noticing they, and her clothes, were damp. Had she slept through a short rain shower? Maybe that ginger beer wasn't as innocuous as she'd believed. Better get back and start writing.

As she shrugged on her rucksack, she noticed she wasn't wearing a bra.

Three:
The Guesthouse

Kirsty had to read the discreet advertisement in the London newspaper twice. The Lachmuirghan Guesthouse was for sale? And at such a low price! She was already reaching for the phone…

Thoughts of returning to Lachmuirghan had been haunting her for a while now, and this felt like the opportunity she had been waiting for. A small legacy meant she was in a position to purchase a modest property, but why was the guesthouse on the market for practically nothing?

The advertisement offered few clues, except perhaps for one: "Elderly owners forced into retirement by too much excitement—"

Excitement?

In Lachmuirghan?

Smiling with disbelief, Kirsty felt buying fever grip her as the estate agent answered her call.

☙

Kirsty Muir and the Guesthouse

By Xandra King

Exchange time for eternity.

It was a strange sign to hang above a bookshop. The peeling paint suggested the sign was as old as the building. Kirsty couldn't remember it being here when she had lived in Lachmuirghan as a child. Everything in the village seemed to have changed.

It was too late to worry whether or not those changes suited her. She had sold her London apartment, burned her bridges, and now she was on her own. Her elderly parents had settled into a retirement home in Florida, and it seemed unlikely that anyone in Lachmuirghan would remember the rebellious teenager who had left the village fifteen years before.

Kirsty was drawn to bookshops. As far as men were concerned, she was hopeless at finding good ones, and found the heroes in the pages of romantic fiction a much safer bet. A little love between the covers of a book hurt no one, and it helped to take the edge off eighteen months of celibacy.

A small silver bell chimed overhead as she stepped over the threshold. She was immediately drowned in the scent of old dust and even older books.

"Good morning. Can I help you?"

There were no lights, and in the shadowy interior it took Kirsty a moment to spot the shopkeeper. He seemed to take shape rather than appear behind the counter, but if that was strange, it was a relief to hear the lilting Highland accent hadn't changed.

"Are you a visitor to Lachmuirghan?" His keen eyes scanned her face with such intensity she felt uncomfortable.

"Yes, and no." She smiled faintly—she wasn't ready for the inevitable interrogation. Life in London had made her cautious and unwilling to share too much of herself with strangers, which was why the idea of returning to a simpler life in Lachmuirghan had held so much appeal. But now she was back...

"Have you been in Lachmuirghan long?" the shopkeeper persisted.

She had to tune in to small town curiosity and stop being so suspicious. "I arrived this morning." She added a smile.

"You'll be tired, then?"

"Not really..." She glanced into the darker interior of the shop. She didn't want a conversation, she wanted a book.

"And hungry..."

Patience and good manners cost nothing. Kirsty smiled again, dismissing the old *duine's* concerns—and then smiled for remembering the Gaelic.

It was hard to believe she had exchanged the craziness of London for this. No wonder she was finding it hard to adapt. She still felt a sense of unreality, a sense of not being quite on the same dimension as everyone else in the world she had left behind.

"No doubt you'll find everything you need in Lachmuirghan." He cocked his head to look at her, as if assessing just what that might be.

When she had left the lawyer's office after signing the deeds to the guesthouse Kirsty had thought the soothing ambience of an antiquarian bookshop just what she needed. That was because she had forgotten the locals' hunger for information.

"I hope you've somewhere to stay..." The old man frowned with concern, but his voice invited further explanation. "The inn is shut for redecoration, and with the guesthouse closing down..." He looked at her expectantly.

"Actually I've bought the guesthouse, and I'm moving in today." Just saying the words out loud made it seem real and right. "So, you could say I'm here to stay."

"Is that so?"

The old *duine* adopted a faraway look as if he was tuning in to some invisible radio station which would give him the latest bulletin on a twenty-eight-year-old red-headed, freckle-faced spinster called Kirsty Muir.

And now she was being fanciful. The *duine* didn't intend to be rude, it was just that Lachmuirghan was so isolated, so cut off from the fast-moving whirl of modern life, he couldn't contain his curiosity.

"I'll go and look at the books—" She wheeled away, reluctant to be drawn into any more revelations. This was a new beginning and she had a lot of things to sort out at the guesthouse—buying a book was just a spur-of-the-moment indulgence.

"No! Not those!"

Kirsty snatched her hand away from the section marked "Romance". How could the *duine* see her when she was out of sight around a corner?

He was so familiar with the shop he could second guess where her footsteps had taken her, she reasoned, reining in her imagination.

"I have something here you'll like," he said.

The old man's voice had turned persuasive, and he might have been smiling, but judging by his tone of voice, his good humor might not last for long.

"I'm sorry," she said, returning to the counter. "Did I do

something wrong?"

"Those books aren't suitable reading matter for young ladies."

"Young ladies..." Kirsty bit her tongue. She knew better than to inflict her own viewpoint on an elder of Lachmuirghan. Now she was back in the village she had to make a go of things and appear to conform to local ways. She couldn't afford to cause ripples if she was to make a success of her new business.

To her relief, the *duine* hadn't noticed her flash of affront, and ducking down beneath the counter, he brought out a book. "This is the book for you," he said, holding it out to her.

Kirsty's laugh was awkward. It was a long time since anyone had prescribed her reading matter—in fact that hadn't happened since infant school.

But the *duine* was only trying to be helpful, Kirsty reminded herself.

As it happened, she didn't even have a chance to turn the book over in her hands before it spoke to her—books had been doing that since she was old enough to read, and this one said quite clearly, "Buy me".

"Thank you, I'll take it," she said promptly.

Kirsty handed the book back to be wrapped, and it was only when she closed the shop door behind her and slipped the slim volume from its bag that she read the title. And groaned. *Life in a Basket.*

Life in a Basket? It was some sort of cookery book, she realized, leafing through it. Every ingredient could be sourced from nature.

Great. It was hardly the comfort she had been looking for in bed that night.

Medlar Puree: sweet indulgence for a dark and lonely night.

She had found the perfect recipe. The night was dark *and* lonely, and Flinty, the elderly housekeeper she had inherited with the guesthouse, had told her about the small, bushy medlar tree in the garden that bore tiny apple-like fruits. Plus Flinty had tapped her nose and winked, declaring medlar fruit had magical properties.

Right now she could do with a little magic in her life.

Flinty had considerately laid out all the ingredients for her. She must have collected the fat brown medlar haws back in November and stored them in the pantry at the guesthouse in order to come up with them so quickly. The reason Kirsty hadn't noticed them before Flinty left was because she was still so tired after her long journey from London.

Flinty lived in a small cottage in the village—a place for casting spells, she said, but had declared that she came with the property and would stay on under the new management.

Kirsty smiled. When she had lived in the village as a child, many of the older inhabitants of Lachmuirghan had credited themselves with being fey. But fey or not, she was glad to have a sensible body like Flinty around—she needed all the help she could get if the new business was to be a success.

She was just securing the ties on the apron Flinty had thoughtfully left out when the lights flickered and went out. Kirsty swore softly under her breath, remembering Flinty had warned her not to be surprised if this happened. There was a good supply of candles and matches in the kitchen cupboard...

But when the lights went out in Lachmuirghan it was pitch black and spooky. The sooner those candles were lit the better.

Kirsty breathed a sigh of relief as the flickering candles bathed the country kitchen in a cozy glow. She turned back to the recipe book and saw that along with the medlar haws, she would need a jug full of rich heavy cream, a mound of soft brown sugar and two fragrant lemons, as well as a flagon of whisky from the local distillery.

Flinty had left everything ready as if she'd read Kirsty's mind. The cream was in a glazed jug, the sugar in an attractive blue and white bowl and the whisky in a flacon that looked as old as time.

"Whip all the ingredients together until smooth..." Kirsty read the recipe instructions out loud, and jumped when she heard another voice.

"That's far too good to eat alone." It was a male voice, as deep and rich as velvet.

With a cry of fear, she launched herself backwards, sending pots and chairs flying. Only the grip of someone tall and strong stopped her tumbling after them.

"Do not fear me," the man said in an accent she couldn't place.

"Who are you?" Hugging herself, she trembled, staring round.

The man stared back at her. At first she thought his eyes were black, but then she saw they were a hypnotic, back-lit gray.

"It doesn't matter who I am. They said you were coming, and I'm here."

She had to be dreaming. He was naked to the waist, and had a bronzed, hard-muscled torso that gleamed in the flickering candlelight. He smelled good, like a forest after a rainstorm...clean, fresh, and woody.

"*Who* told you I was coming?"

"Flinty, amongst others."

Kirsty desperately wanted to look away to collect her thoughts, but she couldn't.

Flinty had warned her to expect visitors—after all, this was a guesthouse. And perhaps there was a fancy dress party taking place in the village. Goodness knew, the locals had to entertain themselves somehow.

'I'm sorry, I must seem rude. I didn't catch your name."

"I am the Teacher of All Things," the man murmured.

The local teacher. That was all right, then. There must be a school show in the village hall, or a fundraiser, perhaps. Kirsty smiled with relief as she gave her visitor a closer inspection. Not bad.

Still, it was all a bit worrying. How had he gotten in, for one thing? Was there a trapdoor, a secret entrance she hadn't noticed? She would have to double-check all the security aspects of the guesthouse first thing in the morning. "Hi, I'm Kirsty Muir—" She extended her hand in greeting. "I just bought this place."

He made no attempt to shake her hand.

"So...is there a fancy dress party in the village?"

Still no response. And now she was frightened. What was she thinking of, holding a conversation with an intruder? And a half-naked intruder at that! An intruder wearing a skirt—even if it was a rather neat little battle kilt... And was that a real sword hanging by his side? Passing a hand across her eyes, Kirsty wondered whether she was dreaming.

"A party?" The man's deep, husky voice reclaimed her attention.

"Yes, you know..." Kirsty's face flushed with awareness, and instead of coming up with some smart remark she found herself staring up at a face etched in harsh masculine lines, and some very firm and attractive lips.

“I hope you’re not frightened of me, Kirsty.”

“Frightened of you?” She attempted to laugh it off, but her throat had closed and she could only stare as he strode to the kitchen table and viewed the ingredients lying there.

“I’m glad I’m here in time to help.”

He cooked?

She watched as he fingered the medlar haws, turning them over with long, lean fingers.

The air seemed to have undergone a subtle change as if he carried an electric charge around with him. Or maybe that was the lights snapping back on. There was definitely something hypnotic in his gaze, but at least she was growing used to his costume. Whatever turned him on—she was broad-minded.

“That’s a great wig you’re wearing,” she commented, feeling bolder now the lights were on.

“Wig?” The frown lines between his sweeping brows deepened.

Not a wig? “I’m sorry,” she rushed out, realizing her mistake. “I love long hair on a man...”

He looked at her in a way that made all sorts of sensations rush through her—and not one of them was appropriate for late night meet-the-neighbor scenarios.

“Are you ready for your first lesson, Kirsty?”

“I, uh—absolutely.” She had better not cause any more offense.

Kirsty gulped as massive hands caught hold of her shoulders. Instinctively, she took a step back, and balling her hands into fists, struck once, halfheartedly, on the man’s rock-hard chest.

She should, of course, have thrust him away, or better still, screamed and called for help. But why? *Why*? When the most demanding mouth imaginable was claiming her lips? Relocating to Lachmuirghan had never seemed a better move.

Thankfully, the man had one powerful arm locked around her waist as her legs trembled and gave way. If this was her first lesson from the Teacher of All Things, then she was eager to progress to the next level.

He tasted incredible, and soon she was drinking him, eating him, devouring him in a way she had never felt the urge to do before. Other men might have pecked at her with their tight, mean mouths, but none of them had known how to kiss like this man.

"Can you taste it?" he demanded.

"What?" She stared into his piercing gaze.

"Teacher," he reminded her sternly.

Mmm... The firm prompt lit a fire that circled every inch of her until it landed with a pulsing throb between her legs.

"Can I taste what, Teacher?" This game she liked.

"I know you can taste it..."

"Yes, yes, I'm sure I can..." She sure as heck wanted to.

"You can taste the magic, Kirsty."

"Absolutely." She shivered with excitement as the Teacher nuzzled his beard-roughened chin against her neck.

"Do you like it?" He searched her eyes.

"I love it," she said with feeling. "In fact, I'd like some more."

"Then let's get cooking. I don't have all night."

"Oh, okay then." This was a cookery lesson? Suddenly she didn't feel quite so thrilled about the evening. "Perhaps you should tell me your name if you're going to stay."

"I've already told you who I am."

"Teacher of All Things? I mean your real name."

"The Teacher of all Things *is* my real name."

And I'm Lara Croft. "But Teacher of All Things is a bit of a mouthful. Don't you have a nickname I can use?"

"How does 'Teacher' grab you?"

Pretty thoroughly, judging by the way her skin was still yearning for his touch. "Teacher," she repeated softly, tasting the word on her tongue. Come to think of it, she loved it—didn't teachers go for discipline and stuff?

"Take the warm medlar pulp and mix three parts to one part of lightly whipped cream..."

Oh, my, he really did cook! Kirsty watched transfixed as her new teacher read from the recipe book. But as she stared at him she noticed that his eyes glittered strangely in the candlelight. He'd mentioned magic—was this enchantment?

Before she could work it out, he held up his hands in a gesture that suggested she should stand back while he took charge. "I'm going to add sugar," he warned, as if it were gunpowder.

She was bewitched, Kirsty thought as he held the tiny sugar bowl aloft. *Definitely,* she concluded as the mixture fizzed and gave off a cloud of smoke. Since when had sugar been combustible?

"And now I'm going to add the juice and finely grated rind from these two plump lemons... Stand back," he warned.

As he squeezed the lemons, Kirsty could swear she felt his hands squeezing her. She felt her nipples rise in response. And when he took a wooden spoon and began to beat the mixture rhythmically, she had to shift position and clear her throat to cover for the way he made her feel.

"Are you a little hot?" he suggested, glancing up at her.

Hot? She was about to self-combust.

"Why don't you take your clothes off?" he suggested innocently.

And she had thought Lachmuirghan behind the times?

"You're wearing a capacious apron," he pointed out. "You'll hardly be in danger of exposing yourself. And no one can see in here."

"You can," she reminded him.

"But I'm too busy to look."

"All right...if you promise not to look." What was wrong with her? Had she gone completely mad? It was as if almost she was staring down at another Kirsty Muir—a stranger she didn't know, and this Kirsty Muir was behaving like she was on the lookout for adventure of the hot, energetic and lascivious kind...

"Perhaps I will not look," the Teacher murmured provocatively, "and perhaps I will."

"Perhaps, isn't an answer."

The Teacher caught and held her gaze. She felt her mouth dry, and then she couldn't look away.

Somehow her fingers started flying over the buttons of her shirt, loosening them, and the next thing she knew she was fumbling frantically with the fastenings on her jeans.

"Let me help you." The Teacher turned to look at her, and as he did, the fastenings jumped free. The next thing she knew, her jeans were round her ankles.

But he was right about the apron. It covered her front, and while she was facing him that was fine.

"There, that's better, isn't it?"

Well, they were both in costume now.

The Teacher turned back to the bowl of ingredients he was blending, and as she stood watching him in silence, a breeze intruded on the pleasant warmth of the kitchen, titillating her buttocks in a way that made her shift from foot to foot

She had to stand and wait until the Teacher was satisfied with his mixture and filled a bowl of water at the sink.

"What are you doing now?" She saw a soft cloth floating on the surface.

"You'll see," he promised. "But first you must lie down."

She was so aroused by this time she would have done anything he commanded, and was completely lost in the Teacher's compelling gaze as he led her by the hand across the kitchen.

The old oak bench had no doubt been put to any number of uses in its long life, but surely never one as deliciously seductive as this.

And had it always been angled towards the fire? And who had lit the fire, for that matter?

Perhaps Flinty, before she left, Kirsty reasoned. Everything was muddled—had to be, because now the bench had changed into a comfortable double bed!

But if she wanted more of those kisses...

The edge of the mattress was pressing against the back of her legs and the down-filled cushions looked inviting. There was a small table next to the bed. The bowl of medlar puree was on top of it, along with a larger bowl of warm water. "How did that get there?"

Putting one firm finger pad over her lips, the Teacher eased her down onto the quilted coverlet.

It felt like being encased in a comfy cradle, rather than balancing on what reason told Kirsty was a hard old seat.

"Not yet," the Teacher murmured as she reached out to him.

As he dipped his hand in the bowl of medlar pudding, she imagined he was about to let her taste some of it.

And he did... The portions of deliciously sweet and creamy pudding slid down her throat so easily. And was she imagining it, or were all her nerve-endings responding? *Could food increase the libido?*

The answer to that had to be yes, Kirsty thought, taking the Teacher's fingers deep into her mouth.

As she laved his supple hand with her tongue, she writhed a little on the bed—she couldn't help herself. She wanted more—she wanted everything he could give her. But when he flicked up the skirt of her apron, she gasped, demanding, "What are you doing?"

The Teacher didn't answer as he scooped up a handful of pudding from the bowl. Smearing it thickly between her legs, he massaged it in with considerable attention to detail.

"Oh, that's..."

"Good?" he suggested.

Good didn't even cover it.

She opened legs a little more, and was rewarded by the Teacher pressing her knees back, exposing her fully to the cool air.

He examined her intently, and then as if satisfied, he reached for the bowl of hot water. Taking out the cloth, he squeezed it dry. Kirsty exclaimed with pleasure as he applied it firmly to her over-sensitized mound, pressing it home so that it made contact with every part of her. He let it linger for a moment, and then peeling it back, he wiped her firmly.

"Would you care to look?" he suggested then.

There was a mirror in her hand she couldn't remember him putting there.

"Don't be shy," the Teacher instructed her.

Her heart thundered as he folded his massive arms across his chest.

"Well? Do you like what I've done?"

She was as smooth as a peach between her legs. Not just smooth—softly pink and sweetly swollen, and they could both see she was pulsing with desire. She decided honesty was best. "I love it. How on earth did you do it so painlessly?"

"How on earth?" The Teacher raised an ebony brow.

Okay, she'd go along with the game—this game, at any rate.

"No more talk. It's time for something else."

"It is?" Well, she was ready.

After positioning her on her hands and knees, he came to stand behind her. She could feel the cold metal of his broadsword brushing her buttocks. She was brazenly exposed, which drew a gasp of anticipation from her throat. He slapped her once, and then began to paddle firmly. The thrust of her cheeks rose to meet the flat of his hand. "That's so good!" she cried excitedly, angling herself as much as she could for him.

Her nerve endings were singing with pleasure as blood rushed to attend the site of the Teacher's ministrations. She had never been more aroused and whimpered to express her need—to show him she wanted more; much more.

"Oh no, don't stop…" She couldn't bear the frustration, but then she felt a cooling balm rolling over her heated flesh. "Oh, that's so good." She groaned and squirmed to let him know how much she appreciated him.

"You are prepared," he said sternly.

"Not yet, surely?"

He laughed, a low and seductive sound. "I shall have to discipline you some more."

"Please..."

She mewled with pleasure as the Teacher's hands continued to tend her most secret needs. "Be stern with me... Be strict..."

She was floating in an erotic web, transported to a place where pleasure ruled. "Punish me... I've been really bad..."

He applied more of the medlar puree, slathering it over her stinging cheeks where she soon realized it made every sensation even more pronounced. Having realized this, she rested her chest on her arms and thrust her bottom in the air so that he could attend most thoroughly to the pouting place between her legs.

"Aaah, that's good." She gasped as his knowledgeable fingers stroked and probed and rubbed. But now she wanted him inside her...deep inside her. "Please...please," she begged him hoarsely, wriggling her bottom to show him the way.

The Teacher's answer was to scoop out another handful of medlar puree, which he smothered over her before licking it off.

"Now, hold yourself open for me," he commanded fiercely.

She felt him rub against her—hot and smooth and firm. Cupping her buttocks, she opened herself, but still he used his tongue, setting up a rhythmical pattern that soon had her groaning. The sensation was so strong she had known nothing like it before. There had to be some stimulant in the medlar juice, but whatever the explanation, she was close...

But the climax would be too big for her... Clutching the cushions, she bit into them, waiting, trying not to think what it would be like.

The first spasm hit like an explosion, while the second made her collapse beneath him, forcing the Teacher to hold her in place so he could help her finish properly. Then it was just a world of sensation where nothing existed outside of sex.

"Was that good?"

She could hardly answer him. As a welcome to the village the Teacher's induction program, it was sensational.

But where were her clothes, Kirsty wondered groggily. And where had the silken throw come from that had somehow found its way on top of her?

"Is it time for this now?"

As he threw back the covers, she saw that the Teacher was naked. And so hugely engorged she knew for certain she would never manage to take him inside her.

He was perfectly proportioned, and his cock was the same heroic build as the rest of him.

"That comes in lesson two," he warned softly as she ducked her head beneath the cover to take a closer look.

"I only..."

"Never mind what you only thought you might do. It's time for this," he said, settling her onto her back.

"If you insist..."

"I do." Pressing her knees back, he spread her legs wide.

Surely she couldn't take all of him... He was far too big...

But she did. Gratefully. He was massive, and he stretched her beyond anything she could have imagined, but instead of feeling pain she was crying out with delight and begging for more.

Sinking deep, he worked his hips firmly against her before slowly withdrawing. By allowing her body to close each time, she had to be penetrated again...and again...and again...

Surely no one could survive this level of pleasure?

The Teacher thrust slowly and rhythmically, withdrawing each time with a teasing lack of haste until her drenched passage was quivering with the urgent need to be had hard and fast. He stretched her wide each time, forcing cries of pleasure from her lips, and it seemed an eternity until he finally he built up speed. When he did, she drove him shamelessly, biting into buttocks of steel with greedy fingers and closing her mouth on his massive shoulders.

The thrusts came thick and fast now, forcing barbaric words from her lips. She needed this. He had to do it and keep on doing it until she told him he could stop. He had to plunge harder, faster, ramming, thrusting, pounding into her— He was saying something. "What is it?" she demanded breathlessly, not wanting him to stop.

"There will be others like you, Kirsty."

"Like me?" What did he mean?

"Many lonely people who come to Lachmuirghan looking for magic to touch them. That is where your guesthouse comes in—"

"My guesthouse?" She was paying full attention now. "Explain."

"Many people will need your help—"

But not yours, she hoped. She didn't feel like sharing him.

"I will guide you," the Teacher promised, sinking into her.

Better.

But was this just a dream? Was she suspended somewhere in that half-world between sleep and consciousness?

Had she sampled too much of the whisky when she followed the recipe for medlar puree, Kirsty wondered, lacing her fingers through the Teacher's thick black hair to drag him down to her. He seemed real enough. "And how will I find these people?" she asked him.

"You won't need to find them...they will find you."

"And you will guide me?"

The Teacher's lips tasted of dreams... Kirsty slept on until the old clock on the mantelpiece started chiming. Turning sleepily, she glanced at the kitchen table. The bowls and the jug used in the preparation of medlar pudding were still there. Sitting up, she pulled the coverlet under her chin. She was naked and her clothes were scattered round the floor.

She'd been lonely and had drunk too much. That was the simple explanation. Any other explanation was far from simple.

But what a dream she'd had!

As Kirsty began piecing her dream together, she smiled and shook her head. Nothing like this had ever happened to her back in London. She would have to steer clear of the local whisky in future.

Squirming a little as she remembered the dream, Kirsty suddenly paled and grew still. Someone had given her the best wax of her life while she'd been sleeping. Now how could that happen? And painlessly? Not even waking her?

She frowned as she stared around the room. Everything looked normal. So what had happened between Flinty leaving for her home in the village and the kitchen clock chiming to waken her?

No... Surely that had been a dream...

ଔ

Kirsty Muir and the Bondage Cellar

By Xandra King

Kirsty shot up in bed. What could have woken her? She had been plagued by restless nights since moving back to Lachmuirghan. She put it down to the highland mists sending her imagination into overdrive. The strange tricks of the *solas,* as the light in the hills was called, could all too often form into ghostly shapes resembling people. But imagination or not, she couldn't afford to take any chances with a houseful of guests in the guesthouse she had so recently purchased.

Snapping on the light, she dragged on her robe. Her concerns for the security of the Lachmuirghan Guesthouse had been growing recently. Doors she was certain she had made sure were safely locked for the night were sometimes found open in the morning. The cellar door, for instance...

The noise had come from the cellar, she was sure of it. She used the basement for storage and had vague ideas of converting it into a spa once the guesthouse became more profitable. She didn't have any reason to go down there, but on the rare occasion that she did, she had a fancy that the cellars hummed with a different type of energy to the rest of the house.

One guest this week had explored the basement, but Mrs. Thorndike seemed such a lonely person. Kirsty hadn't liked to make a fuss and had accepted the woman's apology and explanation that she had lost her way.

Padding silently downstairs, Kirsty opened the cellar door a crack. It was only when she reached up to secure the bolt that she heard the noise. The rhythmic sound of a woman having sex shocked her. And very good sex too, judging by the groans of satisfaction.

But who was down there? And how could they possibly find the cellars a suitable place for their tryst? A mental image of whitewashed walls and bare stone floors sprang into Kirsty's mind. She had to be mistaken. Who would want to have sex in a cellar with a bare light swinging overhead? And her only female guest that week was prim Mrs. Thorndike. It was impossible to imagine Mrs. Thorndike sneaking a man into the guesthouse, let alone having sex with him in the basement.

"Kirsty..."

Kirsty gasped, hearing the voice of a man who hadn't entered her dreams since their first memorable encounter on the night she had moved into the Lachmuirghan Guesthouse. "Teacher?" she whispered.

"Go down into the cellar," Teacher ordered. "I want you to see. Don't be frightened. I am with you."

There was no one with her, but both the voice of the Teacher and the noises in the cellar were real. Kirsty's heart pumped furiously as she went to investigate.

The stone steps felt cold beneath her naked feet, and as she drew closer to the sound, what she heard astonished her. Someone was being spanked. She could hear the swoosh of a paddle making contact with naked flesh, and with each resounding slap there was a corresponding cry of satisfaction and encouragement.

Remembering her own discipline at the hands of the Teacher, Kirsty felt a quiver of desire. But try as she might, she could not imagine Mrs. Thorndike enjoying the same forbidden pursuits. So, who could it be?

"It is possible, Kirsty," the Teacher's voice insisted in answer to her unspoken question.

I will not hold a conversation with a figment of my

imagination, Kirsty thought, hurrying down the shadowy corridor.

"Don't you think you're being a little unfair?" the voice said again. "Mrs. Thorndike has never known physical pleasure at the hands of a man. Surely you agree that it's time she did?"

The Teacher's voice seemed so real—but she must be dreaming, Kirsty determined, balling her hands into fists. She would not give way either to fear or her imagination.

The light of a full moon streamed in through a skylight, and there was an eerie, sensual quality below the house she had not noticed before. She was sure now that it was Mrs. Thorndike being disciplined, and far from complaining after each resounding slap, she was begging for more.

Her hoarse cries, interspersed with whimpers of pleasure, made Kirsty's nipples harden. She was aroused too. Her heart raced with excitement as she drew closer to the heavy wooden door beyond which all manner of wicked things were happening. It was wrong to want to see, but it was an irresistible temptation...

This was the price she had to pay for months of celibacy, Kirsty reasoned. Apart from her incredible dream about the Teacher, she had tried not to think about sex at all. What point was there when no man could live up to the mysterious warrior of her dreams?

She almost envied Mrs. Thorndike, Kirsty realized, as she crept closer to the source of the sound. She could hear Mrs. Thorndike urging her lover on and the man's low growls of pleasure.

It was exciting to rest her cheek against the cool wood, dreaming of sex. She might be returning to a lonely bed, but she would picture the two people beyond this door. She drank in the sounds of their lovemaking, longing to touch herself. It would be even better if she could catch just a glimpse of them while she did so...

Tracing the surface of the door with her fingertips, she searched for a crack.

The sounds changed. Mrs. Thorndike's cries became increasingly agitated. There was the swish of something traveling at speed through the air, followed by the smart report of seasoned leather making contact with naked flesh.

"Oh, yes, yes, *yes*!"

As Mrs. Thorndike's approving cries rang out, Kirsty grew more desperate to see what was going on. She gasped in triumph as her searching fingers identified a tiny knot hole in the wood.

She peered through the hole and was astonished to see Mrs. Thorndike naked and tied to a pole with silk ribbons. But it didn't make sense. The cellar had yet to be renovated...

Someone had gotten there before her. The neglected room been turned into the most opulent bondage cellar Kirsty could imagine. The walls were padded with black satin, and every inch of the cold stone floor was covered in deep fur rugs.

"When you meddle with magic, you must expect the unexpected..."

Doubting her own sanity, Kirsty shook her head. "There's no one here," she said firmly.

"Is that so?"

The warm breath sweeping across the back of her neck proved she wasn't alone, and yet there was no one there...nothing except the evocative scent of lemons and medlar haws. *Which she had been using in a recipe the night the Teacher had first appeared!*

With a sharp sound of fright, she scanned the darkness...

Nothing.

It took time for her breathing to steady enough for her to return to her vigil. When she did, she saw with relief that the silk ribbons holding Mrs. Thorndike had been adjusted to fit loosely and were lined with marabou feathers to ensure the utmost comfort. This comfort extended to a crimson velvet cushion placed beneath Mrs. Thorndike's naked feet. Everything was designed for pleasure as evidenced by the look of ecstasy on Mrs. Thorndike's face, which was clearly visible in the moonlight.

The pace of the discipline was changing, Kirsty noticed breathlessly. The man, who she couldn't see, was holding a feather, and that feather was making slow progress over the swell of Mrs. Thorndike's belly.

Moonlight gave the older woman the appearance of a young girl, and she sounded like one too, Kirsty thought as she listened to Mrs. Thorndike's rhythmical moans.

It was such a shame the hole she had to peep through was so small that it prevented her from seeing Mrs. Thorndike's companion clearly. A tantalizing glimpse of muscular forearms and a powerful chest wasn't enough! That he was bronzed and well muscled, and about as far away from the type of man Kirsty could imagine Mrs. Thorndike taking up with was plain to see. This was no office drone, but a man of action whose honed body gleamed in the moonlight—a man who might fulfill any woman's deepest and darkest fantasy. Naked to the waist, he was wearing tight black leather pants that left nothing to the imagination.

Kirsty gasped as she caught a glimpse of a stern face in profile. She saw little more than a flash of strong white teeth and a thick head of glossy black hair. He was in the prime of life with his musculature beautifully delineated, but perhaps his most attractive feature was the fact that he was attending to Mrs. Thorndike's body with complete selflessness.

Well done, Mrs. Thorndike, Kirsty thought, gasping as the man started licking Mrs. Thorndike's breasts. He was laving every inch of them, paying particular attention to her almost painfully extended nipples. Kirsty could just imagine how good it would feel to have the moist roughness of his tongue teasing her and had to stop herself from crying out to urge him on.

With a strong, sure movement, the man swung Mrs. Thorndike round and Kirsty got a good view of the full swell of her buttocks. They were bright pink from the attentions of the paddle and the whip, and the man's fingernails were so sharp they had left a delicate tracery of poppy-colored weals over Mrs. Thorndike's delicate skin.

Another turn and Mrs. Thorndike was facing the door. The man knelt in front of her and parting her legs, he moved between them.

Kirsty's envious sigh provoked a low laugh. It was coming from somewhere behind her, and it was a laugh she would have recognized anywhere.

But the Teacher was a figment of her imagination. Turning, she scanned the passageway, and just as she thought, she was alone. She waited for a moment to be sure, but then Mrs. Thorndike's cry of pleasure drew her back to the door.

Seeing the man nuzzle Mrs. Thorndike with his stubble-roughened chin was too much for her, and reaching beneath her dressing gown, she found her swollen sex with trembling fingers. She tried willing the arousal to subside, but the pulsing would not obey her commands, and so she began to stroke herself in time to the rhythm of the man's tongue as he pleasured Mrs. Thorndike. Planting her feet wider, she leaned against the door, working faster now. Her hips jerked convulsively as the excitement grew.

"Kirsty!" a voice from the shadows reprimanded her. "You are a naughty girl, and I will have to punish you if you don't stop that."

Snapping her hand away from its pleasant duties, she glanced round. "Who is that?" Of course no one answered. She was alone apart from Mrs. Thorndike and her young companion beyond the door.

Convinced she had imagined the voice, Kirsty returned to the peephole and was soon absorbed in the sights and sounds in the room. While she had been away, the man had entered Mrs. Thorndike and his knees were flexed to allow him better access. He had freed Mrs. Thorndike's legs and these were locked around his waist, and each time he thrust into her, Mrs. Thorndike cried out with pleasure.

It was a privilege to watch him at work. But could this be the same timid woman who had arrived at the guesthouse only a few nights ago, the same woman whose voice had barely risen above a whisper? It was well above a whisper now! Mrs. Thorndike was quite certain with her instructions, and impatient too.

Kirsty had a wonderful view of the man's buttocks flexing as he followed Mrs. Thorndike's instructions, and watching him made her want to touch herself again. But that was wrong. This might be the cellar of her own guesthouse, but she was intruding upon a guest, and respecting the privacy of those who came to stay at the Lachmuirghan Guesthouse was the most important rule of all...

Except she hadn't expected her guests to indulge themselves to quite this extent!

Thinking back to the advertisement that had brought her back to Lachmuirghan, she remembered it saying that the elderly owners were selling the guesthouse at a knock down price because of too much excitement.

Was this the type of excitement they had meant?

When she had first read the advertisement she thought it must be exaggerating the situation. She had lived in Lachmuirghan before as a child and "excitement" was not a word she would ever have associated with the village.

"Kirsty."

All the tiny hairs rose on the back of her neck as she spun round. There was no mistaking that voice. It was the Teacher of All Things, and he was so close, her ears were tingling.

"So, you see me now?' the low, husky voice demanded.

There was no mistake—she wasn't dreaming. This was the man who had appeared to her in the kitchen of the guesthouse when she first moved in. "What are you doing here, Teacher?" Her voice was trembling.

"You called me, Kirsty."

"No I didn't," she argued.

"But there are many ways to call me, and not all of them involve speech..."

Her mouth dried. She couldn't stop staring. He was so much more attractive than she remembered. Rugged and hard, he was wearing nothing more than a short leather battle kilt. There was a great sword strapped to his waist, which was held in place by hide bands that strained across his heroic torso. He was even stronger than the man with Mrs Thorndike, and a great deal more desirable. Kirsty's cheeks raged red as memories of their previous encounter came flooding back.

When they had first met, she had told herself the same thing—that it was nothing more than a dream. But that dream had allowed her to indulge her wildest fantasies. And tonight she was wide awake, and it wasn't a phantom in front of her but a flesh and blood man.

"Have you kept yourself beautiful for me, Kirsty?" the Teacher asked.

She gasped as he moved closer and knew the desire to please him was as strong as ever. He was smiling faintly at her, which softened the firm set of his mouth and made her long for his kiss, but the expression in his eyes was still stern. *Which she loved...*

"Let me see," he said, making an imperative gesture.

But she didn't move fast enough to please him, and found herself bound by his powerful arm. With the other he flipped open her robe, his biceps bulging over the gold bands wrapped around them. She stood meekly, head bowed as he examined her, and then glowed beneath his approval.

"I am pleased with you," he said, "and I shall reward you for keeping yourself ready for me."

"You won't punish me?"

He laughed low down in his chest. "Don't sound so disappointed. Didn't I promise to reward you?"

Kirsty's eyes brightened in anticipation. The Teacher gave the cellar door, beyond which Mrs. Thorndike's moans of delight were reaching fever pitch, a look so penetrating she wondered if he could see through wood.

"It will give you greater pleasure if you watch my young friend at work while I see to your needs," he instructed, beckoning her over.

She hesitated. What the Teacher was suggesting was what she longed to do, but it seemed so wrong.

"Don't you want me to attend to your needs, Kirsty?"

"Oh, yes, I do..."

"Then come here, and bend over..."

Her body was melting into sweet honey in anticipation. Walking up to him, she turned her back on the Teacher and bent over, lifting her nightclothes and displaying herself boldly.

She was looking for the spyhole when the Teacher waved his hand and the door became a window so that everything Mrs. Thorndike and her lover were doing was clearly visible. Even the sound of their lovemaking was clearer—moist, rhythmical sounds, mingling with cries of delight.

"This isn't a dream," She could feel the Teacher's hands positioning her.

"Far from it," the Teacher confirmed. "Mrs. Thorndike's husband was a disappointment to her, and so I decided to put things right."

"In my guesthouse?"

"Don't you remember what I told you on my first visit, Kirsty?" the Teacher demanded, starting to tease her swollen flesh with just the tip of his massively engorged cock.

"Yes, yes, I do. But I thought—"

"You thought it was all a dream."

"Ah..." Kirsty cried softly as the Teacher entered her. This was not a dream; this was delicious reality, and he was so big, so hard—

"But now you know it isn't a dream," the Teacher said with a smile in his voice as he thrust slowly and deeply into her. "Kneel on the stool, Kirsty, and rest your head on your arms on this ledge."

Out of nowhere, a padded stool had appeared, and also a padded ledge on which to rest as the Teacher had suggested she should.

"Thrust your buttocks in the air," he commanded.

The Teacher's voice was stern, which made her hurry to assume the correct position. She lifted her bottom high, exposing her sex fully to the Teacher's appreciative gaze.

"Now open your legs a little wider," he instructed.

She spread them as wide as she could on the stool and was rewarded immediately by a fast flurry of strokes. Just as she thought she must tip off the edge with pleasure, he withdrew and teased her with the silky-smooth helmet, allowing her just the tip. He drew it back and forth several times allowing them both to enjoy the moist sounds before plunging deep.

Now his hands were on the small of her back, firmly positioning her. He encouraged her to thrust her bottom as high as she could. She cried out in ecstasy to urge him on.

"Is this what you want, Kirsty? Is this what you need?"

She could only sob her assent. She was almost standing on her shoulders in an attempt to offer him the very best access she could, and with each thrust she tried to take in even more of him. But with the Teacher's hands on her hips, he was in control.

She was content to submit to his will, Kirsty decided, angling her head so she could watch Mrs. Thorndike's lover at work.

She mewled in disappointment when the Teacher withdrew fully once more, and ordered him to return. He laughed and thrust back deeply, and was she imagining it, or was his wonderfully thick cock vibrating too? "How do you do that?"

"There's nothing I cannot do to bring you pleasure," he said. "I can be anything you want me to be, I can do anything you want me to do, I can fill you anyway you want to be filled. For example, I can stretch you like this—"

At the practical demonstration, she gasped.

"Or I can simply adopt the optimum shape to ensure your complete satisfaction."

As he pulsed and plunged she could feel deep ridges on his cock as well as the insistent vibration of some magical power. The sensations were so extreme, the surge of pleasure beyond anything she could have imagined.

"Now," the Teacher exclaimed roughly, "Shall we all come at once?"

"Oh, yes please," Kirsty begged, working her hips frantically.

"Don't rush now," the Teacher warned. "Let me do the work, and that way you will feel more..."

The Teacher could do whatever he liked with her. He knew exactly what she needed and how to extract the utmost pleasure from every stroke. As he had suggested, she allowed her muscles to relax. Reaching back, she cupped her buttocks, holding herself open to show how greatly she appreciated his attention.

"That's good," he approved, "I'm pleased with you, Kirsty."

He set up a series of fast, firm strokes and the slapping sounds excited her so much she was pushed over the edge at once. She wailed in delight as the climax washed over her and then dimly became aware Mrs. Thorndike was crying out too, as was the man with her, though his cry was more of a howl—a long, high-pitched howl of extreme pleasure.

"I think we had better leave Mrs. Thorndike to compose herself," the Teacher suggested when Kirsty had calmed down enough to understand him.

"But her bonds—she is still tied to the pole," Kirsty protested, thinking the Teacher meant to leave her now. "How can we go until we're sure the man with her will release her?"

"They will disappear as your bench has," the Teacher murmured, dropping a kiss on her neck.

He was right. Where was the padded bench upon which she had been kneeling? It had disappeared, as had the padded ledge where she had rested her head. And what had happened to the door? It was solid again. And where was the moonlight that had been streaming through the window?

"What's happening? Where are you?" Kirsty cried out with alarm.

Silence greeted her. She was alone in the cellar; alone in the dark in the middle of the night.

But just as she started to panic, the Teacher returned.

"Kirsty?"

"How could you leave me like that?"

"Our needs were fulfilled."

"Is that how men behave on Planet Erotica, or wherever it is you come from? Down here on earth when a man and woman get it together—"

"Get it together?"

"For the second time," Kirsty reminded him, refusing to be put off. "You can't just do that and then leave me without saying goodbye to me properly—"

"Like this, you mean...?"

His kiss shot molten honey through her veins. "I can't go on like this," she admitted, lacing her fingers through his hair to keep him close.

"Like this?" He kissed her again and again until she cried. "What is this?" he said, examining the teardrop he had captured on his fingertip.

"A tear," Kirsty sniffed. She tried to turn her head away, but the Teacher cupped her chin and brought her back to face him.

"A tear?" he said. "That is what happens to a human when they're sad. They cry. Do I make you sad, Kirsty?" He frowned as he looked down at her.

Did a man who lived in her dreams make her sad? Did he make her feel lonelier than ever when he wasn't there? Longing washed over her for things she couldn't have, but as if the Teacher could read her thoughts, he drew her close again to plant a tender kiss on her brow.

"Don't cry," he said. "I'm always with you..."

"Always?" Kirsty bit her lip. She wondered if *always* was a concept the Teacher understood. "I thought you knew everything. I thought you were the Teacher of All Things. And yet you don't know how you make me feel inside—"

"No, I don't," he admitted.

"Then let me give you a list. You turn up without invitation and turn my perfectly respectable guesthouse into a bordello complete with bondage cellar. You expect me to me to take that on the chin?"

"We have incredible sex and you're complaining?"

"That's not the point. You can't just arrive unannounced, have great sex with me and then disappear immediately afterwards."

"Why would I stay?" he said, frowning.

Kirsty was glad of the shadows as her cheeks flamed red. She should have known there was nothing more to it than sex. What was she expecting? A relationship with a ghost?"

"Don't fight the magic, Kirsty—"

"Magic?"

"What else?"

"I don't know. That's just it, isn't it? And the next time you come here—"

"The next time?" The Teacher's lips tugged up in a smile.

"You have to have a name—"

"A name?"

"Yes." Without a name, he was nothing, no one, and she had just discovered she wanted him to be a lot more than that.

"You know my name," he insisted.

"I mean a proper name—a name I can call you by."

"Is that it?"

"No. It isn't. Don't leave me here alone in the dark, I don't like it—"

"Don't cry, Kirsty, don't be sad."

But the tears were flowing freely now because he had showed that he could care, which made her frightened of losing him. She was frightened of the moment when he would return to his own world, knowing how lonely that would leave her.

"I promise to give you some warning next time," he said.

She looked up into his eyes. "Next time?" she murmured wryly.

"Next time," the Teacher confirmed softly. "And perhaps I'll be able to stay longer next time. But until I return, you must remember what I've told you—you will never be alone. I'm always with you, so you have no need to be afraid."

As she stared at him, she believed him. "I'd better go and make sure that Mrs. Thorndike's all right..."

"Yes, you had."

Was she imagining it, or was the Teacher's voice growing fainter? She ran her hands down his arms, longing to keep hold of him and knowing that he was as illusive as a shadow.

"Go to your guest, Kirsty," the Teacher's voice instructed

her, coming as though from a far distance.

She returned to the peephole and stared in, finding it hard to adjust her gaze. The Teacher was always surrounded by an aura of light, and that had briefly blinded her. But gradually she could see that the pole had gone, and the man too, and that Mrs. Thorndike was free of all her bindings and was fully dressed. She was just easing on her flat-heeled, sensible shoes.

And the cellar window was open, Kirsty noticed with surprise. So that was how the man had gotten in!

It was too late to ask the Teacher, for he had gone. She should have thought of security while he was with her and perhaps asked him for advice, Kirsty realized, impatient with herself.

Resting her face against the wooden door again, she gasped with surprise and lurched back in horror. She had been just in time to see the back legs of a wolf, and the flash of his shaggy gray tail streaking past Mrs. Thorndike.

With a bounding leap, he disappeared through the window and vanished into the night.

☙

Caleb's Tale

By Maristella Kent

Eileen was enjoying her holiday. The walks were in the morning, and optional, but almost everybody went on each one. The scenery around Lachmuirghan was fascinating and often spectacular, but although she had spent some time searching, she had yet to see another stag.

It was the afternoon of the fourth day and Eileen had the

slightly warm and weary calves that confirmed the walk had been just a little too long for her level of fitness. She didn't regret it, though - seeing the waterfall near the end of the long circular walk had been a magnificent prize for her efforts. Caleb hadn't joined them this time, to her disappointment, but Adam had.

Adam. She wondered what it was about him that made him impossible to ignore. Some sense of how powerful he was, how masculine?

Given the choice, Caleb was by far the easier companion. Willing to join in the conversation, to instigate and laugh at gentle teasing, to be surrounded by female company. Eileen admired his ease with himself and others, though she had yet to manage anything more than a passing-the-time-of-day chat. At the end of the walk he would have made some teasing remark about them all needing to chill.

Adam, in contrast, had stayed remote, though he always responded if asked a direct question. She felt that casual chit-chat irritated him, so she preferred not to bother him. When she had reached their goal, elated that she had managed the walk without too much difficulty, she had turned round with a grin and their glances had collided.

He was looking directly at her, unsmiling and deeply serious, as if she were some sort of object for scientific study. Her smile had collapsed but she hadn't looked away. He seemed to take her look as some sort of confirmation as he had nodded slightly before striding to the edge of the pool and bending to splash some water over his face and neck.

She smiled now as she remembered how the teenage girls had run, giggling, into the shallow pool to stand under the water as it poured down from the lip of the rock. Unable to resist, she had joined them. The water had been gloriously cool.

After a very short while she had realized it was really too cold to tolerate for more than a few seconds—no wonder the teenagers had been half-screaming as well as laughing. Her nipples had contracted and were pushing, braless, at the front of her thin shirt.

She was suddenly much too conscious of her body's reaction. Caleb would have given a knowing smile or wink, and she would have laughed with him, but Adam was quite another thing.

She stepped away from the water and shook her hair. The droplets fanned out in the sunshine, each holding a tiny rainbow. And then she sensed Adam looking at her again—he was not looking at her body but at her eyes. It felt almost as if he was looking into her mind.

Self-consciously, she had gone to her backpack to get her fleece and had wrapped herself in it, swapping lighthearted comments with the young girls as she warmed up. She consciously avoided looking at Adam again, and after a while she began to feel less exposed.

She walked with the group back to their lodgings, aware all the time of her damp walking shorts clinging to her thighs and hotly aware of Adam walking behind them, on his own. He had not spoken with any of them beyond politeness, but she sensed he was more relaxed than he had been at the start of the tour. But as he seemed ever more comfortable, she, perversely, became more tense in his company.

After changing into a T-shirt and her favorite faded jeans, the afternoon was her own. Eileen desired nothing more than relaxation. She had not yet decided how to spend her time, but the Book Shop seemed a good place to start. She'd already finished the novel she had brought with her and it would be great to have something else to read.

She stepped into the store, and it was like stepping back in time. A bell rang as she pushed open the door, and the sound brought an elderly man from his office out to the counter. The fustiness unique to old books permeated the rows of shelves. It was a surprise to see one section of DVDs and videos—they seemed incongruous in that setting.

Eileen made her way to the section marked "local history". Perhaps it would have something about the castle? She had been intrigued by how the light changed the color of the castle walls at different times of day and from different angles. There was a walk to the castle planned later that week—one she'd make every effort to join.

She was looking at a thin volume of local maps, the edges of the book amber with age, when an American voice pierced her study and the book was taken from her hands.

"Too dry and dusty for my taste."

Caleb was holding the volume of maps and smiling down at her. It was, perhaps, the nearest to him she had been all week. Not from choice, but because wherever he went he seemed to be surrounded by the teenage girls or by other women in the group. There was no denying the attraction she felt, certainly not when he was standing this close and leaning casually against the shelving. He was lean, tanned, gorgeous—and grinning. His scent was a mixture of a musky aftershave and pure male.

"You missed the walk today," she said, then cursed herself for blurting out something so obvious. So much for promising herself that she would always be cool and controlled in his company!

"Yeah," he drawled, "I went off on my own. Having so much company was getting a little tiring."

And when she stiffened, thinking that he must have meant

to insult her, he was quick to place a hand on her bare forearm. "I'm not including you, just the jailbait—though it's nice to be idolized!"

Eileen couldn't help but respond to that with a rueful smile of her own

"Come on." He pushed the book back into its place on the shelf. "Let's be just a little more modern."

Amused, Eileen allowed herself to be steered towards the DVDs.

"Now let me guess," he told her, "you love romantic films rather than action thrillers or sci-fi fantasy." He wasn't even looking at her as he thumbed the selection. "Romantic comedy, probably." He took a DVD from the shelf, turned to her, and held it up for her to approve.

Eileen wished she could shock him by denying it.

"You're right," she admitted, "but I watched that one less than a fortnight ago. Can I confess that I love musicals and Westerns, too?"

"Westerns? Really?"

She had surprised him.

He put back the DVD and picked up another, this one starring Antonio Banderas.

"How about this one? It had great reviews."

She gave it barely a glance, more interested in his eyes. They were the color of faded denim and perfectly framed by his masculine features and sun-lightened hair. That his hair was not cut short, but reached past his collar, made him even more attractive to Eileen. He was one handsome man, and the only problem she could see was that he knew that all too well.

"It's probably a great film," she acknowledged, "but as I don't have any way of watching it, it seems a little foolish to borrow it just to admire the cover!"

"Are you staying at the The God in the Valley?"

"Yes, aren't you?"

"I was, but I checked out after one night and three notes pushed under my door."

He grinned again, inviting her to share the joke.

"I tried The Royal Rescue—but they only have one room for hire, and that was booked, so I'm staying at the Guest House now. It's only just reopened. I've indulged in their best room, and I have a DVD player and a TV if you want to watch this with me."

Eileen hesitated. Was she crazy to think that he might be propositioning her? He had been nothing but attentive. She was experienced enough and wise enough to talk herself out of trouble if need be, surely? The frisson of attraction she felt was probably one sided. Hadn't he just said how tired he was of being pursued?

If he noticed her inner dialogue, he was smart enough not to comment. He just waited until she gave a faint nod, then walked to the counter with the DVD.

After Caleb had a brief conversation with the shopkeeper, Eileen realized that he would have to buy the disc rather than rent it since he wasn't able to prove local residency.

The elderly man looked rather searchingly at the both of them, which made Eileen feel a little uncomfortable. Then he left the counter to go into his small office, and on his return produced a sealed copy of the DVD they had chosen. He smiled at Eileen, revealing an incomplete set of teeth. It was a kindly smile, as if he knew something she did not. He looked as if he intended to speak, but then he appeared to think better of it and just handed the DVD to Caleb, before telling him, with a soft Gaelic accent, that he hoped they would both enjoy it.

Eileen shivered, though she was not cold. It was probably arousal, the awareness of just how much she was attracted to Caleb.

And now she was reluctant to leave the shop, which, she realized, was silly. She chided herself mentally and stepped out into the sunlight. If anyone did see them together, it was a totally innocent thing to be doing—walking together and looking into the shop windows they passed, commenting on the goods for sale.

There was so much tangible history here. Eileen paused to look into the windows of the old-fashioned sweet shop. There were glass jars aplenty—each holding sweets that she could remember from her childhood but hadn't seen in years.

She looked round, but Caleb had vanished. And then she saw him through the window, inside the shop, pointing at various jars and getting an awful lot of paper bags filled with the sweets. She walked inside to join him.

"Is there anything you'd like to try?" he asked her.

She pointed to a couple of jars but he laughed and said he had some of those already. Then she saw butter tablet, a golden fudgy brown, in a shallow pan. "Some of that, then, please."

The shopkeeper deftly broke off half a dozen hand-cut squares and placed them in a bag. Eileen looked for her purse, but Caleb stopped her and reached for his own wallet to pay for the sweets.

"Thank you."

The shopkeeper found a larger bag and placed all the packets carefully inside.

They walked on, sucking aniseed balls—something Caleb swore was completely new to him but "Not that bad, really," which made her laugh.

When they arrived at the guesthouse, Eileen's voice failed her in the middle of a sentence. She felt her throat dry with nerves. What was she committing herself to doing? She hardly knew this man, was not by nature flirtatious, and wondered again if it was wise to go with him to his room. But he had already gone to get the key. He returned with a friendly woman who seemed pleased to see them. He introduced her as Kirsty, the new owner of the guesthouse, and she explained there were not many visitors staying yet, since she was renovating the rooms one by one. Eileen was ridiculously grateful when she smiled at her. She had been anticipating disapproval, but Kirsty seemed perfectly happy to welcome them.

Caleb clasped her hand in his, and she was so surprised that she followed him meekly to the stairs.

"I'm on the top floor," he told her.

And he was. He unlocked the door and she went at once to stand by the window. The view across to the castle was marvelous. It was golden in the afternoon sunshine.

Behind her, Caleb placed the carrier of sweets on the bedside table and examined the DVD player and a large-screened television. He tore off the plastic wrapping, placed the disc in the player, then went to arrange the pillows on the bed.

"Come on and make yourself comfortable," he invited.

When she looked round, he was sprawled on the bed, his head and shoulders supported by a couple of pillows, and seemed thoroughly at ease. She saw no way of refusing without seeming prissy. The room was not large enough to hold much more than the king-sized bed, the wardrobe, and one hard-backed chair by the window. Justifying her decision to sit on the bed, she mentally noted that they were both fully dressed. Caleb seemed to have nothing on his mind but relaxation, and he had placed the small packs of sweets enticingly in the middle of the bed. He was already crunching at a lemon sherbet.

She shucked off her shoes and climbed onto the luxuriously silky bedcover.

"I hope you are claiming a refund for the other room," she told him. "This one looks considerably more expensive."

He shrugged. "It's only money."

His casually well-cut clothes supported the idea that he had more than enough money not to worry about spending some on a comfortable place to stay for a few days.

As she settled down beside him, the wonderful pillows light and comfortable against her back, he pointed the remote control at the television and the disc started.

It was at once apparent that the sunlit room was too bright. Caleb hit the pause button, stood up and walked round the bed to the window. He reached for the curtain, but then sought Eileen's permission.

"Are you comfortable with me doing this?" he asked her.

And, just because he had bothered to ask, Eileen was happy that he should shut out the world.

There was still enough daylight through the drawn curtains for him to make his way to the bed. He snuggled back down, and Eileen wondered if perhaps he was a little nearer than before. She was very aware of the male scent from his skin, still warm from the sun.

She tried to concentrate on the film.

Against an empty desert a man on a horse was silhouetted against the horizon. The camera watched them move swiftly into the foreground, dust rising from the horse's hooves. Eileen expected the man to be Antonio Banderas, but it was not—it was a man who looked very much like—Caleb.

Beside her she heard Caleb's intake of breath. She turned

to look at him, but his gaze was fixed on the screen as if he could not believe it.

The camera tracked the man as he rode past the camera to a simple homestead. Dismounting, the cowboy strode to the door and knocked. And the door was opened by a woman in old-fashioned Western clothing. She looked just like—Eileen, though on screen the woman's dark curly hair was loose around her shoulders. Eileen had caught her own hair back, as the day had been so warm.

For the first time the man spoke. He had Caleb's deeply sensuous voice and he asked for water for his horse and whether he could buy provisions for himself. Uncertainly, the woman gave permission for the man to draw water for the horse, and invited him to come back inside when he had finished. She indicated a rail where he could tether the animal.

Although the woman had a Southern accent, her voice was Eileen's.

Eileen turned from the screen to look at Caleb. He had stopped midway through eating his sweet. Obviously they were both seeing and hearing their likenesses on screen. Caleb managed to swallow. She found she had reached out to touch his hand and he had enclosed it in his. They looked at each other in disbelief.

"Does this make any sense to you?" he asked her.

Eileen shook her head, unable to speak. They both looked back at the screen. She drew comfort from how his hand enveloped her own.

The film now focused on the man walking back into the homestead. He took off his hat respectfully and she indicated he could use the chair at the table. He drew it back, and sat on it carefully, as if he were not quite sure how to behave in a woman's company. She took his hat from him and placed it on a low cupboard.

Then she ladled some stew from a pan on the stove and set a bowl of it in front of him, with a hunk of bread and a spoon. He bent hungrily over the food and began to eat. It did not take him long to finish eating, and she offered him more. Eileen found the way he ate, the neediness, very sensual. She could almost smell the aroma of the thick stew—it must have been heavenly to a hungry man.

When he had finished the second bowl, mopping up the last of it with the crust of the bread, he sighed and leaned back a little in his chair.

"Thank you, ma'am. That was just what I needed," he told her.

She smiled, her face shy, and asked what else she could do. And then he stood and reached for her, holding her firmly by the shoulders, and kissed her on the lips.

She seemed stunned, but not more so than the couple watching her. Arousal surged through Eileen, making her stomach tense. Caleb tightened the grip on her hand as if he could not bear to let her go.

After a second, the cowboy drew back to see that her cheeks were stained with a rosy blush. He released her and started to apologize, but she leaned towards him and silenced him by returning the kiss.

Caleb's grip slackened, perhaps in disbelief, then tightened once more. Eileen found herself unable to look away from the screen.

In a gesture totally without shame, the woman reached for the ribbons that tied her blouse and undid them. Now the cowboy could see the slope of her breasts. He pushed down the material and exposed her nipples. Then he bent to kiss each in turn.

Caleb muttered something and shifted a little on the bed, wriggling against his jeans. Eileen, sparing him just a sideways glance—afraid that she might miss something on the screen—sympathized. Her clothes also felt too tight against her aroused flesh.

The woman who was almost Eileen placed her hands on the cowboy's shoulders and kissed him once more. There was a passion and awareness in that kiss that was more sensual than anything Eileen had ever seen. Beside her on the bed, Caleb muttered a curse which confirmed he, too, felt its power.

The woman pushed off the cowboy's sleeveless leather vest, leaving his shirt still buttoned, then dropped her hands and grasped his. Without taking her eyes off him, she led him through a curtained doorway into her bedroom. The furnishings were simple, but clean. A small window illuminated the room and the high bed.

The cowboy knelt to undo the woman's skirt then place it over the bedstead. He eased her blouse off her shoulders and let it fall past her hips to the ground. Her skin was not sun-kissed but tantalizingly pale. He stood back briefly to admire her before returning to his task and removing all of her undergarments. His fingers were shaking with desire and urgency but he did not hurry the task.

Caleb groaned.

The woman stood in front of him, naked and proud of her body. Once more he worshipped her breasts, then he began to kiss down her body, murmuring his pleasure. She stopped him to unbutton his shirt, easing each button from its hole. Then she pulled his shirttails out from his old-fashioned travel-worn and dusty jeans, and bent in her turn to kiss his nipples. Eileen was mesmerized by his lean body, one obviously honed by hard outdoor work, with the muscles well defined. His chest was bronzed by the sun.

Eileen felt so hot she could hardly breathe. Her palm was sweaty in Caleb's hand. She wanted to release her grip, yet she wanted to go on holding his hand forever.

Taking her time, the woman pulled at the cowboy's belt and undid the silver clasp on the leather. Once loosened, she unbuttoned his jeans. Then, having tantalized Eileen to the point where she was feeling faint with the desire to see his arousal, the woman stopped and pushed the cowboy down onto the bed and knelt before him. He sat at the edge, legs akimbo, awaiting whatever she chose, his pupils dilated with desire.

Eileen gulped. Surely she wasn't intending...?

The woman paused just long enough to convince Eileen that she was indeed about to draw the man's cock from his jeans and suck him into her mouth, then she laughed quietly and bent to remove each of his boots, her hair brushing against his jean-clad thighs.

Eileen, who had started to relax as the tension eased, sat up once more as the woman finished her task and boldly put her hand on the cowboy's fly. And then, as he thrust himself impatiently towards her, she drew out his marvelous cock—rigidly erect—and stroked down its hard length. The cowboy sighed.

And so did Caleb, but his was a sigh tinged with frustration rather than pleasure.

The woman bent to kiss away the pearl of liquid at the tip of his cock. The camera showed all of this in a glorious close-up.

She licked her lips and, unconsciously echoing the action, so did Eileen. The cowboy's erection, released from the jeans, was waiting to be kissed again—twitching just a little in anticipation.

With the hand not holding Eileen's, Caleb rearranged his own erection. He moved as subtly as he could, she thought, but Eileen was sensitized to his body now and was feeling the same excitement. He swept the packets of sweets down the bed, uncaring that some spilled, and scooted closer to Eileen. She was perfectly happy to have his body pressed next to hers and noticed, distantly, that they were both breathing quite fast.

The woman pulled the cowboy's jeans down his muscled thighs, he shifted to help her, and she sighed with pleasure as she saw his cock and his balls fully revealed. He was massively erect, and the head of his cock reached almost to his belly button, rearing up from a diamond of tight curls. His balls were tightly contracted against the apex of his thighs.

He stood and stepped out of his jeans and, still kneeling, she took the head of his cock into her mouth. He was too long for her to take all of him in, but she sucked eagerly and tried hard to take in all she could. Then she released his cock and swirled her tongue around the rim of its head. He moaned his pleasure and so did she. She kissed her way down the stalk to his balls and took each in turn into her mouth.

That sight was one of the most erotic Eileen had ever seen. The woman's lips were red and swollen with arousal, contrasting strongly with his paler skin, and his dark blond sex curls tangled with the woman's darker hair.

He raised her to her feet and bent to kiss her, stopping briefly to register the musk of his own scent on her lips, then he plundered her mouth with his tongue.

When Eileen was certain she couldn't become more aroused, the cowboy started nipping at the woman's swollen lower lip with his teeth, then butterfly kissing the place he had bitten.

Eileen could bear no more. She took her hand from Caleb's

and undid the clasp which restrained her hair. Her scalp tingled as she ran her hands through her heavy curls. Caleb shifted on the bed so that he could reach round Eileen, hastily pushing the pillows into place so that he could lean back and take Eileen's weight against his chest. He rubbed urgently at her breasts and squeezed her nipples through the thin knitted cotton of her T-shirt.

Eileen sat up and pulled the T-shirt off. Like the woman in the film, she was not wearing a bra. Caleb ripped open his shirt so that the heated skin of her back was against the tightly aroused skin of his chest. Both were still watching the screen but Eileen felt a connection to Caleb that seemed eons old. Caleb cupped and stroked Eileen's breasts—how swollen they seemed and how distended her nipples were with desire.

He breathed out against her neck, ruffling her hair, causing her to shudder at the moist warmth and press herself even more closely against him.

In the film the man was urging the woman down onto the bed. Unlike Caleb and Eileen, he was able to gaze fully at the object of his desire. He arranged her reverently and the camera followed his gaze down her body. When it reached her sex, Caleb and Eileen saw his fingers move to her clit then stroke her. She mewled with desire and pushed herself invitingly towards him. Encouraged, he ran his fingers once more over her mound. The camera watched as he inserted the forefinger of one hand gently into her moist sex, still stroking her clit with the other.

Eileen felt the heavy heat and wetness of her own cunt waiting to be stroked and worshipped.

The cowboy withdrew his finger and took it to his own lips. He savored the scent of her arousal before he slowly licked her perfume off his finger.

Caleb shrugged off his shirt and scrabbled to undo his jeans. He pushed them down his legs and onto the floor. Eileen removed her own clothes, and when they were both naked, she knelt over him with her legs astride his, both of them still turned toward the screen. She could feel Caleb's cock pressing up against the small of her back. She wriggled against it and heard him moan once more.

On screen the cowboy now arranged himself so that he was lying with his head on the woman's stomach, his legs by her head. For a moment he looked directly at the camera and Eileen felt the shock as if he had looked right at her. He smiled ever so slightly and then bent to apply his tongue to the tender flesh his fingers had prepared.

"Please," begged Caleb as his fingers followed the path the cowboy was making.

She gasped her approval. Caleb kissed her shoulder, and she shivered at the way the kiss zinged to transfer itself to her cunt. She looked over her shoulder to Caleb and he rubbed his face against her cheek.

They looked back at the screen.

The cowboy now held the woman's sex lips apart, starkly beautiful and almost purple inside with arousal, as he licked at the liquid center. Eileen could hardly bear to watch the beauty of it. He looked up once more at the camera and again she felt he was staring at, connecting with, her.

Like Eileen, the woman was shuddering with the need to complete the act of penetration, but she took advantage of the man's position to take his cock into her mouth even as he sucked and licked at her clit and cunt.

The man gently disengaged himself, his cock pulsing and wet with the woman's kisses. He stood up, never taking his hands off her skin, and positioned her so that she was half-sitting, half leaning back, her elbows supporting her body at the edge of the bed. The mattress was high enough for his cock to be level with her cunt. In a stunning close-up, Eileen and Caleb watched him place himself so that his cock entered her sex.

The camera cut away briefly to show the ecstasy in his face and hers as she threw her head back in pleasure.

Eileen raised her own sex and positioned herself over Caleb's cock. With a groan, she lowered herself until she had sheathed him completely. Like the cowboy, he was a gloriously substantial size.

As the cowboy penetrated then withdrew from his woman, Eileen raised and lowered herself on Caleb's cock as Caleb supported her with his hands around her waist so that she felt weightless and cherished.

The cowboy and his woman were very close to coming. The woman broke first but the cowboy came almost at the same time, pulling out of her so that his seed spurted impressively over her belly and breasts.

As Eileen convulsed in her turn, pushing down onto him, Caleb spurted his own seed deep into her body. As he did so, Eileen turned to look at him over her shoulder—her eyes seeking and gaining the reassurance that his feelings were as intense as hers.

The cowboy cried out the woman's name as she called out his:

"Eileen!"

"Caleb!"

The couple in the hotel room were locked in a kiss so deeply and mutually satisfying that they were oblivious to anything happening in the film.

Eventually, when they did look back at the screen, it was

blank.

Eileen felt that perhaps she ought to have been ashamed, but she was not. Never before had she enjoyed sex with two different men in the space of so few days. Each experience had been totally unexpected, but wonderful—and completely irresistible. Smiling at the memories she would take with her from this holiday, she allowed Caleb to lead her into the adjoining shower room where they washed each other tenderly.

Finally they dried each other on the fluffy towels and returned to the bed. Caleb tucked her under the covers and insisted on feeding her pieces of butter tablet through her giggles, so that she could "regain her strength".

They were both tired but Caleb, curious, switched the DVD on again.

This time there was no erotic film, just the Western they had expected to see. Sated and contented, Caleb turned it off. With their arms around each other, Eileen and Caleb fell asleep.

Four:
The Museum

Lachmuirghan has a small museum, though it is not mentioned in any tourist brochure, nor is its location on any map. It is referred to in a couple of the older books in the local bookshop, but no directions are given. In fact it is housed in an old building on the outskirts of Lachmuirghan. In glass-fronted cabinets are some artifacts showing a little of the history of the village. Some say these are genuine, others are not so sure.

Like the museum itself, the artifacts are sometimes there to be seen, and sometimes they are not. The most prized exhibits are in the "Bonnie Prince Charlie Room".

To find the museum, you need either a guide—or to be very lucky. Even the local folk are not always able to find the ancient building. To enter the museum, you need an old metal key, and that is only available from The Guardian.

Some say the key is passed down within a family, others that it is passed down within a coven. Either way, it is always a female guardian who holds it in trust. Whenever it is in the possession of a male for more than a few hours, bad luck accompanies the key.

And sometimes The Guardian will refuse to give it to you. She will never say why.

So lucky indeed is the person granted access to the museum...

ଓ

Ben's Tale

By Maristella Kent

Eileen was wandering through the village of Lachmuirghan when she saw Ben at the far end of one of the narrowest lanes. Her first instinct was to pretend she hadn't seen him. So much had happened in the past week that she had been seeking solace in being alone.

Caleb had left the tour the morning after their encounter.

"Too weird for me, sweetheart," he'd told her. Then insisted she kept the DVD as a souvenir. She half-wondered if it had been a shared hallucination. She had no other explanation for what they had both experienced.

Nobody had said anything to her after his departure, so presumably they hadn't known why he was gone. Eileen was glad that the group of young girls, who had been so disappointed on that morning's walk, didn't connect his disappearance with her. Not that they could have been that upset—after the first few minutes they had concentrated their efforts on teasing Ben, their guide that morning, until he was an embarrassed brick red. Eventually she had intervened and distracted them, leaving Ben to walk behind with the elderly couple in the party and call out directions from time to time.

Adam hadn't been with them. She'd seen him speaking into a mobile phone just before they left, and he had not joined them. She wished he didn't hold such a powerful attraction for her, and could not understand why he did.

It was too late now to pretend that she hadn't noticed Ben. He had been saying goodbye to an older woman, perhaps a family member, and now that he had seen Eileen he was hurrying towards her.

"It must have been fate." He smiled. "My aunt was just lending me the keys to the local museum—if you can call it that."

"I didn't know Lachmuirghan had a museum," she told him. "You've not mentioned it before."

"Ah. Well," he looked embarrassed, "the thing is that—you can't always—it's not easy to—" He cleared his throat. "Some things are best not enquired into too closely, if you take my meaning."

Eileen nodded, though she wasn't at all sure she understood.

"Anyway," he jangled the bunch of keys, "I have these, and now I've met with you, so perhaps we'll be lucky today. Will you walk a way with me?" He offered her his arm in a gesture of old-fashioned courtesy.

Once again, Eileen was struck by his physique. Normally, for driving, he wore a crisply ironed white shirt over a white tee, but today he was in a knitted polo shirt and jeans. She wondered if it was driving the bus that had developed his muscles, or whether he worked out in a gym.

Where Caleb was lean, Ben was muscled, where Adam was dark and brooding, Ben was fairer, sunnier and shorter, but solidly attractive nonetheless. She linked her arm with his strong forearm, loving the warmth of flesh against flesh, and they walked in a companionable silence along the lane. After perhaps ten minutes, the houses thinned. They reached a bend in the road and he muttered something about seeing if it was there.

"Wait here just a minute," he told her.

Bemused, she waited as he walked quickly ahead then saw him sigh and relax.

"It's here," was all he said, but it sent a tingle of anticipation up her spine. When she joined him, he escorted her down the footway beneath some ancient-looking trees. Ahead of them was an old building, set back a little from the path. The leaves offered pleasant shade against the strong afternoon sun, and she could hear a stream as well as birdsong.

If she'd thought the trees were ancient, they were nothing to the age of this building. It was not completely straight or square at any corner. The beams that held up the top story jutted out a little way into the lane, supporting the multi-chimneyed top half, and the whole thing listed a little to the right.

Ben stepped up to the doorway, took the largest key—an ancient iron affair, very plain—and inserted it into the huge door. It turned easily and the door swung open. He moved to the side to allow her to enter first.

The air inside was sweet rather than musty, and cool. She shivered and Ben immediately wrapped his arm round her shoulder.

"You'll soon get used to it. Come on, see what there is here."

He led her through the doorway to the left of the steep staircase. The room was not large, but it was fitted out with floor-to-ceiling glass cases. In each of them was a scene portraying an aspect of village life through the years. In one there was an ancient scythe and a spoked wooden wheel rimmed in iron. Behind these and other implements was a wonderful painted background showing villagers toiling in the fields—the castle behind them.

Another case had fishing implements, a woven reed basket, and an oar. Again there was a painting. This time it was showing a fishing boat and villagers bringing in the catch.

Eileen became very conscious that Ben's arm was still around her shoulders. And that they were alone here. She tried to move away slightly and stumbled over the uneven flagstone floor. Ben caught her, showing quick reflexes, and saved her from tripping. Eileen gave in to the feeling of being cared for.

When they had finished looking at that room, they walked to the door, and Ben seemed anxious as they turned back into the hallway. She felt the breath he took before walking her into the opposite downstairs room. He was suddenly so tense that the easy conversation they'd been having dried on her lips. Why was he so worried?

As they walked into the room he relaxed.

"We are honored, lassie," he told her. "I promised my aunt I'd lock the front door if we were able to visit this room. I'm not sure why she was so insistent, but I have promised."

Eileen nodded her permission and missed his warm, strong, body as he went to lock the front door. But then her eye was caught by the exhibition of artifacts of Bonnie Prince Charlie.

She went nearer to the case to get a better view. Ben joined her and explained that sometimes jewelry and letters were here and sometimes they were not. This time they were not. A hooded cloak, a leather-bound prayer book and a dirk were arranged against a painted background of a croft. A rowing boat could be seen—with two figures in it—through the small croft window.

"Did that prayer book belong to the king or to Flora?" she asked him.

He smiled.

"It might not have belonged to either! My aunt is a firm believer that these cases contain the genuine things, but I am not so sure."

He did not look away from her, and although she thought it might be wiser to do so, she did not break their glance either. This time it was definitely a sexual tension which made her shiver.

Gently he leaned down to claim her mouth in a kiss. His male scent, mixed with aftershave, was potently attractive. Drawing back, he told her, "I didnae mean to do that, but I confess that I've wanted to since I first saw you."

He kissed her again, and this time Eileen was the one to prolong the kiss. She was quite shaken by the intensity of the moment. Perhaps she could blame it on the history around her? The hushed atmosphere seemed to magnify her awareness of her body—and his. Without taking her eyes off his gentle face, she took his hands in hers and moved him down towards the far end of the room. In the middle of the space was a narrow bench, beautifully upholstered, evidently intended for the weary visitor. At one end it had a scrolled wooden and padded rest. She had meant to sit there for a while with him, but the glass case on the end wall snagged her attention.

It was quite small compared to the other case—there were no painted backdrops here, just a deep blue velvet cloth, and on it, a stunning half-mask.

They gazed at the mask.

"Strange," he murmured, "I remember that as being made of wood and yet..."

It glinted, golden in the light. He chose a key on the ring and unlocked the case. Picking up the mask, he turned it in his hands, puzzled.

“Are we allowed?” Eileen whispered in awe. She was sure that this item was centuries, eons old.

“Oh yes, if we do not intend harm,” Ben told her. He handed the mask to her and she took it, reluctantly at first. But the polished metal was warm to the touch and heavy as she turned it over in her hands. It was sized to fit a human head, the eyes were removed to allow a wearer to see through it, and there were tears dropping from each eye socket. It was plain other than for a suggestion of stylized curls of hair around the top edge. It reminded Eileen of a Greek mask—one used for drama. Surely that was not its origin?

“How old is it? What is its purpose? Does it really belong here?”

Ben shook his head in amusement. “If you asked my aunt she would tell you it was worn by a high priest and related to The God in the Valley, or the grieving god. I have to agree with her that it does seem very old. But why don’t I remember it being metal? Is it bronze, do you think?”

“Well,” Eileen shook her head, “I know I’m being fanciful, but it seems as though it might be solid gold—just from the weight of it and the detailed craftsmanship.”

He took it from her and hefted it in his palms.

“Mmm, you could be right, or it might be lead covered with gold plating, I suppose.” He offered it back to her, but she held her hands up against taking it.

“Tell me about this god first.”

Ben smiled at her. “It’s just a legend, and nobody really knows its origins. Apparently a god once loved a mortal woman in this very village, and when she died he grieved for her. He cried so many tears that he filled the loch, turning the water salty. It’s still a little salty, you know, though nobody has ever found a place where it is joined to the sea. He’s meant to haunt the village, waiting for her return."

"And this mask—what do they say about that?"

"Will wearing it bring you unimaginable wealth, you mean?" he teased her.

"No! Of course not!" Eileen was horrified. "I have no intention of wearing it—it seems such a sacred object."

"It probably was, once, and they do say it was worn by a priest to the god, but those days are centuries past. Are you not curious?" Again he offered it to her, and gently smiled. "I'll make sure you are not harmed."

It was a strange thing for him to say, but Eileen lifted the mask from him and traced round the polished edges with her finger.

"Whether it's precious metal or not, it's still special," she told him, "and it is definitely meant to be worn by a man."

She reached up and fitted it to his face.

It had been an innocent gesture, but in that moment the world seemed to lurch. She no longer saw the display cases—the light around them dimmed as if they were caught in a spotlight. In what seemed a painfully slow gesture, he led her to the upholstered bench and stood behind the scrolled end, just looking at her and not speaking. She went willingly, though she wondered if some part of her brain was trying to stop her. Then she stopped worrying as her leg bumped into the turned wooden leg.

His masked face mesmerized her. He seemed so remote. From his lips came the words of an ancient tongue. She did not know much Gaelic, but it seemed not to be that. Certainly, she had no idea of its meaning. It was a prayer—or an incantation, perhaps. She allowed herself to be positioned, unshod, on the bench, kneeling up on it, facing Ben—who was no longer Ben, but a priestly wise man. This much she knew.

He raised his hands in a summons as the words flowed from his lips. And then she felt the first touch.

It wasn't Ben whose hands were raised in supplication. It wasn't somebody from the lane, as she had heard Ben locking the outer door. It wasn't somebody from upstairs, as she would have heard feet descending on the bare treads.

The touch was not frightening. It urged her, helped her, to undo her clothes. Willingly she obeyed. The room was warm now and flickered as if lit by a hundred candles. Ben's clothes were being peeled from his body by other unseen hands. He was magnificently formed and tanned all over. He must sunbathe naked. It flickered through Eileen's mind that she ought to be frightened, but she was not. If she was to be a sacrifice, then she was a willing sacrifice.

The touch came again. It stroked down her arms to the tips of her fingers and then repeated the action. The second time it happened, another pair of hands cupped her breasts and she leaned forward into the caress. The touch on her arms steadied her as she moaned in pleasure. A third pair of hands joined in, massaging her naked back. As they touched, they warmed. And still Ben chanted, looking heavenward.

A fourth pair of hands joined the others. These parted her legs, gently but firmly, spreading her thighs so that she felt exposed. She was conscious of the perfume of her arousal.

She relaxed as yet more hands rubbed her shoulders and neck and massaged up into her nape whilst another pair stroked her inner thighs.

Now the hands made her bend forward towards Ben. She would have been helpless to resist, but she had no thought of resistance. In front of her, Ben was massively erect. She ached to take his cock into her. Into her mouth or cunt. She wanted to, had to, serve him.

The chanting grew stronger, deeper.

Now the hands were oiling every inch of her. It was a sweetly perfumed oil that was at first cool, then warming. No part of her was neglected. Again she moaned out her pleasure, feeling the probing fingers at her inside lips—where she was already moist and really needed no oiling.

The sensation of being stroked by so many willing hands was exquisite. She wished it would last forever, and yet she wanted it to end now. Somehow she must find the energy to go to Ben or, rather, the Priest-who-was-Ben.

Fingers were swirling around her puckered bottom hole now, spreading her cheeks and rubbing the oil over and around the entrance, and she was aware of how she must look to any viewer—utterly submissive and so close to a climax.

A finger slipped inside her cunt and she cried out and spasmed. She did not want to come before she had pleasured Ben—she knew, somehow, that she must wait for that. All the same, she nearly orgasmed as another finger joined the first. And then a third finger—or perhaps a thumb—carefully inserted itself into her bottom. It was a gentle violation, but the pressure in that forbidden passage as the digit pushed against the resistance then, once inside, massaged itself against those fingers in her cunt made her throb. She cried out and leaned forward even further, intent on taking Ben's hugely erect cock into her mouth.

As she moved she saw his cock turn golden. Perhaps it was a trick of the light, or perhaps it really did turn to gold? She thought she heard a voice whisper in her ear: "Yes. Worship me."

And when she took him into her mouth at last—eager fingers still pinching her nipples and cupping her breasts, and urging her forward—he was velvet on her lips rather than metal.

She pulled slightly back and kissed at his delicate skin, taut with arousal. Oh how good he tasted! She took as much of him as she could into her mouth, and as she licked and sucked, she felt the probing fingers withdraw and something rather larger than a finger take her cunt. She gasped around the cock filling her mouth—it felt so wonderful.

As she continued to suck she felt yet another cock enter her. Somehow she was being doubly penetrated from behind—one huge cock in her cunt and another in her rear. She was unused to feeling such complete fullness. Then, as she allowed herself to relax into the sensation, a finger began to circle her clit and she cried out her pleasure, muffled by Ben's cock. It was with a joyful urgency that she pressed against that skilled finger, allowing her mouth to cherish Ben-the-Priest's phallus as she circled him with her lips and took him alternately shallowly then deeply. With her tongue she pressed against his tip, then teasingly under his rim, then strongly licked where the root met his balls.

She could feel him tensing and his balls gathering tightly up beneath his cock. He, too, was close to coming. Then his voice cried out to the god, unable to stop his sperm spurting into her reverential mouth, and her senses whirled as he came. She closed her mouth tightly over him and took what she could of their offering to the god.

The cocks in her cunt and rear began to move then, pushing, bumping at her and urging her to a violent climax. She felt her muscles clench around the invading cocks. And she could not now prevent the spasms of absolute pleasure. Releasing Ben's cock from her mouth she cried out her own satisfaction, loudly, to the god.

Just when she thought that she had experienced the ultimate climax, the fingers and hands began to stroke her insistently to a second, devastating orgasm. They supported her weight as she came—contracting over and over again—until, spent, she was allowed to sink onto the upholstery. She thought she heard a deep voice whisper once more. This time it said, "We are pleased."

She did not know how long she remained there, though when she looked at her watch later it seemed that some hours had passed. When she stirred she found that she was fully dressed, and that she was lying on the bench with her head in Ben's now-trousered lap, his hands gently stroking her hair.

She looked up at him and he looked down and smiled at her, though it seemed to her that his mind was still half in another time. When she carefully sat up, she saw that the mask had been replaced in the case. It looked nothing more than a wooden artifact now.

Ben gathered her to him, encircling her and kissing her, breathing her scent.

"Thank you," he said, and seemed unable to say any more.

She leaned into his broad chest and savored the quietness of the moment. She was happy, she realized. Happy, but exhausted.

"Are we far from the village?" she asked.

Ben shook his head and told her they were far closer to the village than it had seemed. Sure enough, as they walked back, his arm round her shoulders once more, it was only a couple of minutes before she saw the comforting lights of The God in the Valley glowing in the dusk.

Ben held up the key ring.

"I'll have to return these to my aunt."

Eileen nodded. She smiled as he kissed her then walked away into the gathering darkness of Lachmuirghan.

Five:
The Castle

So many rumors and fables surround the origins of Lachmuirghan's castle, that it is hard to separate truth from fiction.

According to one well-documented fable, the castle was originally the creation of a sea god who caused it to appear overnight. Some say that survivors from the mythical island of Atlantis built the castle and invested it with special magical powers. Whilst yet another states that the castle was built at the same time as the pyramids and beneath its dungeons lie stairs and tunnels which once led to the tomb of a great and powerful king.

In more modern times it has even been suggested that the castle was built to disguise a spaceship and that the strange pulsing light locals swear they have seen radiating from the castle really comes from the hidden craft.

Others say that the fairytale style of the building shows that it was the faeries themselves who built it, and that they return every Midsummer's Night to reclaim it and to hold their revels there, at the command of the Lords of the Universe. It is further said that all manner of faery folk attend these revels—warlocks and witches, spellbinders, shapeshifters and vampires; that Herne the hunter blows his horn to start the revels; that one may see the mysterious sea kelpies; and that it is the fire from the Welsh dragons that lights the ancient hall.

Local legend has it that every magical creature of earth and sea must come to the castle at Midsummer to swear allegiance to their lords and that their names are then written in an ancient and magical book. There is a foolish fear amongst some of the locals that to go near it on Midsummer's Eve is to risk the anger of those who gather there.

Such stories are simply that, of course. Historically and architecturally, it is perfectly clear that the original ancient fortification was rebuilt in the French château style, during the reign of Mary Queen of Scots' father, James V.

And as for the fact that its walls glisten as white as icing sugar and its roofs glint warm gold—why that is merely a trick of the light reflected by the loch and the hills and nothing more, for it is certainly true that the roofs are not gold but mere slate and the walls are not icing sugar but granite. This has been proved when samples of both have been removed from the castle and taken to laboratories for testing.

And as for those who swear that they have actually seen the whole castle lifting from its foundations and hovering above the ground only to change into a different building—let us just say that some of the natives of Lachmuirghan possess an ancient "still", hidden away out of sight, where they brew a spirit strong enough to make a man think a whole village is hovering above the ground.

In recent times the castle has been modernized and is now a luxury spa hotel.

ൠ

Bed of Roses

By Clarissa Wilmot

"So, how does it feel to be the world's greatest rock star?" Crass question, but the one the punters wanted to hear.

"How do you think it feels?" Leo Cathar's tone was teasing, even gently mocking. The famous long, fair hair was flicked casually over broad shoulders, and he sprawled nonchalantly across the sofa, so that Gayle Harper was quite aware of his sheer masculinity—an effect he no doubt intended.

Gayle swallowed hard. There was something so earthy and sensual about Leo Cathar, the latest rock sensation, she was finding it difficult to concentrate on the job in hand, namely to get the exclusive her editor was after. Particularly when the equally gorgeous wine waiter would keep filling her glass. If she wasn't careful, she was going to get squiffy.

"I don't know, you tell me," she said, neatly batting the question back. She flicked her own jet-black hair over her shoulder (not natural of course, but along with her crop top, tight leather jeans, black leather jacket and fuck-me boots, it made her look and feel the part of the rock journalist, and not the ugly gawky kid she had so recently been).

No you're not.

"Excuse me, did you say something?"

Leo looked at her, those deep—were they yellow? Unusual, anyway—eyes bored into her and made her feel hot and bothered in a way that she oughtn't like, but was really quite pleasant.

"No," he said. "I think I was still avoiding answering your question."

Gayle laughed, knowing she was beaten.

"Ok, then, tell me about the vampire stuff. It's all an act, right?"

It was the "vampire stuff" which had first attracted Gayle to Leo Cathar's particularly individual brand of rock music and made her so eager to accept this assignment. He had made his reputation on his ability to shock—performing "sacrifices" on teenage virgins, releasing bats into the crowd, taking part in "satanic" rituals on stage. Most of it was hammed up to get the media's interest, but rumors continued to abound of wild orgies and blood-soaked drug fests. No doubt kept fueled by Leo's PR people. Sales had rocketed as a result. But still it made you wonder, no smoke without fire and all that.

As a teenager, Gayle had been fascinated by vampires and must have read Dracula a dozen times. Since then, she had seen nearly every vampire flick going, and part of her had always hoped they really existed. In fact, and this was something she very rarely admitted, even to herself, the idea of sex with a vampire was a secret fantasy, and one which she was finding increasingly compelling of late. She'd even had dreams about it.

Sick, I must be really sick, she thought to herself. It was something about this place—she was interviewing Leo in the plush surroundings of the Castle Hotel in Lachmuirghan. It was a soft, silent place, with an air of sumptuous luxury. The carpets were so deep, they deadened any sound, which had the odd effect of making people seem to appear from nowhere. Gayle had already been startled by the waiter in this way, and the woman who had led her to this room had positively seemed to glide across the floor. Most odd.

The lights were low and sensuous, and every room was decorated in varying hues of red. The room she was sitting in now, for example, had deep red curtains, two plush red sofas (she was sitting on one, and Leo was sprawled on the other), and a pale pink carpet. A fire burned in the grate—but it didn't seem like a normal fire. It was too fiery red—almost the color of blood. And weirdly, it didn't give off any heat. The rosewood table between them had a vase filled with roses. The perfume was heady and made her dizzy, and she felt herself being overcome by a curious languorous sensation. It wasn't unpleasant but it made her head throb slightly, her arms and legs felt loose and floppy, and she was starting to feel—well—horny. What was it that she had been thinking? Oh yes, that she was pretty sick to fancy vampires. Not even her closest friends were ever going to know that.

Not sick at all.

"I'm sorry?" Gayle blinked and looked at Leo, who was sitting silently in front of her. It was carefully staged without a doubt. Be enigmatic, say nothing. Just look the part. And that he certainly did. His long, fair hair flowed over the baggy white shirt which was undone slightly at the top, revealing a smooth chest.

Good, I don't like chest hair. The thought popped into Gayle's head without a by-your-leave. Good God, what was going on? She didn't normally swoon at the sight of rock stars, but this one—this one was different. His slim legs were encased in leather trousers which left little to the imagination, and the effect was finished off with a pair of cowboy boots. He really was magnificent.

"I don't recall that I said anything," Leo responded. "But you were asking about the 'vampire stuff' as you so quaintly put it. If you believe it, then it is real and if not, then it is just an illusion. Come, let me show you."

He stood up, and in a daze, Gayle found herself standing too. It was as though she had no will of her own. He held out his hand, such a long, beautiful hand, with the sharpest fingernails she had ever seen in a man. The hand of an aristocrat, she thought to herself dreamily.

"Come," he said again. "Let me show you my world."

And suddenly the world was shifting, changing on its axis. She felt herself spinning round and round in a dizzying dance which was not unlike vertigo. He still held her hand and pulled her to him, and she was overcome with the most overwhelming desire to kiss him, to hold him, to let him come to her. And in the midst of it all she could detect the smell of roses, stronger and more potent then ever, which heightened her senses and made her wish for—what exactly? She didn't understand what was happening but she was experiencing a sense of longing the likes of which she'd never known before.

Gayle blinked.

"Well, my lady, would you care to dine?" Leo let go of her hand and motioned her to sit down. The room had changed. The sofas had vanished and been replaced by an enormously long table made of rosewood. And Leo was dressed differently. Instead of black leather, he wore the dress of an eighteenth-century gentleman—or at least how she imagined an eighteenth-century gentleman might look. And he was wrapped in a dark cloak. Okay, now she got it—this was part of his act. The cloak was a staple part of his stage shows.

But then, why was she dressed differently too? She was wearing the most magnificent dress, of a deep crimson, shot through with purple thread. It shimmered and sparkled in the candlelight. It pinched her tightly at the waist and she noticed with some embarrassment it made her breasts swell and thrust forward in a most provocative way—lord, she even had cleavage. Her hair was piled on her head, and round her neck was a locket containing a single ruby.

She looked across at Leo. He was—incredible. He had an

animal presence; was sensuous in a way she had never experienced before. He only had to look at her with those penetrating—yellow, they were definitely yellow—eyes and she was lost in a web of hot desire from which she never wanted to escape. She was his, pure and simple. And he had known it from the first moment they met. And now, so did she.

As if in a dream, she sat down and took in her surroundings. The fire still burned fiercely red in the grate, but above the mantelpiece was a huge mirror decorated with fleur-de-lis. The ceiling of the room was magnificently painted with pictures of cherubs and angels—or so she thought at first. A closer inspection revealed them in somewhat less-than-angelic poses.

She blushed and looked instead at the candelabra which hung from the middle of the ceiling rose. It was very ornate and covered in what she could only imagine was gold leaf. The room felt incredibly luxurious, and—well, soft. Gayle felt as though she could sink into it and allow the sweet, lingering smell of roses to wash right over her, giving herself up to all manner of sensual experiences.

Leo snapped his fingers and a servant appeared as if by magic. Gayle found herself having the strangest and most sumptuous feast of her life. She was presented with oysters, prawns, lobster. Little dishes of capons appeared, sprinkled with coriander; plates piled high with roast potatoes, carrots, leeks and parsnips; trifles and cheesecakes which melted in the mouth.

And every time she turned around, the mysterious manservant would fill her glass with wine the color of blood. With every drop that passed her lips, she felt a growing sensation of desire. She felt sensuous and wild, a woman in control of her destiny, and yet one completely at the command of the man who sat opposite her saying very little.

"Shall we dance?" It was an order, not a question.

Gayle assented, but it was a willing assent. Her heart was beating faster than she thought possible when he took her in his arms and began to swirl her around the room. She was vaguely aware that the table had disappeared and they seemed to be in a huge ballroom, but all else was lost as she let her senses take over. Her body strained towards his, yearning for those soft hands to touch her all over. Underneath the constraints of her dress, her nipples hardened, and as his firm erection pressed against her, her cunt became wet with desire. The dance became faster and faster, and as she swirled around the room, she caught a sudden glimpse of them in the mirror. Only it was a glimpse of just her. It looked as though she was dancing by herself.

"You don't have a reflection," she said, weakly.

"If you believe, then it is real," he whispered, and spun her even faster, until suddenly she was aware the room was thronging with people. They were in the middle of a masked ball. Women with gold metallic masks and long, red ball gowns partnered men in black, whose masks were pure white. They danced stiffly, to a slow beat. Gayle glanced back at the mirror. Apart from her, the room was empty. It looked as though she were standing alone in this vast room.

Leo pulled her towards him, kissed her seductively on the mouth and then ran one long, slow finger from her neck to the tip of her breast. She longed for him to carry on, but he stopped, merely whispering, "You are nearly ready."

The music changed. It became faster, more frantic. Suddenly Leo spun her forwards into the crowd and Gayle found herself being flung from person to person in a wild and erotic dance. She was aware that the women's dresses were diaphanous and clingy, and was conscious of the men's animal virility. As she passed among them, soft hands touched her breasts and her back; delicate kisses were planted on her neck and her mouth leaving her craving more, and she had a growing sensation of wanting to rip off her clothes and let them come to her, all of them, and take what they would.

Because, now she knew without a doubt, she had found her vampires, and before the evening was out, they would turn her.

And it was what she desired most of all.

Just when she could stand it no longer, the crowd parted to reveal Leo standing before her.

"You are ready," he said.

She nodded, weak with desire. She knew she would go wherever he wanted, do whatever he wanted. To be with him forever was all she craved. The room reeled and changed. Gayle felt the same dizzying sensation as before and suddenly, she was falling, down, down into a bed of roses.

She awoke lying in the middle of a four-poster bed. Rose petals were scattered on the pillow, and she was wearing a simple white nightshift. A single candle burned by her bedside. All was quiet and still.

Where was she? And where was Leo?

Her bedroom window suddenly blew open and the curtain billowed inwards.

She got out of bed to shut it, and the candle blew out.

And then he was there, beside her, and she knew what she must do, what she was destined to do.

Gently he led her to the bed and laid her down on it. He kissed her on the lips, first softly and then with a deep and hard passion which sent small shots of desire right through her. His hands caressed her body, reaching down into her secret places. Panting with desire, she tugged at his shirt and found his firm flesh. She ran her hands over his taut body which further enflamed her. As if sensing her mood, he ripped at her nightdress until he exposed her breasts, and massaged them roughly. He kissed her on the mouth, the neck, her breasts, until finally he found her nipples. They hardened at his touch and she screamed her pleasure as he caught them with a slight nip.

She worked her hands down his body, until she found his penis. A single touch was enough to make it hard, and she pulled it urgently towards her wet cunny.

As he sucked her nipple, Leo worked his hands down her body towards her thighs. He pulled up her nightshift and gently parted her legs while his fingers stroked and teased her until they found her clit. She moaned slightly as she pulled his cock inside her. As they came together as one, Gayle had the strangest sensation of flying. She wrapped her legs around him and pulled him deeper inside, urging him on to the inevitable conclusion.

Just before she was about to come, he whispered, "Now?"

Unable to speak, she just nodded, and shut her eyes as the climax washed over her.

She felt his mouth hot on her neck, and the slightest of pin pricks which shot through her, making her body buck as the orgasm went on and on. She looked up to see him, blood dripping from his mouth. He proffered his neck to her, and she bit gently into it. Then they kissed, their blood mingling softly and silently as rose petals rained on them.

Gayle loaded her bags in the car. It was already dusk. She had spent the whole day rather lethargically in bed, and hadn't felt like leaving until now. A fact for which she had no explanation. She wasn't entirely sure quite what had happened with Leo the previous night, but she suspected hallucinogenic drugs might have had something to do with it. Oh well, at least he'd paid for dinner, and the sex had definitely been worth it. For a moment there, she had nearly been convinced she'd really had sex with a vampire. But as that was clearly impossible, she concluded that a combination of her feverish imagination, Leo's own brand of showmanship and the aid of some mind-altering substances had altered her perceptions of the events of the previous evening. It was the only logical explanation.

She got in the car, started the engine, and then adjusted her rearview mirror. She slowly started to drive out of the hotel car park. Lachmuirghan. Funny place. Funny name. If every visit was like this one, it might be worth coming back some day. As she set off on the main route out of Lachmuirghan, she noticed some headlights dazzling her in the rearview mirror. It must need adjusting. She went to move the mirror and noticed something odd. She couldn't see her hand. But that couldn't be.

She passed her hand over the mirror. Still nothing. Shaking now, she stopped the car and adjusted the mirror once again so she could see her face properly. But there was nothing to see. Not anymore.

Because she no longer had a reflection.

cR

The Return of the Prince

By M.A. duBarry

It was the anniversary of his death. The death of the warrior prince exiled from his beloved homeland for falling in love with the wrong woman. Killed when his betrothed destroyed the necklace carrying his soul. Killed when he betrayed the one woman who loved him...

Abigail O'Neill ran her fingers over the tattered page of the romance novel she'd been carrying in her purse for the last twenty years. The author knew nothing of her prince, the magnificent warrior she'd fallen in love with, nor did the woman know anything of her. In fact, for centuries, scads of writers had been penning the tale of her union with warrior prince Conall Dunmore, and never once had a single one of them gotten the story right. Of course she couldn't really blame them. She was the sole person who knew the truth of that day. The last survivor of magic gone wrong.

With a sigh, Abigail dropped the novel into her tote bag and approached the hotel's front desk. It was a bold move, coming to Lachmuirghan. Setting foot on land where she had no right to be. But Conall Dunmore's soul belonged as much to her as it did to his people. Perhaps even more so to her. However, tonight wasn't about rekindling an ancient squabble. She came here to make amends with the past and to be free of the pain she'd carried for centuries. This was a matter between her and her dead prince.

Tomorrow, she'd tell the curator of the Lachmuirghan museum the true facts of Conall's death. Of how no one knew what became of the man, and how the necklace carrying his soul hadn't been destroyed as the myths proclaimed. Then she'd donate the necklace to the people of Lachmuirghan and move on with her life. Her broken heart would finally mend. At least she hoped it would.

A female clerk appeared behind the front desk, breaking Abigail's thoughts. "Welcome to the Lachmuirghan Spa and

Hotel. May I have your name?"

"O'Neill. Abigail O'Neill."

The front desk assistant worked the computer. After several seconds she looked up and placed a printed sheet of paper on the marble countertop. "I have a reservation under your name for the Dunmore Suite for one night. The rate is listed at the bottom."

Abigail looked over the confirmation. "That's correct." She signed her name on the signature line and handed over her credit card along with her passport for identification.

The woman processed the reservation and gave Abigail a copy accompanied by a small map of the castle, a gold key and her credit card and passport. "The Dunmore Suite is on the fourth floor in the wing overlooking Lachmuirghan," she said. "The view is lovely, especially at dawn. It's simply breathtaking."

Abigail studied the map the woman had outlined on the reservation sheet and found the room's location. "Thank you."

When she arrived at the room, Abigail unlocked the door and stepped inside. Faint traces of citrus and clove teased her nose. The fragrance reminded her of Conall. If only she knew how he truly fared. Did he rest in peace? Was his death painful? Did his father's men kill him because she was part Fae or did he die of natural causes, peacefully in his sleep? Endless questions pounded her brain. She sighed, her heart still aching. Despite knowing the past could never be recaptured, Abigail found little solace in the thought of letting go.

Shaking her head, she flicked the light switch on, closed the door and headed toward the bed. She tossed her tote and duffle bag on the chair next to the window. With the drapes parted, the enchanting view of Lachmuirghan caught her eye. The lush, rolling hills surrounding the loch reminded her of the last time she'd seen Conall. Dressed in a tunic and breeches, he'd brought her outside to their favorite place on the hill surrounding her father's keep and handed her the necklace. His instructions were to keep the sapphire charged with moonlight. Then he told her he had to leave. But he'd promised to come back that night. Unfortunately, that promise was a vow he couldn't fulfill because she'd failed to keep her end of the bargain.

Pain twisted in her heart. She'd prayed for centuries that in death Conall would understand what she'd done, how she sacrificed their union for the sake of his survival. When he'd first left her, she was angry. But when she'd heard rumors of his death several days later, guilt settled on her soul and had remained there ever since. If the gods favored her, tomorrow's meeting would ease some of her torment.

Abigail walked away from the window. Maybe coming to Lachmuirghan wasn't the best idea, but she could think of no better way to finally leave the past behind. She kicked off her shoes and slipped out of her mini-dress. Tonight she planned on relaxing, ordering room service and taking a hot bath. And if she were lucky, she'd sleep soundly, undisturbed by the taunting dreams that had haunted her for centuries.

Reaching into her bag, she retrieved her favorite bubble bath and white terry robe, and headed for the bathroom. As she filled the tub, she poured a capful of bath gel under the faucet, reveling in the sweet aroma of freshly cut roses. She removed her lace bra and panties and lowered herself into the warm water.

The familiar fragrance stirred him to the core. Conall Dunmore suffered the lack of a physical form but his soul remained very much aware of his surroundings. He watched in silence as his Abigail lingered in the tub. Small rivulets of water lapped at her creamy white flesh and parted the rose-scented bubbles gathered near her breasts. He crouched at the tub and stared at her. Why, after all these centuries, had she come to him? Was it not enough she'd betrayed him, condemned him to the ethereal plane and forced him to remain no closer than a hair's breadth from her skin, forbidden to make his presence known to her? In his present state, he was capable of capturing her scent—an intoxicating aroma of rose mixed with a divinely feminine musk—of watching her and of hearing her. Everything, save for touching her. The harsh sentence tormented him. And now she'd come back to him, set foot on his sacred land, dangled her tempting body before him. Curse the woman. She had no right.

He balled his right hand into a fist and pounded the tub's edge.

A bottle of bath gel fell into the water.

Abigail gasped, her lips slightly parted. A look of shock mingled with fear glazed over her bright green eyes.

That wasn't supposed to have happened. Conall rose to his feet and stepped back, confusion rattling his brain. For centuries he'd remained undetected in the mortal realm. Allowed nothing more than the right to sit back and watch, he could do naught but observe man and his modern ways from a distance. Obviously, something had changed.

This canna be happening.

Mayhap his immortal Irish witch had put yet another curse upon his soul. He swore a vile oath under his breath. The woman had no mercy.

Abigail rose from the bath and reached for a towel on the rack next to the tub. As she moved, trickles of water slid down her body and pooled at her feet, slowly twisting through the marble tile grout and inching closer in his direction. The cool liquid teased his bare toes. Bloody hell. Something was definitely wrong. As a hexed soul, he couldn't touch or feel the world around him, especially the elements. And water was definitely a sacred element he hadn't felt in ages. He remembered the first time he'd taken a bath after he'd been banned from living with a physical form in the mortal world. The sensation of splashing his body with water yet feeling nothing made him freeze. Over time he'd gotten used to living without the ability to touch, going through the routine of a daily bath but feeling not even so much as a single droplet of water upon his body.

But now the lass before him made a mockery of his curse, and by the gods, he wasn't going to let her get away with that too. Perhaps it was time to tease his Irish wench as she'd taunted him for centuries.

He thought about the curse enslaving his body. His fist had shaken the tub and he'd felt water on his toes. Perhaps his ability to sense things was starting to return. If so, something as light as a towel had to be easy prey. And then his lass would feel him. Sense him. He followed her to the sink and stepped up behind her. The heat of Abigail's towel-wrapped body radiated through his invisible form. For a brief second, Conall closed his eyes and reveled in the warmth.

As Abigail undid the towel, Conall slid his fingers against the terry fabric.

The towel held a firm grasp upon her breast, even after she dropped her hand from the cloth. Abigail froze. The towel remained in place. A slight moan purred at her ear as the fragrance of citrus and spice danced through the air. Both the throaty, velvet-smooth purr and the intoxicating scent were familiar to her.

It couldn't be.

The towel stroked her breast.

It had to be.

Loops of white terrycloth caressed her nipple.

It was.

"Conall?" She spun around, the towel falling to the floor. Facing an empty bathroom, she frowned.

That time she heard more than a throaty purr. "Ah wumman, but did ye na miss me?"

"Where are you?"

"You canna see me?"

She shook her head.

"This isnae the way I planned our reunion."

"What reunion?"

"The one where I get my bloody vengeance on you."

The man had nerve. "As if you have a reason for revenge. I'm the one who was left at the altar. I'm the one who you ran out on."

"I didna do such a thing. Ne'er."

Abigail grabbed her robe from the back of the door and slipped her arms through the sleeves. She headed into the bedroom.

A strong presence followed her, making her spine go all tingly. She stopped mid-stride and turned around to face her invisible prince. "You never came back. Why?"

"Mayhap I did but you never noticed."

She'd have noticed. Even invisible, her strapping warrior had a presence hard to ignore. "I think I would have known if the man I was to marry had returned. You left me."

"At least I didna kill you or toss away your soul as if it were nothing more than a fancy sparkle in a gem made of paste."

Shock washed over her, coursed through her veins like a raging river. How could she have not sensed Conall's return? "You know about the necklace?"

"Look at me," he said. "How could I not know? You made me bloody invisible, wumman."

She swallowed, her nerves teetering on the edge of falling apart. "I didn't do this...this thing to you." She fluttered her hands in the air, gesturing at Conall's invisible body.

"Ah, but you did," he said. "You crushed the gem and gave it to the old hag on the hill. I saw her with my own eyes, ogling the shards of sapphire and running her crooked fingers through the pieces while she basked under the moon. The very bits and pieces that carried my soul."

"I never destroyed the necklace," she said.

"You canna lie, Abigail. My formless body is proof."

"And I have proof I didn't destroy the necklace holding your soul." She turned away from Conall and went for the tote bag. As she padded across the carpet, a hard tug loosened the belt of her robe. She slapped at the air, her fingers skimming the terrycloth. "Don't do that."

"I was only testing the sudden return of my ability to touch. You dinna know what it's been like for me all these centuries."

No, she didn't, but she did know what it was like to be missing the only man she ever loved, to be betrayed by her warrior prince. She reached into the tote bag and retrieved the velvet-lined box carrying the Dunmore Sapphire. "I've kept the necklace hidden since the day you left, taking it out only long enough to energize it in the moon's rays each new cycle as you instructed the night you gave it to me. Just once I failed to charge the stone." She opened the box and gazed at the sparkling gem. The deep blue jewel sat nestled in a circlet of gold, dangling from a thick linked chain. She turned and placed the case on the bed.

Conall ran his hand over the sapphire. A zap of electricity shot up through his arm as his fingers caressed the smooth gem. He staggered back, his body forced by the charge of the Dunmore magic contained within the stone.

Abigail brought her hand to her mouth.

Conall needed no mirror to know what his Irish lass saw. The sense of his body shifting to a physical state overwhelmed him. His nerves tingled. Bloody hell. He hadn't counted on returning to a state of substance tonight, so he never bothered dressing. After all, having spent centuries undetected by the human eye and having no sense of the weight of clothes upon his flesh, he'd gone nude more often than not.

"Are you okay?"

Abigail's question surprised him. "Why the sudden concern, lass? You dinna care what happened to my soul before."

"I always cared," she said. "Why do you think I kept the necklace all these years?"

The notion puzzled him. He knew what he saw that night on the hill. "What sort of magic are you playing with, Abigail? Did the old hag teach you her curses?" He went into the bathroom and retrieved a towel to wrap around his waist. Abigail followed him

Conall's body had remained exactly as she remembered it. He stood at over six feet tall and was all muscle. In the days when she first came to know him, he'd looked stunning in his tunic and breeches and his shift and kilt. Envisioning him in the modern world was even more bewitching—he had the type of body made for black leather or worn denim. In fact, she almost wished he was clothed, as seeing him butt naked only made her senses stir. And for a woman trying to convince herself she was better off forgetting about him, her body's betrayal didn't bode well.

Conall stared at the mirror. He thought he'd never see his reflection again. And while he wasn't the sort of man who spent hours admiring himself, he couldn't help but take a long look. Then he saw Abigail watching him. "You haven't changed," he said. "You're just as beautiful as the day I first laid eyes on you."

Conall's words made her heart skip. She stood next to him and reached out to touch his long, silky black hair. With his wild, slightly windblown look, he reminded her of the ultimate bad boy. She toyed with one of the two thin braids framing either side of his face, his chiseled features staring back at her through the mirror. "I've missed you, Conall Dunmore." Her words came as no more than a whisper.

Conall turned around and pulled her close. With his free hand, he slipped the bathrobe from her shoulders, forcing the terry garment to the floor. "And love? Do you still love me, wumman?"

She didn't answer him. Centuries of believing she'd been betrayed caused her emotions to plummet into a state of torment. Emotions she hadn't yet sorted out. A single tear fell down her cheek. "I..."

He leaned in and brushed his lips across hers. The burning sensation sent a zing coursing through her body. Conall lifted her into his arms and carried her from the bathroom over to the bed. Setting her down, he then moved the necklace box to the nightstand and joined her on the mattress. "Mayhap talk will come later," he said, settling himself between her thighs. "For now I will prove to you I didna have any intention of leaving you forever."

Abigail moaned as Conall's tongue swirled around her right nipple, the plump bud betraying her instantly. By the gods, it felt good to be back in her warrior's arms, even if they did have unfinished business between them. She'd never forgotten the wickedness of his touch, especially his mouth, but in her wildest dreams she never imagined him fucking her again. She'd given herself to him way before they were to be married, so letting him in again tonight, the first time they'd met in centuries, really shouldn't be surprising to her. In her heart, she knew they were meant to be together regardless of what Fate had tossed their way.

Conall closed his lips around her puckered nipple and tormented the aching peak even further. He rolled it against his tongue. Nipped it gently with his teeth. While he worked her nipple, his hand roamed over her flesh, down to her belly and then to the thatch of hair at the apex of her thighs. His fingers dipped lower, teasing the nub between her nether lips. He stroked her clit with first a soft flick and then a more vigorous touch.

She squirmed beneath him, wanting more of what he offered.

Conall released her nipple and slid down her body. His hot tongue trailed wet little circles over her flesh, a line from her breast to her navel and then below. He teased her clit with a single flick of his tongue as a spasm shot through her.

"Please, don't stop," she cried.

The mighty Scottish warrior did her bidding. He worked her clitoris with his mouth, licking and teasing until he closed in on the aching bud and sent her senses over the edge.

Abigail moaned.

Conall lifted his head and pulled away. He moved upward and lowered his body between her legs. His hard cock nudged the opening of her hole. With a slow push, he inched inside her, his thick rod blissfully caressing her slick walls. As he moved back and forth, Abigail met his every motion, her body enjoying the frenzied dance. She gripped the headboard and raised her legs high, allowing Conall to ram deeper.

After several more thrusts from her wondrous Scot, Abigail's orgasm peaked, sending waves of spasms through her body. The intense ripples of pleasure forced her eyes closed.

"Abigail," cried Conall, his body quivering as he came. He pumped his seed into her womb and then collapsed on top of her.

They remained silent for several minutes before Abigail spoke. "Why didn't you come back that night?"

Conall slipped out of her body and rolled onto his back. Beads of sweat glistened across his muscled chest. "I was forbidden to return to you. The Fae, your own people, were about to hunt you down for falling in love with a mortal. I couldn't let that happen. So I stayed away," he paused, and reached over to pull Abigail toward him, "until I knew certain members of your father's clan who were not of kind heart ceased their stupid beliefs. But when I finally convinced the Fae council I meant you no harm and I loved you, it was too late. I was granted the right to marry you, but on my return, my physical form vanished. I'd been cursed and had no substance."

"I'm so sorry, Conall. I had no idea."

He pulled his arm away. "Sorry for betraying me or sorry I survived the Fae council?"

Shock washed over her senses. "What?" Abigail sat up, her

mind reeling with anger. “How can you say such a thing?”

He glared at her. “You stripped me of my physical form. If you wanted me, if you had loved me, you would never have done this to me.”

“For the last time, Conall, I did not curse you.”

“Then explain, wumman. Tell me who was responsible for my centuries of misery.”

She took a deep breath and recalled the lonely nights at the hilltop. “I feared the old hag would know I had the necklace. I didn’t want her to steal your soul, so I kept the necklace hidden and instead brought the witch shards of a shattered gem made of paste. A fake trinket my father had purchased for me when I was a child. The hag was satisfied with my trick, my father was satisfied in knowing we wouldn’t be together and the Fae who had come to look for you called off their hunt. I didn’t know then that you’d lose your physical form if I refrained from charging the sapphire with moonlight. I only failed to do so that one night. I also had no idea the Fae were trying to kill both of us. But even if I did know, I would have sacrificed my own life for the sake of yours.”

She paused. “I thought you were dead. Killed because I failed to charge the sapphire.”

She saw the pain in his eyes. “We’ve been forced apart, love,” Conall said. “Both forced to live separate lives due to the actions of a small group of misguided Fae.” A look of confusion crossed his brow. “But why did the sapphire give me back my body tonight if it lacked moonlight?”

“Once I knew I’d be left alone on the hilltop, I took to taking the necklace with me as you instructed. And I continued to do so every night the moon stood high in the sky until now. Having physical contact with the necklace again, must have broken the curse and given you back substance.”

Abigail straddled Conall and looked down into his deep blue eyes. "My mother was all Fae and my father half Fae. I had no idea the council would be so angered by my falling in love with a mortal. If I'd known, I'd never have caused you any grief."

He smiled at her. "I'd sacrifice anything for you, lass. The pain I've suffered over the last centuries is nothing if I can still have you. If you'll still have me."

She only managed a moan, for Conall reached up and cupped her breasts, the pads of his calloused fingers grazing her nipples. She licked her lips and reveled in the heightened sensation. Under her bottom, Abigail felt Conall's cock twitch. She nudged her body to the right position, and still wet from their recent lovemaking, she easily slid her pussy over his aroused rod.

Conall's shaft filled her to the brim. Between his length and thickness, the sense of being stuffed and stretched enticed her. Abigail toyed with her clit as she rocked her bottom against Conall's cock. She rode him until they both came simultaneously, until the sweet essence of their sex lingered in the air.

Sliding up off him, Abigail nestled against Conall's body. "I almost gave you away."

"What do you mean?"

Spent from their lovemaking, she had no energy to lift her head. She nuzzled his neck and whispered. "I came to Lachmuirghan to give your necklace to the museum. It was to be my way of making peace with your people for the loss of their favored warrior."

A surprised look crossed Conall's face. "By the gods, wumman. If I hadn't come to this old castle, curious as to the meaning of your presence, and if you hadn't decided to spend the night at Lachmuirghan, we may never have been reunited."

"I don't think I could have survived another century without you."

He let out a soft chuckle. "Neither could I. But what do we do now? I canna just walk out of this place as if I've existed in the flesh all these years."

Abigail laughed. "Well, you definitely can't walk out of here naked. First I'll have to get you some clothes. Then we'll see about making you legal again. My Fae kin owe me for having misjudged you and now would be a good time for them to work a bit of magic for us."

"As long as you'll still have me, lass."

Abigail felt the hands of sleep covet her body. "I'll have you for all eternity, Conall Dunmore. And then some." Abigail slowly drifted off, her heart and her body finally content and well sated. The magic of Lachmuirghan was something she'd never be able to explain, but if it wasn't for this wondrous and mysterious Scottish village, she'd never have known her fierce warrior Conall and she never would have been able to get him back.

ଓ

Adam's Tale

By Maristella Kent

"I need a woman's comfort. Can you—will you—offer me that, Eileen?"

She had thought herself unobserved but she went willingly forward to where Adam stood at the castle battlements, his gaze fixed on the loch. In silence she stood by his side and together they basked in the late afternoon sun gilding the castle.

She offered him her hand and he twined his larger fingers through hers. When she finally found the courage to turn to him she saw, with shock, that he was crying. Silent, fat tears were running down his cheeks.

"Morag was so fond of this view. It was three years ago today that she died."

Eileen was so shocked she was unable to speak, even to offer the customary "Sorry". She squeezed his fingers, offering him mute support.

He turned to her, smiled a little, then looked back out at the loch, so serene before them.

"Cancer," he told Eileen.

She was held silent by his grief.

"On the first anniversary I revisited the crematorium, thinking I might find her there, or at least some comfort, but her spirit had left the place. Last year I resolved to come to her birthplace—and here I am."

Eileen had to clear her throat to speak through the tears welling in her own eyes. "Morag was a local girl?"

Adam nodded. "Lived here until we were married. Then, reluctantly, she moved with me to England when I was offered a hugely well-paid job. But she always wanted to return. We spent most holidays here."

"I won't want to leave here myself, and this is the first time I have ever seen Lachmuirghan." Eileen realized, as she spoke, just how much she regretted that her time here was almost over.

Adam nodded. "Neither of us will find it easy to leave."

She looked at him in surprise. "You speak as if we might both stay on here."

He smiled again but said nothing, turning back to his

contemplation of the view.

"Perhaps it's the loch?" she wondered aloud.

"Ah yes, you do have an affinity with water."

Eileen blushed, certain he was teasing her, remembering how he had stared at her. "The waterfall," she murmured.

"Indeed, the waterfall, but I have an earlier memory."

She looked at him, surprised, unable to judge if he was remembering something she could not.

He met her glance and told her, "I have a memory that seems real but might not be real. It was the night before we came here by coach. You were in a shower and I had the privilege of seeing you unclothed."

"But that's not possible! I was in my own house and certainly on my own."

"I tell myself that many things are not possible and yet they are and were. Morag's death was just one of them."

Eileen shivered. "You were imagining it, though, my shower."

"It was very real in many ways, right from the blue and green tiny wall tiles through to your fluffy cream towels."

It had to be a lucky guess. Had to be.

A thought struck her. "Was that the only time you, um, saw me?"

He smiled, and this time there was a laugh as he answered, "Oh, Eileen, I have been with you so many times over this holiday, but I would not embarrass you now."

"So you have seen...?"

"You being pleasured and giving pleasure. Yes." He spoke quite definitely.

She turned her face and would have moved away, but he

held her tighter in his grip. "You are a beautiful woman and I felt privileged to have shared some of your adventures."

She could not face him.

"Shall I mention what I have shared so that we start with no more to hide? I saw you on the hillside that first afternoon," he ignored her gasp, "and watching that film, and in the museum." He drew her gently towards him and tipped her face so that when she opened her eyes she was looking directly into his.

"There is nothing to be ashamed of in any of that. I am not sure why I was destined to share your joy with you, but I cannot say I was ever unhappy."

"You must think—"

"Nothing more than that you are a highly sensual and sexual being and attract attention and very special adventures because of that. It was a privilege to see things through your eyes."

"Have you, um, seen anyone else that way?" Eileen was bewildered and struggling to understand exactly what had happened.

"Never before and with nobody else. I did wonder if I was just imagining things, but I don't think I was. Am I right?"

Eileen nodded, disconcerted. That he had shared things she did not understand herself was so shocking she could barely comprehend it.

"The stag?" she asked.

Adam nodded.

"The mask?"

"Oh yes! And above all, the feeling that we were somehow destined to be together."

Before she could stop herself she spoke. "You too?" Then

she felt embarrassed.

Again he refused to let her turn her face from his. He planted the lightest of kisses on her brow. "Never ever feel ashamed of what has happened," he admonished.

He kissed her, more warmly this time, on her lips. She reached up and twined her fingers in his hair and deepened the contact. She was responding instinctively and it felt so completely right. This was what she had longed for from the moment she had first seen him standing alone at the edge of the loch.

"Eileen." His word was a plea.

She nestled into his strength and took his lips once more in a kiss that was as fiery as the sun.

"We were made to be together. This I believe," he stated. It sounded like a vow.

Her breath caught. She felt too emotional to say anything and feared breaking the spell.

"Do you trust me?" he asked.

She nodded, certain that her future would involve his future.

"Then..." He took her hand and turned her once more towards the loch. Keeping his body pressed to hers, he raised the hem of her dress. Her thighs were exposed and she trembled, though she was warm in the sunshine. Then Adam pushed the hem further up until the dress was at her waist and he sighed his pleasure as he stroked her bare thighs.

"What if...?" Panic sharpened Eileen's voice.

"I doubt we will be disturbed by other visitors to the castle so near to closing time," he soothed. "And anybody looking up will see only your top half between the stones."

As he spoke he slipped his thumbs between the silk of her

panties and her buttocks. Caressing her, circling her with his strong hands, he moved his fingers round to the flesh of her sexual mound.

She moaned and was granted the blessing of his fingers caressing the delicate insides of her thighs. He stood back from her. His thumbs hooked at the elastic waist of her panties and eased them down. A cool breeze fluttered against her nakedness and she gasped.

At once he nuzzled her neck. "You are so very beautiful. There is nothing to fear from me."

"No, I have no fear," she agreed, and gave herself up to his embrace.

His fingers worked their clever way back under her dress and stroked the heated flesh until she thought she would melt.

"Have you ever heard the tale of The God of the Valley?"

He seemed intent on talking when she was rather more minded to make love. His hands stilled until she nodded, reluctantly. "I was told there was a legend, about a god who loved a mortal—she lived right here, in Lachmuirghan."

Adam nodded. "When she died, he grieved for her. His tears turned the loch to saltwater, and he is meant to haunt the village waiting for her return. Will you think I am completely mad if I tell you how much I relate to him?"

"Oh, Adam, of course you will see parallels to your own life!"

He smiled. "Thank you for that. When I look out on this scene I can almost think I created the loch with my tears. I have wondered if you are the one for whom I have been waiting."

Impulsively Eileen told him, "Perhaps I am. I want there to be nobody else in the world right now. Just the two of us to enjoy this glorious afternoon sunshine." She looked into his eyes and felt once more the tug of connection between them.

"There is nobody looking, I am sure of it," he promised her urgently, and brought his hands up to unbutton the top of her dress. She allowed it, dizzy with desire to share her body with him.

Today she was wearing a bra. She regretted that until she heard his unsteady breathing and realized it was adding to his enjoyment, delaying gratification for them both.

Taller, as well as infinitely stronger, he was treating her with a gentleness that was seductive beyond belief. Her nipples hardened even further as he nuzzled her neck and whispered how beautiful he found her. His hands cupped her and gently but insistently pinched the nubs of her breasts through the cloth until she was desperate to be naked.

He pushed down her bra cups, exposed her to the sunshine and murmured his admiration. She was past caring that anyone might see him worship her body in this way. He left one hand there to adore her and moved his right hand down to stroke once more at the sensitized flesh between her legs. She was glad that she was wearing heels for once as that gave her a few crucial inches of height to equalize the difference between them. As he pulled her against him, murmuring his intentions in explicit detail, she could feel how aroused he was.

At his instruction, she leaned forward over the broad ledge between the uprights of the battlement. She rested her elbows on the almost-smooth stone, bleached with age, and gripped the front of the ledge. Now she was precariously leaning out, her head, shoulders and breasts beyond the profile of the battlements, and she was completely exposed should anybody in that part of the castle gardens look up.

The sun and Adam were caressing her breasts alternately. She felt so cherished. Her trust in him could not have been more clearly demonstrated. She was aroused by how high they were—if he had not been holding her so securely, she would never have dared lean out so far. She felt both fragile and invulnerable in his arms.

He could hear how quickly she was breathing, he could sense her heightened agitation, he could feel with his fingers how ready she was to admit him. Her buttocks jutted towards him, exposing all of her intimate places to his sight. He readied himself and urged himself into her woman's warmth. He did this so slowly—pushed then stopped, pushed a little more. She was slick and ready for him, but he was so large—and conscious that he must not rush their joining.

Eileen, stretched and awed by his size, was glad she had not yet seen his arousal—she wanted nothing more than for him to be deeply inside her, but she was aware of his huge length and breadth. She guessed he must be as large as the circumference of her wrist. Slowly he continued his progress, making small gains each time he pressed carefully into her. It was so exciting. He was so exciting.

She pushed back against him, eager to help his ingress of heated flesh into willing flesh. Moaning, she felt she would explode from the waiting.

His breath caught as he laughed gently. "Oh, Eileen," he sighed, and applied himself once more to their union.

Finally he was fully inside her.

She expected him to begin to move, but he did nothing, just held her immobile and safe between his strong, broad hands. She could feel him looking but he seemed content just to be there.

At first she felt the same, but then she was overtaken with an urge to move. She tried to rock backwards, but he was filling her completely. She attempted to writhe, to inspire him to move, but still he seemed reluctant to oblige.

Finally she pushed back enough to be able to rub her pebbled nipples against the ancient stone, to try to obtain release that way.

With a grunt that could have been amusement, he began to rock her against him. He barely moved, just pulled her back to him then released her. She sensed that he was holding back in case he hurt her.

She was so overwhelmed with need and lust that she reached back and pulled his right hand forward. Trapping his fingers between her hand and her clitoris she ground his hand over her flesh. "Adam," she insisted. He needed no further urging.

His fingers played with her heated flesh and, at last, he began to move against her. As he surged in and out, she cried out her increasing pleasure and he moved his left hand to her mouth to capture her sounds.

His unaccustomed largeness within her, together with his insistent clever fingers, moved her towards a climax that was shattering. She cried out her pleasure, muffled by his fingers, then, as she lay slumped with happiness against the stone, he started to move fiercely inside her, his fingers splayed over her hips to hold her safe.

She was ecstatic—in turn he was almost withdrawing, then filling her so hugely, that she plateaued and orgasmed once more. As she convulsed around him, he came, spurting strongly inside her. And then, without breaking their intimacy, he encircled her with his arms, holding her upright against his chest, and sighed his pleasure.

For a minute there was no sound other than their breathing as it slowed. Then, "Come with me," he urged.

Gathering the edges of her clothing together, but not

stopping to fasten them, or to pick up her underwear, he swept her up into his arms and carried her back through the ancient wooden door towards the stone staircase.

She thought he would put her down, but the staircase was just wide enough to allow him to carry her down the steps. He did not hesitate in his sure-footedness, and she felt completely safe in his embrace.

Reaching a second door, he stopped and she took the opportunity to kiss him. He felt in his pocket and withdrew a large key. Fitting it into the door lock, he opened it and carried her through into what was obviously a private bedroom. It was a large and old-fashioned room, complete with a comfortable sofa in rose chintz, and an ornate four poster bed within the curved turret walls.

"What...?"

"I'll explain later about being the new owner, but for now..."

He placed her gently on the bed, retrieved the key and locked the door from the inside, then returned and removed what remained of her clothes. "Oh, Eileen."

Unable to wait for him to undress himself, Eileen reached up then knelt to unfasten his shirt. As she savored undoing each button, kissing the flesh she exposed, he groaned his frustration and removed the rest of his clothes so that he stood there in front of the bed in his shirt and nothing else.

She was desperate to see just how wonderfully equipped he was, but at the same time reluctant.

Naughtily, she slowed her pace, and he took hold of the edges of the cotton and ripped, sending buttons shooting. In turn she pushed the sleeves of his shirt impatiently off his arms. Both of them were now equally naked.

"You deserve to be punished for making me wait."

His tone was light, but Eileen chose to respond.

"I am willing to be punished as you see fit, Master." She bent her head submissively, so that he might not have seen the glint of excitement in her eyes. She offered up her hands, palms together, as if in prayer. Her tongue betrayed her nervousness and flicked round her suddenly dry lips.

He growled and encompassed her wrists with one strong hand, and at the same time reached for his ripped shirt. He wrapped one sleeve around her wrists and she allowed her hands to be knotted together. Using the rest of the shirt, he tugged with it as if she was on a leash. Eileen was forced to stumble off the bed, his superb arousal nudging her as they stood and he urged her hands above her head.

He tied the body of the shirt high up to one of the bed posts, so she was forced to stand on tiptoe, her posture pushing her breasts out towards him, inviting and inciting attention. "Oh," he groaned. "These are so ready to be adored. I'm sure they haven't been *too* naughty."

He bent his mouth to suck her nipples, taking each of them into his mouth in turn, and swirling his tongue around them as they hardened exquisitely. Eileen whimpered.

"You disagree? Perhaps they have been disobedient?" He sucked hard on her right breast then took the nipple and gently tugged at it with his teeth. Eileen moaned loudly. He bit gently at the nipple and then just a little harder before licking the pain away. He repeated the process with her other breast, making her cry out her need.

"Oh no, Eileen. You have confessed your guilt, and the punishment continues until I am satisfied. The more you protest, the longer this will take." He looked convincingly stern.

He cupped her breasts with his hands, taking each nipple between a thumb and forefinger and rolling them gently until

Eileen thought she might explode with desire.

"Please," she moaned, "take me now."

"But you admitted you had to be punished. I would not be correct in releasing you until I was sure you were never going to keep me waiting again."

Eileen begged him to make love to her, promised that she would do whatever he wanted. Her eyes were fixed on him: he was hugely erect and proud and his phallus was jutting forward as though waiting to be kissed.

Adam pretended he had not understood. "You are not yet ready, then," he sighed.

Over her protests that she would never be so ready, he flicked her nipples with his fingers. He silenced her by fastening his mouth to hers in a heart-stopping kiss. Then he flicked her nipples again.

He must have sensed that his touch was nearly enough to make her orgasm because he bent and whispered urgently in her right ear that if she had the temerity to come before he did then he really would punish her. His arousal was rearing towards her as if it would defy him and take her anyway.

Eileen's toes and wrists were aching with holding her weight, and her breasts were throbbing where they had been stimulated almost beyond the point of endurance. She knew that she was as moist and as ready as she was surely ever going to be. With great difficulty she stopped herself from demanding release.

She tried to be a supplicant. "Please, Master."

"A slave does not ask," he hissed. "A slave is grateful to take whatever is offered, whenever it is offered." And with that, he released the knot so that she was free of the post.

Before she could draw a grateful breath, he had pushed her

back onto the bed. She made herself lie there submissively under his greedy gaze before he turned her onto her knees, pulling her towards the headboard, and then making her arch her back so he could fit pillows beneath her body.

Then, tethering her once more, he pushed her knees apart. She was left exposed and panting with anticipation.

Tentatively she pulled at the shirt anchoring her to the bed-head. It gave a little as she tugged, but she realized she was effectively tied. She looked back over her shoulder but he shook his head at her.

She was exquisitely aroused. In the past she had always been the one to call the shots, but now she was thrilled to be dominated by a man who was both playful and masterful. She felt completely exposed and...

Smack!

His hand landed on her right buttock. It was the shock rather than pain that made her cry out.

"Oh yes," he told her, "that leaves a red handprint which looks very pretty against your pale skin."

And then he swatted her left buttock. This time his aim landed just a little under the curve and was as arousing as it was painful. His fingers found their way into her crack and she wriggled appreciatively as he caressed her for a moment. She moaned—partly from pain, more from pleasure, and most of all that he had taken his hand away.

"Not yet." He laughed. "I've not finished with you yet!"

Another smack heated her skin. And then another. He seemed to sense that her cries were those of ecstasy and excitement, and he sped up his next two smacks.

Then he stopped and bent over her and she felt his breath cooling her skin. She sighed her relief as he traced his tongue around his handprints, leaving the skin to cool deliciously where he had licked. “Perhaps you have been punished enough now,” he told her.

“Oh yes,” she agreed.

As she relaxed onto the pillows, he landed another two blows—one on each buttock. She yelped her surprise as he chuckled.

While her flesh was still stinging, he straddled her and pushed his magnificent self back into her. She was very wet indeed and he was soon imbedded. Pinching a nipple in each hand, he began to ride her.

Eileen was so close now to release. She began to spasm when he rubbed at her clitoris, and as she came—gloriously and without reserve—so did he.

When Adam had recovered a little, he released her from the headboard and untied her and cradled her in his arms. They lay on the bed in a loving embrace. Eileen felt both completely exhausted and supremely happy.

“I didn’t hurt you, did I?” he asked, softly.

“No, Master,” she reassured him with a grin. “I think I can promise you that I might be naughty again one day soon...and for the rest of our lives together.”

Six:
The Teashop—Sweet Cream and Honey Cakes

When the newly widowed Beryl McDonald opened her teashop just after the Great War, she named it "Flora MacDonald's Tea Rooms", partly to claim connection with her dead husband's courageous ancestor, but mostly to irritate her mother-in-law, who considered it improper for a widowed young mother to go into business.

Beryl's venture was a success, and soon became known in the village as "Beryl's Teashop". Some years later, when Beryl requested telephone service to her shop, she listed it under "B" for "Beryl's".

Beryl's ownership continued through her daughter and granddaughter, with cousins and nieces and nephews filling in over the years. It was Beryl McDonald's great grandson, Ian, who, for his Art GSCE coursework, decided on a sign-painting project. He wrote "Beryl's" in smaller letters, and added his two favorite items on the menu in larger, bolder print and the new name stuck. Visitors and villagers alike stop, especially on dreary winter afternoons, for a pot of tea and the famed honey cakes. The serving of sweet cream is an optional extra.

ଓ

A Teashop Tale

By Madeleine Oh

This had not been the holiday she'd expected. Gina looked around as she strolled up the village High Street. Lachmuirghan was nice enough, picturesque, unspoiled and the weather had been fantastic for this time of year, but that was pretty much that. Obviously all the whispered tales she'd heard about wild goings on and incredible sex were just that—stories. Fiction!

So what? Nothing wrong with fiction, might as well find something to read in the bookshop and spend the afternoon reading by the river. She'd found a lovely sheltered spot where she'd taken off her T-shirt, and hiked up her skirt and basked in the sun a couple of afternoons.

The bookshop was dark after the bright sun outside, but her eyes quickly adjusted as she strolled between the dim stacks and inhaled the smell of old paper and...coffee. The wizened owner was seated at a table drinking coffee from a thermos and munching on a slab of pork pie. It made Gina realize she hadn't eaten since breakfast.

The old man's eyes were bright in his wrinkled face. He nodded at her, pausing with his cup halfway to his mouth.

"Came in to browse, did you then?"

"Yes," Gina replied. 'I just wanted something to read."

"Mmm," he pondered a moment or two, his eyes intent. "You might find what you're needing against the back wall on the right." And turned back to his coffee and pork pie.

Might as well look. She passed the rows of travel books and

history, almost stopped as her eyes caught a dark green book with “Tales of the Young Pretender” on the spine, but something drew her to the far wall and the mixed hard and paperbacks that filled the shelves to the right. A yellowed sign, fixed to the middle shelf with rusted drawing pins, read, “Erotica”.

Really! Had she looked that desperate? True, she’d not had the sexual fling she’d half-hoped for and okay, there were few things more fun that a sexy read, but did she want to take one of these up to the beady-eyed old man? She scanned the titles—an interesting mix of old dusty volumes and newer paperback erotica titles. Lots of anthologies and on the bottom shelf, bound copies of *Forum* and *For Women.*

Heck, there had to be something here. Something she wouldn’t find in a station bookshop. Yes, tucked between two battered paperbacks was a slim, leather-bound copy entitled *The Diary of Mata Hari.* Gina pulled out the book, noticing the worn gilt edges and the cracked cover...and turned the yellowed pages. That it truly was the one-time spy’s reminiscences? That Gina rather doubted, but headings like “A Night with the General” and “Dreams in Istanbul” piqued her interest. Might be a big fat fraud, but the penciled-in price on the flyleaf was more than reasonable.

The old man looked up from his coffee.

“Found something? Good! My customers almost always find just what they need.”

As she paid him, he looked out of the window. “Looks as though we’re in for a wet evening. Better get back quickly.”

He wasn’t joking. In the past few minutes, the blue sky had turned gray and a few heavy raindrops hit the small panes of the bow window. When Gina opened the door, it almost blew back in her face. This wasn’t a summer shower but a full-scale storm brewing.

Two minutes later it was obvious she'd never get back to The Royal Rescue without being soaked to the skin. Best option was to nip into the teashop and wait out the rain. She shut the door behind her just as a nasty squall slashed rain against the building. She shook her hair, glad to be out of the weather.

The tearoom was empty except for a dark-haired man adding a log to the blazing fire. As he straightened, brushing his hands together, he looked her way and smiled, his clear blue eyes crinkling at the corners.

"Seeking safety and refuge from the god's fury, eh?"

"Trying to avoid drowning in the High Street."

He laughed, the sound echoing in the close room.

"You're safe here. You'll need something to warm you up, no doubt."

'Yes, tea would be nice, but—" She looked around at the empty shop. "Are you closed?"

"We are now," he replied, crossing the shop to flip the sign on the door. "But we always serve customers who are in by closing time."

A flicker of unease crossed her mind. She was locked in a deserted shop with an unknown man, an attractive man, a rather intriguing, sensual-looking man. A man who—

"Have a seat by the fire." He indicated a small table pulled up to a heavy oak settle. "I'll get your tea and something to warm the cockles of your heart."

A sharp gust of wind rattled the windowpanes. Sitting on soft cushions by a toasty fire was infinitely preferable to braving the elements and getting soaked to the skin before she made it down the hill. Feet warming by the fire, Gina opened the little book and flicked through the pages. Interesting, it was written as a diary, and appeared to recount Mata Hari's exploits after her husband abandoned her—a liaison with a French diplomat in Istanbul, others with a Polish General and a Hungarian Feldmarschalleutnant. Between her adventures were sad little notes on how she missed her two children and feared they would forget her. These entries were followed right along by amorous exploits in detail. Seemed a particular English industrialist carried his own satin and leather manacles with him on his travels, and a certain German munitions engineer enjoyed—

"Interesting read?" He towered over her, tray in hand. "Sorry to interrupt, but I brought your tea."

"Thank you…" She paused.

"Torval," he replied, "Torval MacDonald."

"I'm Gina Jackson."

"Welcome to Lachmuirghan, Gina. I brought you some honey cakes. Nothing like a sweet cake with a good cuppa."

"Thanks."

She hadn't expected him to sit down and pour for her, but she wasn't about to complain. In fact his company was a distinct addition to the dreary afternoon.

"Milk and sugar?" he asked.

"Milk, no sugar."

This was not the conversation she really wanted, but she could hardly ask him to take off his shirt so she could see what his chest really looked like. Could she? He handed her the cup. Their fingertips brushed and she was certain it wasn't an accident. Good.

"Thank you."

"My pleasure, Gina. It was a dull, dreary afternoon until you walked in."

A bit obvious and clichéd, but somehow he made it sound

sincere.

"Do you live here in Lachmuirghan?" she asked.

He shook his head.

"Oh! No! Wouldn't have the stamina." Odd comment that—by the look of his broad shoulders and the strong forearms visible below his rolled up sleeves, he was all solid muscle. "I teach at Glasgow University, just back here for a few days and my gran put me to work."

"Gives you a hard time, does she?" Forward, yes, but by his grin he was not offended.

"Oh, it's so hard, you'd not believe it! But it has its compensations."

She bet it did.

He held up his cup, and looked at her over the rim as he sipped the steaming brew. "And what do you do, Gina, when you're not strolling our village streets?"

"I'm a writer."

Perfectly true—she wrote instruction manuals for a software manufacturer. She sipped the tea: Lapsang Souchong. The smoky, tarry taste hung on her taste buds.

"And what do you write, Gina Jackson?" He rested his arm on the back of the settle, not quite touching her, but close enough to feel his warmth on the nape of her neck. "A treatise on Mata Hari?"

That was a thought!

"I'm researching a book on famous lovers and courtesans." A white lie, yes, but operating manuals weren't sexy.

"Ah!" His mouth curled at both corners and his lips parted slightly. "Fascinating."

She didn't think he was talking about research.

They sat in silence for a few minutes—the only sounds the shifting of a log on the fire as it burned, the tick of the clock on the mantelpiece and her racing heart. At last she was face to face with one of Lachmuirghan fabled lovers.

"More tea?" he asked, lifting the pot with its knitted cozy.

"Please."

"My pleasure." He took her cup and refilled it, shifting a little closer as he handed it back. His knee wasn't quite touching hers, but if she moved just a little...perhaps stretched her leg. "Ah, Gina, but you haven't had one of Great Grandmother Beryl's honey cakes. You cannot leave here without tasting Lachmuirghan sweetness." He picked up one of the tiny cakes and held it out to her.

She opened her mouth and he popped the morsel inside. It was rich, sweet and wonderful.

"Delicious!"

He smiled, his eyes meeting hers as he very deliberately licked his fingers.

"I thought you'd like that."

If the cake had been any bigger it would have lodged in her throat. As it was, the tiny mouthful slipped down.

"Wonderful!" she said and deliberately reached for another. This one she bit in two. Aware he was watching, she shut her eyes and sighed as she chewed and swallowed. She gobbled the rest if it and smiled at him. "Very good. Worth coming all this way for."

"Oh! Yes, Gina Jackson," he said, patting her on the knee. "Enjoy your tea and the warmth. I have dishes to do"

And he disappeared through the narrow door at the back of the tearoom.

Damn! How dare he walk out just when she was getting in

the mood? She was tempted to leave, but the wind and rain lashed against the windows, even though the heavy velvet curtains were drawn tight. When had that happened? Torval hadn't walked past her. Had he? They hadn't been drawn when she came in. In fact she didn't remember any curtains at all.

Too bad. If he wanted to play tease, she'd survive. She poured another cup and proceeded to gorge herself on the rich honey cakes.

In the distance, she heard water running and china clinking. Let him do the dishes! She was comfortable by the fire, in fact she dreaded leaving the warmth for the wild night outside. She poured another cup, put the saucer on the table and, for just a minute, closed her eyes.

As she dozed, a voice whispered, "Oh, Gina! My sweetness!" Warm hands rested on her shoulders, then stroked down her front, cupping her breasts and easing down to rest on her belly. She tried to open her eyes, but warm lips kissed her eyelids. "No, sweetness. This is your dream. Your pleasure in the dark."

She wasn't sure she could open her eyes and knew she didn't want to. In the dark of dreaming, his touch was magnified. The flat of his hand on her belly stirred sensation right through her. His lips on her neck, she felt right down to her cunt. His fingers unbuttoning her blouse had her sighing with anticipation. She was naked above the waist, but warm from the heat of the fire and his breath on her skin. His mouth closed over her nipple and she cried out. She reached out, wanting to touch him, to run her hands over his chest and taste the warmth and heat of his lips on hers.

"No!" he commanded. "Be still!" He stretched her arms over her head until they rested against the back of the settle. "You cannot move. You cannot touch me. I will do the loving."

He stroked her arms, brushed his fingers over her breasts

and teased her nipples with his tongue until they ached with pleasure. She was distantly aware of her sighs and little moans in the quiet, but the only sounds from Torval were his steady heartbeat and his breathing as he put his mouth against her skin.

She was held immobile in the dark. Lost in his sensual caress. His hands were on her skirt now, easing down the zip, moving her clothes until she was naked. Exposed to him like this, she pictured how she looked, spread on the old settle, her skin bathed in firelight. She imagined his eyes feasting on her nudity. Was he hard for her? Ready to fuck her? What next?

She lay there, aroused and quiescent.

Waiting.

She felt a hand on each thigh as he gently spread her wide. She was open, exposed. The thought set her cunt flowing.

"Yes, my Gina," he said. "Yes." And cupped her pussy, pressing hard as he ground the heel of his hand against her clit.

She gasped and fancied he smiled.

As he took his hand away, he whispered, "Patience," and she felt him move away.

Why? Where? He couldn't be doing more dishes! Could he? Leaving her like this! She wanted to open her eyes but she was lost in the dark and not only were her arms immobile, her legs were fixed apart.

She called his name but it came muffled as if he'd gagged her.

"Hush!" he said in the dark. "This was worth waiting for wasn't it?" He thrust something—a finger? Two? Three?—deep into her cunt. As her hips rocked with sheer bliss, his thumb rubbed her clit. She was sighing, lost in his sensual assault, and then he added to her sensation by fastening his mouth on one breast then the other. This was wonderful but oh, she wanted, needed his cock. In the dark, she pictured it—hard and stalwart, angling out from his toned body. Erect, and ready to fuck her. She hoped.

"What do you want, Gina?" he whispered.

"You. Inside me." It came out rough and hoarse as if through a fog or a gag.

"What part of me, Gina? My fingers? You like my fingers in your cunt?"

"Your cock!"

"And what should I do with my cock, Gina?"

"Fuck me! Fuck me until I scream!"

"Mmm." He sounded as if he were contemplating the possibility.

With a movement so swift she gasped with shock, Torval grabbed both her ankles and raised them high, spreading her even wider. Her ankles rested somewhere strong and warm. His shoulders? His naked shoulders? Over his arms? Before she could decide for sure, his hands cupped and lifted her arse and his cock invaded her. He was even harder and larger than she'd imagined. He was immense, filling her with his need and his male power.

As she gasped with satisfaction and anticipation, the wind outside roared against the little shop, rattling windows and doors. With a groan that seemed to come from his soul, Torval began pumping. He was strong, seemingly tireless, as he fucked her in rhythm with the rain and wind.

She was crying out, her body twisting with her mounting sensation as he continued his sensual pounding. He didn't stop when she screamed out her climax, nor with the second or the third, or...she lost count, her body and mind caught in a wild spiral of orgasm that continued until she was too exhausted to do anything but whimper with happiness.

She wasn't sure when he left her. She remembered kisses on the inside of her thighs and the brush of his lips on her breast before she fell into the sweet sleep of utter satiation.

She was still dreaming of wild ripples of pleasure when she heard Torval's voice and felt him shaking her shoulder. "Gina, Gina, wake up."

Her eyes opened slowly. She was stiff from sleeping on the oak settle and one leg had gone to sleep. And she was dressed.

"Sorry to disturb you, my dear," he said, "but I really do have to close up. Got to go pick up my Auntie Moira from Largs. It's stopped raining."

It had. No more rain slashing against the window or wind whistling around the house.

"What happened?" Silly question. She knew what had happened. Or did she?

"You must have dozed off. It was warm in here."

She must have. But how much of the dream was a dream? Gina stood and gathered up her handbag and picked up her book off the floor. "What do I owe you for the tea and honey cakes?"

Torval shook his head. "It's on the house. We were closed anyway."

She tried to insist but he refused her money, all but shooing her out the door and locking it behind him before driving away in a bright red Fiat.

Gina walked back to The Royal Rescue. It was a pleasant

evening and the streets were surprisingly dry after such a heavy storm.

It wasn't until she was in the bright foyer of the hotel that she noticed her blouse was missing two buttons and her skirt was back to front and her hair no doubt looked as tousled as it felt. She did get rather an odd look from the doorman, but smiled. What matter? She was leaving in the morning and taking with her a very satisfying memory.

଼

Rainy Day Encounter

By Madeleine Oh

I wasn't too sure what I was doing in Lachmuirghan. Other than taking advantage of my cousin Chloe's birthday present. "A weekend at The Royal Rescue is just what you need," she'd insisted. "Have some fun and cheer yourself up. I had a smashing time there. Just what I needed after Martin dumped me."

Maybe, but Chloe is as heterosexual as they come and no doubt did have a great time with some of the brawny, lusty men-of-the-soil types who strolled around town, pulled pints behind the oak-beamed bar, or hefted my cases up the wide staircase. Since I'd arrived Friday afternoon, I'd not encountered anyone who struck my fancy. Not that a casual weekend affair had been my only reason for coming. But to be honest, it was the main one. Chloe had waxed long and enthusiastically about the weekend of near orgy she'd spent in the little town. What the heck? If the eligible populace wasn't my sort, I could live with that. Besides, I could appreciate scenery as much as the next person, so on Sunday I donned my stout hiking boots and set off to walk around the lower end of the loch.

With a bit of luck I might come across a mermaid in the saline lake.

No mermaids.

No lovely water sprites, of either sex.

No primal creatures lolling in the heather.

There was an old shepherd, complete with shaggy black and white dog, off in the distance, and I sat on a handy boulder and watched as he and the dog drove a flock of sheep across the hillside. By the time the team had ushered the sheep out of sight, I'd finished the last of the really excellent packed lunch The Royal Rescue had provided. Shaking the crumbs off my clothes, I decided I might as well head back to Lachmuirghan if I wanted time to change before dinner.

I thought I'd taken the same path back, but I didn't remember seeing the little stone cottage by the side of the trail, and I certainly hadn't encountered the old woman on my way up. She looked like an old crone out of a fairy tale. You know, the wizened, ugly old woman who offers the youngest (and politest) son a magic ball, or three wishes, or a goose to lay golden eggs...because he shared his bread and cheese with her.

There was nothing left of my lunch to share, except the rubbish I was carrying back with me, but I did pause to wish her "Good afternoon," and agree that, yes, it had been a beautiful day.

"There's more for you here in Lachmuirghan than watching Alistair bring the flock in," she said—right out of the blue, as far as I was concerned. And how the dickens had she, with those cataract milky eyes, seen me a few miles away across the countryside?

"It's been a great day for walking," I said. Sort of making

conversation.

"It'll rain before you get back to the Rescue. You'd best be stopping at the teashop. Fiona's expecting you." And with that enigmatic pronouncement, she turned on her heels—darn sprightly for her age she was—and disappeared into the cottage.

What exactly to make of that, I had no idea, but I was headed down to the village anyway, and she was right about the dark clouds scudding across the sky that had earlier been a perfect summer blue.

I had just made it to the outskirts of Lachmuirghan when the skies opened. I was drenched in minutes. The streets were like a shallow stream and all sensible people fast disappeared indoors.

I was a good half mile from the hotel at the far side of the town so, as I turned the corner, head down against the blinding rain, I nipped into the comparative dryness of a shop doorway.

A teashop doorway.

I sure as heck didn't remember seeing it earlier, but in this rain, I'd no doubt taken a wrong turning. Lights were on and the door opened to my hand on the knob.

Inside was deserted, but the blazing wood fire was more than enough encouragement to come right in. As I closed the door, a woman appeared from behind a curtain. She was beautiful—dark hair tied back but with soft curls loose around her face, eyes as blue as the loch water before the clouds rolled in, and a smile that lit up her eyes.

"Come in," she said, crossing the room to me and taking both my hands in hers. "Old Meg told me to wait for you."

Now I had a name for the weird old woman on the hillside. "What's your name?" I asked, as if I didn't I already know.

"Fiona," she replied with a smile that enticed and intrigued.

"You're soaked to the skin, let me lend you something dry to wear." She handed me a long housecoat of soft wool and locked the door and pulled down the window blinds. "So no one disturbs us."

At that point, I was standing there, bemused, dripping on the floor. "It's all right," she said, "you're in Lachmuirghan, and I'll be sure you get what you've missed all weekend. You'll catch your death if you don't take off those wet clothes."

She leaned in and kissed me, just a brush of her lips on mine but the brief contact stirred every shred of my pent-up need. Maybe Lachmuirghan was as magical as Chloe insisted.

"I don't know who you are." I did retain a little bit of sanity, after all.

Fiona shrugged and grinned. "Isn't that the whole point? People come here for what they don't find in what they know. Get your wet clothes off and warm yourself. I'll put the kettle on."

I still wasn't sure of anything other than the fact I was chilled and wet and vastly intrigued...and aroused. By a kiss from a total stranger? What the heck? I took off my wet jacket, undid my sodden shoes and proceeded to peel off my jeans and sweater. I hesitated over my bra and panties—they were pretty much dry and I was not quite ready to get down to my skin. I reached for the housecoat Fiona left for me. The silk lining slid over my skin as I pulled it over my head and pushed my arms though the sleeves.

I was dry, and the fire beckoned. I settled on the high-backed sofa and curled my feet under me. This beat trudging through driving rain. As if to convince me the warmth in here was infinitely better than staying outside, a sudden squall sent rain slashing against the leaded panes of the shop window.

"Here you are!" Fiona crossed the shop bearing two

steaming mugs. "A nice cup of tea. Just what you need to keep out the cold and warm the cockles of your heart, as my gran used to say."

Some mug of tea! I caught the whisky aroma even before I tasted it. Hot toddy, more like! Sweet and smooth as Highland honey and about as potent as the wildest sex I'd ever imagined. Wasn't that what I wanted?

"Good," I said and took a good, deep taste. Sheesh! It was! I moved over and made space for Fiona on the sofa.

Watching her over the rim of my glass, I drank. So did she. I took another taste, holding the potent brew in my mouth and working it over my tongue before swallowing.

"Feeling better?" she asked, snuggling close. "Anything else you need?" She wrapped an arm around my shoulders and her fingers separated the tendrils of my wet hair. "You are staying, aren't you?"

Why not? I was probably dreaming this anyway. I smiled and reached for her. I might have kept my bra on, she hadn't. Her breasts were soft as I reached under her sweatshirt to touch her. As my fingers found her sweet, hard little nipples, she smiled.

"Do stay. Why go out in the storm and get drenched?"

"Why indeed?" I replied and reached over and pulled off her scrunchy so her long, dark hair fell about her shoulders like a cascade of black silk. "Lovely," I said as I let it drape over my fingers. "Are you alone here?"

"Not now."

I liked her. She might not even be real. Just a figment of Lachmuirghan magic. But who gave a damn?

"Drink up," she told me, putting her own empty mug down with a soft clunk. "A warm bath will help stave off the cold."

In a teashop?

Oh, yes!

In a large room up the narrow stairway was a vast, claw-footed tub. Steam rose as Fiona turned on the taps. I pulled off the borrowed woolen housecoat and she reached over and unsnapped my bra. I saved her the trouble of getting off my panties and helped her off with her sweatshirt. Her breasts were small and firm and her nipples pink and sweet. Her legs were long, her thighs smooth and the hair between her thighs trimmed in a neat Mohawk.

"Lovely!" Smiling with anticipation, I eased my hands down her belly and watched her. Fiona smiled back. I didn't wait any longer. Cupping the back of her head with my hand, I pulled her face to mine. I started soft and slow, just a brush of lips on lips, but she opened her mouth and swallowed the kiss and kissed back with a passion and enthusiasm that was nothing short of delightful. I made the best of it, trailing my other hand down to between her shoulder blades and holding her steady in my arms.

As I broke off the kiss, she whispered, "Let's get in the bath." Brilliant idea! As she stepped in, I couldn't resist skimming my hand over the curve of her lovely, smooth bum.

I stepped in after her and she reached for a bottle and poured fragrant oil into the bath. The room was now filled with lavender-scented steam. Perfumed water rose to our breasts as we sat down. As I soaped Fiona's breasts with scented foam, she closed her eyes, sighing as my fingers trailed lower. I soaped her all over, having her kneel up as I washed between her legs and down her thighs.

After I rinsed her with a damp washcloth, she washed me with a touch that left me impatient and ready. Damp and heated, we patted each other dry with warm towels that wrapped us from shoulders to knees.

Fiona raised her fingers to my face. “What must I call you?” she asked, her voice tight and her eyes bright with curiosity and need.

What a question as we both stood there naked. ‘Margaret,” I told her.

“A fine Scots name.”

I hadn’t the heart to tell her I came from Yorkshire.

“Come on!” I grabbed her hand. “Where do we go?” I wasn’t against sex on the bath mat but hoped for somewhere a little more comfortable.

She led me to a narrow, low-ceilinged room, pretty much filled by a wide oak bed. She yanked back the covers and pulled me beside her. As she rolled onto her belly, giving me full benefit of her back and lovely curvy bum, I had a brilliant idea. “Don’t move! I’ll be back in a minute.” I was down the hall to the bathroom and back with a jar of lavender lotion in less time than it takes to tell.

“What’s the matter?” Fiona asked, looking over her shoulder as I walked back in.

“Absolutely nothing.” Far from it, in fact. I squeezed out the scented lotion and rubbed my hands together to warm it before easing my palms across her shoulders and down her back to the curve of her waist. She sighed with pleasure so I reached for the lotion again. I anointed her. Kissing her neck and shoulders as I stroked lotion into her back and arms... Fluttering my tongue on the soft pale skin behind her knees as I massaged her thighs and bum... She went limp and relaxed under my touch. Lovely. But I didn’t want her too loose. I needed her sweating with want as her body arched under me and her eyes blazed her need.

I rested a hand on the curve of her hip and nudged. “Roll

over."

She didn't need asking twice but flipped onto her back, giving me an uninterrupted view of her delicious, firm breasts. I ran my tongue up from her rib cage to her nipple and felt her excitement as I worked it between my lips. She gasped as I pulled it into my mouth and let out a slow moan of contentment as I worked my lips to her other nipple.

"Don't stop," she whispered as I pulled away.

"I won't," I promised.

I could smell her arousal over the scent of lavender but I took my time, running my fingertips over her curves and tasting her skin. As I rested my hand on her neatly-trimmed bush, she was whimpering with need. I spread her legs with my shoulders and opened her with my fingertips, reveling in the scent of her sex. Gently I breathed on her moist flesh and ran the tip of my tongue from fore to aft. Her head came off the pillow with a jolt, and the eyes that met mine were wide as her cunt.

"Margaret!" It came out on the tail of a gasp.

I didn't say anything. My tongue was busy.

She was sweet and lovely and as ardent a lover as I'd ever known. She climaxed with a series of little cries and frenzied jerks of her hips as her frantic hands grasped my hair.

She was still gasping, her breasts rising and falling with each pant as I eased up the bed and took her face in both hands. I kissed her very gently, letting my lips linger before opening her mouth so she could taste the joy I'd given her. She was halfway to fainting when I let her go. I settled for gathering her close, delighting in her warmth and scent.

"Margaret?"

"Yes." I smiled at her as I ran my hand over her hair.

"You haven't come?"

I shook my head. "Not yet. It's your turn."

It truly was!

Propping herself on one elbow, Fiona bent her head to my breast and carefully worked her way down. When she reached my cunt, she delved in with enthusiasm and ardor. I came three times before she finally paused and I was loose, spent and definitely warmed up.

Staying beside Fiona until morning didn't seem a bad idea, but after a long and decidedly pleasant cuddle, she sat up and swung her legs over the bed.

"We both have to go," she said, regret clear in her voice. "I can't stay and you have dinner waiting at The Royal Rescue."

Frankly, I could have happily skipped dinner, but she was out of door and back in moments, dressed and carrying my clothes—all dry and ironed! Something had clicked out of reality here, but with a thank-you kiss to her still-tempting lips, I got dressed.

She gave me a lovely hug as she opened the shop door and I stepped out onto the narrow street and a crisp, clear evening, but when I paused at the corner to look back and wave goodbye, the street was shrouded in mist.

Next morning, enjoying a leisurely breakfast before I set off home, I was reading the *Lachmuirghan Morning News*. There was an announcement on the front page saying Beryl's Teashop was still closed as the repairs from the fire three months previously were more extensive than first estimated. The planned reopening would regrettably be delayed until the end of the summer.

Seven: The Book Shop

The inhabitants of Lachmuirghan have long memories and an even longer history, but no one can say with certainty just when the Book Shop first opened.

True, there is a date chiseled into the stone lintel above the door, but it is not one that anyone can truly recognize. Like so much else about the Book Shop, the origins of the stone are a mystery. Some say the strange markings come from an ancient civilization, others, more fancifully perhaps, say it is from another world. Certainly the stone is different in color and texture from the granite surrounding it, but over the years the inhabitants of Lachmuirghan have grown accustomed to its strangeness and even, some might say, rather proud of it, and the fact that it brings so many visiting "experts" to the village to study it.

And then there is the Book Shop itself. Some say that in a long-ago time, it was the home of an alchemist and caster of spells and horoscopes, a friend of the great Master Dee who cast the horoscopes of Henry VIII's two daughters and who was thought to be a sorcerer. Others even more boldly claim that the old gnarled shopkeeper who guarded his precious books so fiercely and had so many visitors who arrived late at night and in secret was Master Dee himself. And there are those who say that the Book Shop is magical and that it suddenly appeared one Beltane night, in the middle of an otherwise nondescript row of similar dwellings, its shelves heavy with ancient books.

Whatever the truth may be about the Book Shop's past, it is now a "must see" place for visitors to Lachmuirghan, but one word of caution: There are those who say that to enter its portal can change a person's life forever.

Dare you?

ꟹ

Shapeshifter

By Pandora Grace

Prologue

Ellie heard the cat's terrified yowls the moment she opened her front door. She had been intending to go to the post-box to post the considered, measured, and yes, begging, letter she had so carefully composed pleading with Eric to give their relationship a second chance. With a letter so intimate there was no way she was going to email it to him.

Now despite the darkness and the rain, she could see the three boys bending over the terrified animal, aiming kicks at it as they laughed at its plight. Poor little thing, how could they be so cruel? The yellow fuzz of the streetlight became a red mist as Ellie dropped her letter and hurried to the rescue.

There were, after all, some advantages to having a brother who had practiced his martial arts on her whilst they were growing up. Within seconds, the trio had fled.

Ellie bent down and picked up the cat as gently as she could, tenderly checking it over for broken bones. She had always loved cats, unlike Eric who disliked all animals.

"Oh, your poor little thing," she crooned tenderly to it.

The cat mewed plaintively and tried to crawl up her shoulder. It had a handsome face and huge amber eyes, despite its thinness. It fixed its gaze on her and stared unblinkingly at her. Its fur was wet and matted. With blood? Ellie searched for a collar, wondering where the cat had come from, but it wasn't wearing one. By rights she ought to leave it here—Eric would certainly have said so. The cat made a strangely angry sound and dug its claws into her coat.

"Okay, then, I'll take you in with me, but you can't stay, you know, and first I need to post my letter."

Her letter. Where was it? She looked down at the pavement and saw the envelope lying a few feet away. Relieved, she hurried to pick it up but to her dismay, just as she reached it, a sudden gust of wind blew the envelope out of her reach. Still holding the cat, she hurried after it, gasping as the force of wind increased to such an extent that it drove her backwards through her open front door. Too out of breath and scared to risk continuing to pursue her letter, she slammed the door shut.

Chapter One

Congratulations. This voucher entitles you to a free stay at the luxurious Castle Spa, Lachmuirghan Village, Scotland. Directions as enclosed.

For the umpteenth time since she had received the letter over a week ago, Ellie studied the bold black print on its expensive cream background. Initially she'd assumed it was a sales gimmick and had intended to throw it away, but the cat had insisted on sitting on it and she forgot. He'd even given her a small warning growl when she'd gone to pick him up, although he had allowed her to stroke his now lovely clean, glossy fur.

Then she'd had the weirdest sort of dream in which somehow the cat had turned into an eagle and was holding her tightly beneath one wing whilst he muttered about the ingratitude and stupidity of humans in general and herself in particular and commanded her to look down as he flew her over the rooftops. Through the open window of a house, she saw a man lying in bed asleep—asleep and completely naked, his body making Eric's look like a pallid caricature. She wondered if she were suffering from some kind of burnout and maybe a few days away from the rat race could well be a good thing.

She had still hesitated, though—wary of anything that sounded too good to be true, even though the helpline she had telephoned had assured her that the offer was genuine. But what had finally decided her had been seeing Eric and his new partner walking hand in hand right past her. Eric had a silly besotted look on his face she'd never been able to put there, and he had been totally oblivious to her presence. Since she and Eric shared the same local pub, she decided there and then that a few days of cosseting in a luxury spa would equip her far better for facing Eric than those same few days spent comfort eating and sobbing into a glass of merlot.

So here she was, although it had taken her much longer to drive up to Scotland than she had expected. And now it was dark, a thin mist blurring the landscape. It felt like hours since she had seen any signs of inhabitation. Had she taken a wrong turning somewhere?

"What do you think, Puss?"

In his basket in the backseat of her small car, the cat made a sharp sound of male contempt. Ellie smiled. He looked so handsome now, his black coat brushed and gleaming with good health. In the few weeks since she had rescued him, he had become her unwitting confidant.

Sitting down with him on her knee whilst she enjoyed the sensual pleasure of stroking his thick warm fur, she had told him all about how miserable her relationship with Eric had made her, how afraid she was that the less-than-orgasmic and at best mediocre sex she had had with Eric, was going to be the only kind of sex she ever had.

Getting up and holding the cat tightly, she had paced her small kitchen, thinking wildly, *I want more than that. If someone gave me three wishes, I'd wish for wild, uninhibited, thrillingly orgasmic sex. The kind of sex that all women dream and fantasize about: mega, multi, heart-stopping, breathtaking, no-holds-barred, physical passion. And what's more, I'd wish to have it with a man so sexy and gorgeous that I get wet just looking at him. A man who's a world away from men like Eric. A man who loves me and wants me, a man who's my soul mate.*

The cat had stared so hard at her that for a moment she wasn't sure if she had actually spoken her thoughts aloud. Just in case she had, she added, "That would show Eric." Before he had walked out on her, Eric often complained that she was not as skilled in bed as his previous lovers.

"Oh, Puss," she had sighed as she bent down and scooped him up. "I wish more than anything else that for once in my life something magical and special could happen to me."

But of course, as her late grandmother had been fond of saying, "If wishes were horses, then beggars would ride."

She just hoped that this spa place, when she found it, didn't object to her bringing the cat.

Through the mist she could see a sign up ahead of her which read: *Welcome to Lachmuirghan—Please fly carefully through our village.*

Fly? The village children had obviously altered it.

Suddenly the mist cleared and she could see the glen down below, its loch a glistening teardrop at the far end of the valley. Beyond it she could see where a river ran like a silver ribbon toward high cliffs and beyond them the rolling breakers of the sea itself. The steep, winding road she had climbed led toward the cleft-shaped entrance to the glen. The narrow road lay between smooth rounded walls like a sleek tongue, its pointed tip curling round a sprinkling of buildings which she assumed must be the village.

She could see the castle too, a shining sugar-white fairytale of a place, or so it seemed to her, all slender turrets and steep gilded roofs, surely more fantasy than reality, and enough to lift any daydreamer's heart.

"It's so pretty."

The cat yawned, obviously bored.

Smiling to herself, Ellie headed toward the village.

Chapter Two

"Thank you, that was lovely."

The spa really was the oddest place, Ellie reflected as she thanked the same woman who had greeted her the previous evening and then shown her to her beautiful baroque suite, with its sensually exotic décor and furnishings and murals of bacchanalian scenes painted everywhere. She even had her own personal sunken spa pool on the balcony outside her bedroom.

She could see no sign of any kind of heating anywhere and yet the air was warm and balmy. She hadn't seen any other guests either, but surely there must be some? She couldn't be the only person to have been invited to enjoy all this luxurious splendor. In her room she had found a program with her name printed on it, informing her that she had the morning free to explore the village and that her treatment would begin after lunch. With the program was a map of the village, on which its visitor attractions were clearly marked.

And her breakfast. Exactly what she had most wanted to eat had appeared as if by magic out of nowhere, or so it had seemed.

"My cat—" she began.

"The shapeshifter you mean? Out about his own business."

Ellie's forehead crinkled. *Shapeshifter*—was that a local name for cats? The woman disappeared before she could ask her.

She felt something soft and silky moving against her legs and immediately recognized the soft sensuality of the cat's fur.

"So there you are, 'shapeshifter'," she teased as she bent down to pick him up and stroke him. "I'm going to go for a walk now and explore the village, and you, my handsome one, are going back to your basket."

He purred as she tickled his chin and then licked her hand.

"If only I could find a man as handsome and loving as you," she whispered to him.

Lachmuirghan was exactly what she had expected from a Scottish village and yet at the same time very different. Take the loch, for instance, whose bank she walked along on her way to the village. It was everything a loch should be, complete with its own small island. When she gave into the urge to kneel down and trail her fingers in the water, she had discovered it was saltwater—warm saltwater.

And then there were the villagers themselves, oddly silent as they turned away from her so that she couldn't quite see their faces, but the village was obviously a popular tourist spot because she had seen a sign saying: *To the Guesthouse.*

The pretty café with its offer of cream teas had tempted her, but the moment she had touched the door handle, a closed sign appeared in the window.

Up ahead she could see a small old-fashioned bookshop, the kind that tempted one to go in and browse. She hurried toward it, eagerness and excitement quickening her step. Its door, happily, was not displaying a closed sign. She pushed it open and walked inside. The shop appeared empty, apart from the small old man seated behind the counter, frowning over something he was reading.

She cleared her throat self-consciously and he looked up at her. His eyes were shaped like a cat's—green, gold and unblinking. Ellie couldn't look away from them.

"I...I..."

"Your book is on the seventh shelf, thirteen volumes along."

What on earth had he meant by that?

She walked uncertainly between the high shelves until she found the book he had described. The bookshop was so warm, too warm almost.

"Pick up the book."

The words felt like the stroke of warm fur against her ear, the disembodied voice reminiscent of the purr of a big cat. She wanted to turn round, sure she had just seen the tip of a long black tail, but instead she felt compelled to reach for the volume in front of her.

It was thick and heavy, the binding slightly worn. A

mythical heraldic creature was emblazoned on the front of it in gold, a griffin's head on the winged body of a hunting cheetah. She traced its outline with her fingertip.

"Open it."

The words were rough velvet now, the sensual rasp of a knowing tongue against bare skin, or rather how she had imagined such a sensation must feel since Eric had refused point blank to indulge in anything other than plain quickly-over, missionary-position sex.

She heard a soft snarl and the lash of a whip thin tail on the dusty floor. As she jumped, the book slipped through her fingers, falling open.

A most peculiar scent rose from the open pages, a mixture of spices and musk and something else that made her skin prickle with heat and her tightly closed sex cleft suddenly start to relax and expand.

She knelt to retrieve the book, her eyes widening at the photograph lying on the open pages. Just looking into the face of the man in the photograph made her dizzy with excitement and longing. Tall, dark-haired, broad-shouldered, with white teeth and a smile that sent her heart bouncing into her ribs and swelled the love-starved lips of her sex with excited anticipation. He was everything she'd have created in her own imagination if she'd only known how.

But even as she focused hungrily on his image, a thin, fine mist rose from the pages of the book, swirling slowly around her, its movement mesmerizing her as it swirled faster and faster, whirling round her until she felt so giddy she could hardly stand...and suddenly it sucked her into its dark center.

Chapter Three

"What on earth—?" Ellie stared up at the two beautiful girls standing beside her luxurious bed. She struggled to sit up and then clutched pink-cheeked at the thin silk wisp of fabric lying on the bed beside her as she realized she was completely naked.

"Who are you? What's happening?" she demanded anxiously.

"We are here to prepare you for your fate," one of the girls explained with a smile.

"My fate? What do you mean? I don't understand."

"The shapeshifter has granted your wishes and we are to prepare you to receive them."

"The shapeshifter? Are you talking about the cat?"

The two young women exchanged wary looks.

"He has many different guises."

What on earth was going on?

"Where is he now?" she demanded.

"You ask too many questions. It is not given to a mere mortal to question a Lord of the Universe. You are honored indeed that he has granted your desire. And now we must make you ready to receive it, and he who will bring you the pleasure you have asked for."

He? The pleasure? Ellie's head was spinning. How was it possible that the thin, starving, battered cat she had rescued could be responsible for all of this? He couldn't be!

"But I am."

The words purred through her.

She looked round quickly but only she and the two girls were in the room.

She heard the low growl of satisfied laughter, and a feeling stroked over her as though cool, silky fur had brushed her naked body.

"See, you are thinking of what lies ahead already."

One of the girls laughed teasingly, calling out to her companion.

"Look sister, how the little buds of her pleasure globes have grown."

Ellie gasped as they both stared interestedly at her breasts.

"Your face grows red. Is that another sign of female human readiness for pleasure?" the second girl asked Ellie curiously.

"No," Ellie denied indignantly. "It is because I am embarrassed."

"Embarrassed? What is that?"

"It is-it is how anyone would feel—how you would feel if you were naked and I wasn't and-and we were strangers," Ellie struggled to explain.

"Naked?" The girl's forehead creased in bewilderment.

"If your body was like mine and you were not wearing...anything..." Ellie persisted.

"Wearing anything? But we are as we always are," the second girl told Ellie.

"I know what it is, sister, she sees us as she wishes to see us," the first one explained to her companion. "Close your eyes," she instructed Ellie.

Reluctantly, Ellie did so.

"Now you may open them again."

Ellie gasped aloud in shock. Both girls were now completely naked. Their skin was very pale, their bodies completely free of hair. Their erect nipples were a deep dark pink and the outer lips of their sex were swollen and slightly parted.

"First we must bathe you."

Bathe her. Ellie gulped uncertainly, and then gasped as suddenly she discovered that she wasn't lying on the bed anymore, but instead she was seated in the huge sunken bath on the terrace, and her two companions were with her.

"Close your eyes."

She didn't want to obey the silky, purred command, but she did all the same.

Warm water lapped at her skin, stroking it, surging intimately against her so powerfully that the force of it parted the lips of her sex and then rubbed against her clit. A deliciously sensual feeling of arousal raced through her.

Soft hands stroked and soaped her body. Her body began to heat, erotic pulses quickening through her. Sensuality, she realized, was so very different from mere sex. She felt as though her body was waking up from a very long sleep, sloughing off a dead unwanted skin to awaken revitalized and quivering in every pore with expectation and excitement.

She tried to open her eyes but her eyelids felt too heavy to lift. Images formed inside her head—a photograph; a man's face; a man's body, sleek-fleshed, taut-muscled, naked, his cock proudly displayed for her enjoyment.

She wanted to touch it. She wanted to run her fingers up his thick shaft and then around the rosy head.

He smiled, his hand reaching out to cup her breast, the pad of his thumb rubbing excitingly against the tight peak of her nipple. She heard herself moan and then whimper with desire as she opened her legs and silently invited him to take his pleasure and enjoy her.

A low growl broke into her fevered thoughts, breaking their sensual spell. She opened her eyes, her face burning as she realized that her own nipples were now as engorged as those of the two girls sharing the bath with her.

In the blink of an eye, she was transported from the bath back to the bed, her body miraculously dry, whilst equally miraculously a small table had appeared beside it on which stood an assortment of different crystal bottles, containing what looked like creams and lotions. Like the girls, her own quim was now free of hair, her flesh smooth and naked.

Her two handmaidens stood on either side of the bed, passing the crystal containers to one another and removing the bright jewel-colored stoppers. The brilliance of the sunlight bouncing off the bottles and the rich décor of her room with its ornate plasterwork, dazzled Ellie so much that she had to close her eyes.

She could feel their hands on her body, the cream they were massaging into her skin soft and warm, the strength of its musky scent dizzying.

She had smelled it somewhere before. But couldn't remember where.

The girls turned her over onto her belly. Their clever, quick hands softened the stiff muscles of her shoulders, one girl taking hold of one of her arms and one the other, stroking down them and then back up again.

They kneaded the length of her spine and then the soft roundness of her cheeks.

Her whole body began to relax.

As they worked their way right down to her feet and then turned her over again, their touch suddenly became much harder and firmer.

Reluctantly, Ellie opened her eyes.

The girls had gone and in their place stood two handsome young men, garbed much as the girls had been, their bodies equally free of body hair so that their erect cocks were intimately visible above the swollen sacs of their balls.

They were massaging her legs without looking at her, each one totally focused on what he was doing. They had opened her legs, and their cocks reared up harder in recognition of her desirability.

How very strange it all was. And how very enjoyable. Eric had always insisted on them having sex beneath the bedclothes and with the light off.

Sex. Just looking at their hard cocks was making her ache.

The cream they massaged into her smelled as musky as sex and Ellie could feel her body responding to it. Their hands stroked up the insides of her thighs now, their ardent gazes fixed on her breasts. A small bead of pearly fluid rose from the head of one cock as its owner's hand brushed against her quim.

She was lying propped up against a bank of pillows so that she could watch them ministering to her and look down at her own body. At it, but not intimately into the wet excitement of her sex.

"You want that?" The purred question stroked against her skin.

She shuddered hotly. She could have sworn she had actually felt the touch of hard fingers parting her lips and stroking the length of her. But she had seen nothing.

"You want to see now?"

A mirror appeared at the bottom of the bed. Her two attendants gently eased her legs further apart so that she could see her own sex reflected back at her. The right hand of one and the left hand of the other massaged the inside of her thighs with slow stroking movements that made her tremble violently. In perfect unison, they reached for her breasts, cupping one each so that her nipples stood proud, and then in equally perfect unison they both bent their heads.

Ellie was shuddering with excitement even before she felt the hard flick of their pointed tongues against her nipples.

The hands massaging her inner thighs moved upwards. Over their heads she watched them carefully folding back the lips of her sex to reveal the glistening pink flesh surrounding her slit and the delicate shape of her clit.

"You are ready to give yourself over to me and to your fate."

"Yes, oh yes..."

She looked up. And saw a man.

His face was that of the man in the photograph from the bookshop. A huge surge of passionate longing filled her.

She knew at once he was her soul mate, and they were bound to one another for all eternity.

Emotional tears filmed her eyes. She closed them and saw another image. One with green-gold eyes, and sleek dark fur.

Chapter Four

She had been having the most extraordinary and even shocking dream, Ellie acknowledged, burrowing down into the warmth of her bed. In fact, by rights she ought to feel ashamed of just what she had been dreaming, instead of feeling like a female animal in heat, all satin-skinned and sexually turned on, longing for her male counterpart to claim her and satisfy her hunger for him.

A small movement in the night shadows beyond her bed caught her attention and she froze in shock as she saw the man from the photograph, the man about whom she had just been dreaming so sexually, walking toward her. He was naked, his body gleaming in the thin silver light coming in through the castle's narrow windows.

"What—?"

"Why do you draw back from me in fear?" he asked her softly.

"Who are you? What are you doing in my room?"

"I am he whom you told The Lord of the Universe you desired, and I am here only to pleasure you in every way you desire to be pleasured. His minions have made you ready for the banquet of sensual delight we are to share.

"Your every thought and wish is known to him, and through him to me. You tremble, and with your eyes you try to show me fear, but I can see beyond that pretense to your excitement and longing."

Ellie stared at him in disbelief. This was some kind of joke. It had to be. And as for him reading her mind, her desires—he couldn't possibly know about the hidden hot-sweet ache decorously and primly concealed from him beneath the bedclothes.

"Of course I know about it," he laughed. "And your quim is not so decorous or prim now—see for yourself."

There was a small flurried sound and the bedclothes disappeared, leaving her lying naked in front of him. Outraged color stormed her face, intensifying when she glanced down at herself and saw that her mound of Venus and the lips below it were indeed ripely swollen.

Another few minutes and her lips would be parting wantonly of their own accord to show him the eager readiness of her opening.

"I daresay they will be but I intend to tease them apart myself because I know that this is what you are wishing for just as I know that you want me to—"

"No!" Ellie denied angrily. "I do not want anything from you. All I want is for you to leave."

But not before I've reached out and touched your cock to see if it feels as hard as it looks. Its head is so swollen and slick with your man-heat that already I can imagine the pleasure it would give me to have it sliding slowly in and out of me.

How on earth had such thoughts entered her head? They were not her thoughts.

"But they are your desires. Already your woman's passage grows wet and eager to know my shaft. But there are other pleasures you desire to taste before that one, and more you will wish to experience after."

"I don't believe this. It isn't happening," Ellie protested weakly.

Only it was.

He walked toward her and lifted her from the bed, taking her into his arms as he gazed into her eyes. Setting her on the smooth sheets, he raised his hands and cupped her face, his fingers stroking the delicate flesh just behind her ears so that she quivered from head to foot.

A small smile curled his mouth as his thumbs brushed the corners of her lips.

"Believe," he told her softly. "Believe and it will be so. Just as you have always wanted it to be."

He bent his head toward her, obliterating the light, and she remembered how as a teenager she had spent hours fantasizing about what it must be like to be kissed properly. Then her virgin body had been on fire with passion and longing for such a kiss, but she had quickly discovered that the kisses she had longed for did not exist.

"Oh but they do..."

The words were a warm breath against her lips as his brushed them. A sweet melting heat slid slowly through her veins. He brushed her lips with his again, and she sighed and leaned against him. The third time his tongue eased them apart, and the fourth, his hands dropped from her face to her hips and then up to her breasts as his tongue moved rhythmically against her own and his thumbs and fingers drew the same excited pleasure from her begging nipples as her lips were drawing from his tongue.

She had longed so much and for so long for this pleasure that she had begun to think it could not exist, that only her own imagination could provide her with the lover who would take her to such heights. But she had been wrong. She knew that now.

If just having him touch her nipples could make her feel like this, though, what would it feel like it he were to caress them with his lips?

“It will turn your body liquid with passion and you will open your legs to me and cry out to me that you want to feel my touch against your quim—”

“No!”

He laughed gently again.

“You are afraid that if I touch you intimately, your pleasure will be so intense that it will be over too quickly. But you need not fear. That first pleasure will be but the small foothills of the highest of high mountain ranges. And even when you reach its pinnacle there will be other pleasures.”

Ellie couldn’t contain her shudder of arousal.

“Yes, of course I shall prove it.”

He got on the bed beside her. He parted her legs and kissed the flesh of her inner thigh, slowly stroking her skin as he did so.

Surely pleasure such as this was too intense to be endured? She didn't just want to endure it, though, she wanted more of it. Much more.

But to her disappointment he moved away.

"This way? Very well then," he told her, smiling as he arranged her so that she was arched over him. Positioned thus, he laved her nipple with his tongue tip and then took it into his mouth to tease and suckle. The surges of erotic intensity jerking from her nipple to her clit felt as though he was actually tugging on some magical secret thread that linked them. Each tug of his mouth on her breast caused her secret self to pulse with pleasure.

His fingers stroked her inner thighs, making her cry out in urgent need and shudder excitedly. Parting her pussy lips, he slowly dipped one finger into her wetness, rubbing across her slit, and back again slowly, and then faster, until she began to pant and moan, her hips writhing as she responded to the rhythm of his pleasuring.

In her dreams she'd imagined this tight coiling urgency, but her imagination fell short of the reality. How could she have known to dream of the hard pointed tongue of her soul mate circling her clit as he eased long fingers deep into her? Now though, she knew her dreams fell short of reality, and she cried out her need to him as she trembled on the edge of that place he had called a foothill but which to her seemed to be the highest mountain she would ever climb.

"Sweet. So sweet, the way you take your pleasure, and I shall give you more, so very much more."

As her shudders subsided, he stroked his fingers over her sensitized clit and kissed her smooth flat belly before pulling her to him and lifting her to place her on top of him.

"Now you are ready to begin to climb the mountain. Open

yourself fully to me and take my cock into you. Rub its head against your quim so that they may get acquainted with one another, and when your wetness matches my heat, let him thrust up between your lips and into your slit."

Ellie curled her fingers round his stiffly erect cock. Its head burned with heat as she rubbed it against her quim.

Unsteadily she lowered herself onto it, moaning with hot longing when he reached out and held her pussy lips open.

He fit her so perfectly, her woman's passage stretched sweetly tight to hold him, his breadth such that her every nerve ending that surrounded him flooded with delight. She took him into her, and then deeper still, her short panting breaths matching her increasing speed as she rose and fell.

The rosy head and thick shaft were hers, his cock her prisoner. She would keep him so until he had paid his lover's dues to her and left his treasure within her womb.

Faster and faster her body moved, her head thrown back in exultation as she saw how desire corded his muscles when she took his control from him, He reached for her hips, holding her down on him whilst he thrust higher and stronger. A wild, wanton sound of pleasure burst from her lungs as his thrusts brought her to that peak he had promised her, and then miraculously took her beyond it.

Chapter Five

Ellie thanked the woman at the cash desk as she handed her back her debit card. With her car refilled with petrol, there was no need for her to linger in this garage she had pulled into several miles outside Lachmuirghan.

Lachmuirghan! She could feel her face starting to burn and

her body starting to heat. She would never be able to explain or understand the sensually wanton person she had become in that bedroom in the castle when she had given herself over to pleasure. And what pleasure. Even now her body sang with it. Just walking from the car to pay for her petrol had been enough to make her aware of her secret wetness and the ache inside that was a mixture of the last three nights of sex, and a desire for a lifetime more of them.

A car pulled up next to her own. The door opened and a man got out.

Ellie stared at him, her eyes widening in recognition. The man from the photograph! The man who had been her lover!

A thin mist blew in from the sea, and the garage and the surroundings seemed to quiver and somehow melt away, but Ellie didn't care.

Her soul mate was looking back at her, his austere look giving way to a smile.

Ellie took a step toward him and then another.

"Excuse me. I think you've dropped this."

Ellie stared down at the envelope the tall, dark-haired, gorgeously sexy man standing in front of her was holding. It was grubby and wet from lying on the rain-soaked pavement outside her flat, Eric's name almost illegible where the ink had run.

"Oh, thank you..."

"I've seen you a couple of times, and wondered how I could introduce myself. I've just moved into the area. Now it seems that fate has taken a hand and given me the perfect excuse. Look, I was wondering...could I buy you a cup of coffee?"

A cup of coffee and a wedding ring, Ellie thought dreamily, screwing up the envelope and pushing it into her bag.

"Yes. I'd like that," she answered him.

He hadn't stopped looking at her and his eyes, she was relieved to see, were a lovely warm shade of blue.

ଓ

The Ride of Your Life

By Clarissa Wilmot

Mary Montagu put down her glasses, rubbed her eyes and sighed. She glanced at her watch. Eight o'clock. It really was time to put her books away, leave the library and get home. Not that there was anyone waiting for her. Not anymore. Not now that John had finally pushed off with the blonde bombshell from the office rumored to be a sexual athlete, with a parting shot about how a bluestocking like her would never be any good in bed.

She looked at the notes she had made for the chapter of her PhD entitled *Sea Kelpies: Fact or Fiction*, and turned back to the book she was reading. She had been working on her thesis for a couple of years now, and sometimes even she had to admit, this was no way for a grown woman to earn her living. Immersed as she had become in fantasy and myth, she had begun to feel that she had forgotten how to live. John certainly thought so, and he was always on at her to put her books away and think about getting a proper job.

"I have a proper job," Mary had argued, but it was true part-time lecturing at the local college of further education while helping her fund her PhD research didn't exactly amount to a high-flying career. Which was exactly when she and John had started to part company—he was heading for the top of the career ladder at the swishy firm of accountants he worked at, whereas she was still swimming in the shallows. Presumably Brenda the Blonde Bombshell was more up for social climbing than Mary—well, if so, she was welcome to it. Mary would rather keep her kelpies. In fact, she had to admit she was developing something of an unhealthy interest in them.

Perhaps John was right and she did live in a fantasy world, but there was something dark and mysterious about the kelpies that drew her to them. She felt greedy for knowledge and wanted more. Sometimes when she was wrapped up in her research, she had to pinch herself to remind herself that they didn't exist. No wonder John had teased her about being an uptight academic. It was as though nothing else seemed real to her.

But the stories about kelpies were so fascinating. A stranger would see a horse, black as midnight or gray as rain-tossed storm, grazing by a river or by the sea. Perhaps drawn out of greed, as the horse always sported a golden bridle, or perhaps mesmerized by the horse's piercing blue eyes, the stranger would feel impelled to ride it. What happened next varied depending on the malignity of the kelpie. Sometimes the rider would merely be unceremoniously tossed in the water, but in the darker tales—the ones Mary found herself increasingly drawn to—the rider would be taken on a wild ride out to sea, and never heard from again.

The rumors said that male kelpies feasted on human flesh, and yet the female ones seemed to choose men to mate with. Mary had wondered why that was, and had found herself searching for evidence of a story in which the legend was subverted and a male kelpie had found himself a human lover. And tonight she had finally found the story she was after, in the library book she was now reading.

A male kelpie who lived on the shores of a village called

Lachmuirghan had fallen in love with the daughter of the local laird. The love was reciprocated and so the myth went, they consummated their union in a passionate ride across the waves. But when the girl became pregnant, her father said she had bought shame to the family and, taking her to the standing stones which stood on the cliff high above the beach, stabbed her through the heart. The kelpie, unable to rescue her, keened a wild lament below. And for revenge, he had enticed the laird onto his back and thrown him into the depths of the sea. Legend still had it that on stormy nights you could hear the sound of the kelpie's lament.

Mary shivered, thinking about it. There was something so unutterably sad about that story, and yet its poignancy had a certain beauty. She found herself staring at a picture of the kelpie. He was in his human form, dark and handsome, and the face looked out from the page with brooding blue eyes. Staring into them, she could almost smell the brine of the sea and hear the sound of the waves. She could feel strong arms sweeping her away and a fleeting kiss across her lips which left her with a yearning for something more.

It was late. Even she had to admit she was getting fanciful. Shutting the book with a snap, she started packing her things away to get ready to go. She went to return the book to its shelf, when a piece of paper dropped out of it. She picked it up, curious. It was a picture postcard showing a village. The village appeared to have a bookshop, a castle, a beach and standing stones. *Welcome to Lachmuirghan*, it said. Mary frowned. She hadn't realized Lachmuirghan actually existed. But turning over the card, she saw it was a promo.

The Lachmuirghan Book Shop welcomes you to an evening of mystery and suspense. Find out the truth behind the local legends. And meet Conor McLaughlin, author of Lachmuirghan: Village of Secrets, *who will be talking about his latest book,*

Lachmuirghan: The Devil's Lair. *Dare you enter?*

The date was soon—*I could go,* Mary thought for one mad moment, and Conor McLaughin sounded mysterious—sexy even. *After all, who is there to stop me?*

"Only yourself..." Mary turned round, startled—she could have sworn somebody whispered those words, yet there was no one there. But as she made her way down the library steps, ever so faintly she heard the sound of a distant seashore, and blowing on the breeze was the merest hint of brine.

What am I doing here? Not for the first time, Mary asked herself this question as she drove down the country roads towards Lachmuirghan. To her surprise, it did exist, and she had found the place easily on a map. When she mentioned it to her tutor, he had thought it was a good idea to go and visit. "You might find something out about your kelpie," he had joked. Mary, drawn by the memory of piercing blue eyes and brooding looks, and as usual at a loose end for the weekend, couldn't think of a reason why she shouldn't go.

And now she was nearly there. She seemed to have driven the hundred miles or so from Edinburgh in a daze. The road she had taken followed the coastal path, and suddenly as she turned a corner, she saw a golden strand where a sparkling sea gently lapped the shore. At the far end of the beach, she could see the silver snake of a river winding its way from the sea up into the distant mountains. And ahead of her lay the village of Lachmuirghan.

High on the cliff above the beach stood a ruined kirk, and in the distance the castle stood atop a hill. But there seemed to be no sign of the stones—strange, they had been on the postcard, and the kirk was in exactly the place the stones were meant to be in the legend.

Stopping the car for a moment, she looked again at the card, which was propped up on the dashboard. That was weird. The postcard looked exactly as it had before, but this time there were no standing stones—only a picture of the kirk in its place. A slight frisson of not exactly fear, but something close, ran through her. What was this place? It seemed otherworldly, somehow. The last line of the postcard seemed to taunt her. *Dare you?* it whispered.

A sound halfway between a sob and a wail caught her by surprise. She got out of the car and looked around her. There was nothing but the sound of crashing surf and the faint keening of the seagulls. The wind caressed her face, almost like a kiss, and her dark curls blew in her eyes. *What would it be like to ride with a lover here?* she wondered, then mocked herself for even thinking it. She was imagining things. Something to do with the haunting nature of this place. That was all. But as she got in the car, she thought she caught sight of a dark shape racing down the beach. A horse-like shape, with the glint of a golden bridle. And suddenly the most intense of yearnings pierced her heart and a desire she could barely begin to articulate filled her body. She looked again, but the horse—if it had been there—was gone.

"Get a grip, Mary," she muttered to herself, and got back in the car and drove on.

The talk at the bookshop proved rather dull and uneventful. Conor McLaughlin turned out to be fat and fifty. He had nothing of great note to say about the area. He was certainly nothing like Mary's vivid imaginings and when pressed, didn't even know the story of the kelpie. "That's a new one on me." He had coughed rather apologetically and then turned to answer a question about the strange geographical anomaly that led the loch to have saline water in it.

"If it's kelpies you're after, there's no point asking him," a voice whispered from behind her.

Mary turned to see the wizened features of the bookseller, whom she had vaguely noticed on her way in.

"He's not even local, he doesn't understand our ways," continued the bookseller. The session seemed to be winding up now, and Conor McLaughlin was signing books. "I think you'll find what you're looking for on that shelf. I'm sure you'll find it most illuminating."

Mary wandered over to the shelf in question, and her eyes immediately alighted on a book entitled *The True Storie of the Lachmuirghan Sea Kelpie.* That was more like it.

She picked it up, and opened it. And immediately was hit by the smell of brine—lord had it been dropped in the sea?—and then the sound of roaring waves overpowered her. She felt dizzy and the room seemed to be spinning. Her ears filled with the haunting, keening sound she had heard earlier. Again, it filled her with an ache of desire and longing—she wanted to go and comfort the author of that sound, drown in the depths of his sorrow. For she was certain it came from a *he.* And at the same time, she could feel the wind on her face, blowing her hair away, and beneath her legs the wild thrumming of a horse. The combination made her feel wild and wanton, her whole body prickled with desire, she wanted to tame him and be tamed by him—this stranger, this mysterious lover who set her soul on fire...

...Mary came to with a start. The bookshop was deserted, and in her hands she held an open book. Not entirely sure what had happened but thankful there was no one to see her shame, Mary quickly closed the book and beat a hasty retreat. Coming to Lachmuirghan had been a waste of time. She hadn't learned anything new, and had just escaped making a fool of herself. It was time she headed home.

As she walked to the car, which she had parked by the jetty, she passed by a few fishermen mending their nets. One sat, feet over the side of the quay, lounging in an arrogant yet appealing way. He had a kind of smoldering beauty, and as he looked up, she realized with a shock that he had eyes of the most piercing blue. They seemed to look into her soul and see her innermost desires. Remembering the strange episode in the shop, Mary blushed and hurried on. But as she got to the car, she had a sudden thought. What was she rushing back for? There was no one at home waiting, and it was a beautiful sunny day. Why not take a stroll down to the beach while she was here? It couldn't do any harm, could it?

The path from the village down to the beach was further then she had thought. Panting slightly, she wondered whether or not she should turn back. Dark clouds were gathering and a mist was rolling over the sea. But just as she was about to turn around, she heard the faint whinny of a horse. That decided her. She would carry on. If only to prove to herself there were no such things as kelpies.

The path led over the dunes and to the beach, and there by the seashore, a majestic-looking horse pounded the surf with his hoofs. He was magnificent: his coat a midnight black, his eyes a bright piercing blue, and round his neck was a golden bridle. As if in a dream, Mary stumbled forward. She pulled off her shoes and fell into a run. This couldn't be happening, and yet it was. Here was her kelpie in the flesh. If he was real, she shouldn't go to him—all the stories said not to, and yet those piercing eyes filled her heart with such longing she couldn't have resisted even if she wanted to.

The dark clouds she'd noticed earlier were racing across the sky as a wild wind blew up, and rain fell in sharp shards, soaking her to the skin but at the same time invigorating her.

The strange wanton feeling from the bookshop returned and, throwing her inhibitions to the wind, she ran towards the horse, her whole body tingling with anticipation. This would be an adventure beyond compare. She didn't dare to think how it would end, but she could see the challenge in his eyes, and would take up the chance of the ride of a lifetime.

Despite never having mounted a horse before, she jumped up with ease, grabbed hold of the bridle, and suddenly they were off, racing down the strand, the wind whipping her hair, the stallion's magnificent body pounding the sand beneath her own. They were in perfect rhythm, perfect harmony, at one with the landscape and each other. But she wanted more. As if he read her mind, the kelpie suddenly changed direction and plunged into the sea.

"This is what you want?"

The question framed itself in her mind, and yet he hadn't said a word.

"Yes, oh yes." The answer burst out of her, from a body hot with desire, a body that for too long had spent time in dry and dusty books, and was aching to be held and caressed in all her secret places.

"Then we begin."

It was a command, and she felt it. She was no longer in control. The kelpie held her at his mercy. But how she reveled in it. How she wanted this as she had never wanted anything before.

They plunged headlong through the foam, further, further into the sea. She clung to him, and as she did so, his body seemed to change. They dove together under the water, she realized she was holding onto a man. A man whose every touch was sending her mad with desire.

Down, down, down they plunged into a green and swirling

world, lips locked onto one another in a kiss which sent a fire coursing through her body. It was unlike anything she had ever experienced. She had never felt this wild desire rage through her, this desperate need to have her lover inside her riding with the waves.

Soft voices called her name, and as they reached the bottom of the seabed, hands pulled her gently away from the kelpie.

"Worry not, my love." His voice was in her head again. *"They will make you ready for me."*

Gently they removed her clothes and laid her on the softest bed she had ever been in. She felt herself in a sort of stupor, drowning in desire, as their fingers trailed across her body, finally alighting on her quim. She moaned aloud with wondrous pleasure, only idly wondering how it was she could breathe down here.

The thought was sent instantly from her mind by the sight of him entering her watery boudoir, and pulling back the cover that only half exposed her. He was magnificent, his cock rising to greet her lips, and while she greedily took him inside her mouth, he gently caressed the bud of her nipple until she thought she would weep. She was hot and horny, and taking control of the situation in a way she could never have imagined, she pushed him away from her down on the bed. Seemingly compliant, he laughed a deeply sensual laugh, and she climbed on board for the ride of her life.

With their bodies entwined in a perfect rhythm and harmony, physically it could never get better, but before she thought she would explode, he turned her over and his shaft penetrated her deeper then ever. They melted together, bodies pounding against one another until wave upon wave of desire crashed over her, and the pounding of the waves matched the pounding of her heart, and she lay with her lover's head in her arms in perfect peace.

Mary sat up. The walk must have tired her. Because she had fallen asleep and had the weirdest dream. It had been the most erotic experience of her life, and she felt hot just thinking about it. Quickly, she gathered her things together. It had been the strangest day. This place was very unsettling. Very. The sooner she got back to Edinburgh the better.

Still barefoot, as the path was sandy, she made her way back to Lachmuirghan, when up ahead of her she saw a man. It was the fisherman from the village, carrying his nets down to the shore.

He stopped and smiled a greeting, those piercing blue eyes looking right through her.

"Is that seaweed in your hair?" His soft Scottish lilt making her heart beat faster than normal.

Mary realized with a start that not only did she have several strands of seaweed tangled in her curls, but they were also rather damp. He gave her a secretive grin and plucked the seaweed from her head in a gesture that was both endearing and sexy. He smelled of the sea, and hot prickles of desire shot through her. In the distance she could hear the keening of seagulls.

"Are you staying long?" he asked.

Mary looked at him with a most un-Mary-like twinkle in her eye.

"Do you know, I think I might," she said.

Afterward

How exactly did Lachmuirghan come about?

Like so many good things, by serendipity.

After an online discussion on writing "hot stuff", we decided to create a shared world for our erotic stories. During a fun, online brainstorming, we tossed about ideas, suggestions and wild inspirations, and Lachmuirghan emerged from the mists of our (admittedly rather fertile) imaginations. We chose as our setting the warm and hospitable west coast of Scotland, added the legend of the heartbroken god, the mysterious and ever-changing town and the myriad sexual adventures of the contented inhabitants and happy visitors.

We continued our online venture between deadlines and other writing commitments, until we had enough rather naughty stories to fill the book you've just read.

We hope you've had as much fun visiting Lachmuirghan as we've had creating our mysterious, erotic world.

Enjoy the fantasy.

Madeleine

About the Authors

Madeleine Oh

Madeleine Oh is a woman of mystery. Some say she is the granddaughter of an odalisque from the Bey's harem in Algiers, others that her father was a direct descendant of the line of Welsh princes. It's been said that her parents met whilst working for the French Resistance during WW2. There have even been claims that she was born on a farm in Ohio and/or that Madeleine is a pseudonym for a best-selling author. Perhaps all of this is true. But truth or fiction, readers love her wildly imaginative, erotic tales. Visit her website www.madeleineoh.com.

To keep up with new releases join Madeleine's announcement list: news-madeleineoh-subscribe@yahoogroups.com.

Isabo Kelly

Isabo Kelly has a gypsy soul, which she's indulged wholeheartedly over the last fifteen years, living in Las Vegas, Hawaii, Germany, Ireland and New York. There's no telling were she might end up next—but Oregon, Italy and Argentina are at the top of the list. She's the award-winning author of numerous sexy science fiction, fantasy and paranormal romance novels, short stories and novellas. Currently, she lives in New York City with her hunky Irish husband. You can visit Isabo at her web site www.isabokelly.com.

Send an email to isabo@isabokelly.com or join her Yahoo! newsletter to join in the fun with other readers as well as Isabo!

http://groups.yahoo.com/group/isabokellynewsletter

M.A. duBarry

M.A. duBarry is an award winning author and digital artist. Her erotica titles have garnered numerous awards and nominations including the P.E.A.R.L. Award and Bloody Dagger Award. Ms. duBarry is also the recipient and two-time nominee of the Dream Realm Award for Best Cover Art. Her digital art renders have been featured at Daz3D's Monthly and PC Galleries. For more on her books and artwork please visit: www.madubarry.com.

Clarissa Wilmot

Clarissa Wilmot: Despite being orphaned young, Clarissa always knew she was destined for greater things. And so it proved, when she met and fell in love with the dashing Sir John Rochester Wilmot, who completed an erotic education which had begun with reading Fanny Hill. Sadly Sir John eventually left her for a young model, so Clarissa now spends her days penning erotic fiction in her boudoir, putting to good use everything he taught her.

Maristella Kent

Maristella Kent is a vibrant redhead who lives in a tiny village in the south of England. Under other names she contributes stories to magazines and to anthologies of erotica. She likes to claim that the research for her stories is far more arduous than the writing. Maristella lives a rich fantasy life—and that's the way she likes it.

Xandra King

Xandra King loves hearing from readers, so please contact her at: xandra_king@yahoo.com or visit her web site: www.xandraking.com and her web diary at: http://xandraking.bravejournal.com.

Pandora Grace

Pandora Grace is a bestselling writer who hides behind a pen name when she's writing erotic tales that would shock her family and horrify her employers. She keeps Pandora Grace safely hidden away so her nearest and dearest have absolutely no idea that Lachmuirghan even exists and, sadly, have no idea of the fun they are missing. Pandora Grace invites readers to visit Lachmuirghan and enjoy the fantasies.

Printed in the United States
148878LV00005B/1/P

9 781599 989839